"Senor, you are being foo̲l̲i̲s̲h̲.̲ ̲I̲t̲ ̲w̲a̲s̲ ̲n̲o̲t̲ our plan to come and kill you. But now, because of what you have done to our friends, we must. You have no chance, so why not step out onto the porch so we can be done with this?"

Jennings's reply to Ignacio Garza was a shot that splintered bark from the corner of the smokehouse.

"We will now make your death a slow and painful one," Garza shouted.

When the two Mexicans suddenly abandoned their cover and began running toward the cabin, shouting and rapidly firing their pistols, Jennings was caught by surprise. The attackers made sure they were separated by a considerable distance, forcing him to aim at one at a time.

He fired at one and the man dropped. Then he felt a searing pain in his shoulder and fell backward onto the floor, his rifle skidding away. Before he could get back to his feet, Garza was standing in the doorway, breathing heavily, his eyes aflame, his gun pointed at Jennings.

"It pleases me that my previous shot did not go into your heart," Ignacio said. "Now it will be my pleasure to see that one does."

As he took aim the front wall of the cabin reverberated with a loud boom and the doorway filled with smoke. There was a look of disbelief on Garza's face as he tried to brace himself against the doorframe. He fell forward, his pistol still in his hand. The back of his head had been blown away.

When the smoke began to clear, Jennings was able to make out a familiar form standing over the dead man. Ira Dalton, wide-eyed and shaking, was holding a shotgun.

Jennings tried to stand but fell back to the floor, unconscious.

Ralph Compton

PHANTOM HILL

A Ralph Compton Novel
by Carlton Stowers

A SIGNET BOOK

SIGNET
Published by New American Library,
an imprint of Penguin Random House LLC
375 Hudson Street, New York, New York 10014

This book is an original publication of New American Library.

First Printing, March 2016

For more information about Penguin Random House, visit penguin.com.

ISBN 978-1-101-99022-3

Printed in the United States of America
10 9 8 7 6 5 4 3 2 1

Penguin
Random
House

THE IMMORTAL COWBOY

This is respectfully dedicated to the "American Cowboy." His was the saga sparked by the turmoil that followed the Civil War, and the passing of more than a century has by no means diminished the flame.

True, the old days and the old ways are but treasured memories, and the old trails have grown dim with the ravages of time, but the spirit of the cowboy lives on.

In my travels—to Texas, Oklahoma, Kansas, Nebraska, Colorado, Wyoming, New Mexico, and Arizona—I always find something that reminds me of the Old West. While I am walking these plains and mountains for the first time, there is this feeling that a part of me is eternal, that I have known these old trails before. I believe it is the undying spirit of the frontier calling me, through the mind's eye, to step back into time. What is the appeal of the Old West of the American frontier?

It has been epitomized by some as the dark and bloody period in American history. Its heroes—Crockett, Bowie, Hickok, Earp—have been reviled and criticized. Yet the Old West lives on, larger than life.

It has become a symbol of freedom, when there was always another mountain to climb and another river to cross; when a dispute between two men was settled not with expensive lawyers, but with fists, knives, or guns. Barbaric? Maybe. But some things never change. When the cowboy rode into the pages of American history, he left behind a legacy that lives within the hearts of us all.

—*Ralph Compton*

Preface

I'm of the notion it was hiding out in a cave down by the Concho River for so long that made Ira Dalton a bit feeble of mind. The only person he spoke to during the entire time was his grandpa, who would occasionally visit in the middle of the night to sneak him flour and beans.

Later on, long after he came out of hiding, there would be days when Ira seemed to have most of his wits about him. But there were times he would be reminded of hiding away from these who had come looking for able-bodied young men to join the Confederate army and he'd talk to nobody, except his dog, which he'd buried after it was bit by a snake and died.

My guess is Ira was privately cursing himself for what he later judged cowardly behavior, choosing to hide and continue living rather than fight in a war that got just about every friend he'd known killed by Union soldiers. He'd managed to survive and eventually grow to manhood, but I can't help thinking that deep down his was a life of constant regret.

Still, I liked him. And he seemed to take to me. But even with our friendship being what it was, he rarely spoke of the demons that caused him such torment.

He did tell me it was just days after his sixteenth birthday when word came that the Confederate government had decreed it mandatory for all men in Texas to join up. Some who had no taste for fighting quickly fled south of the border into Mexico to avoid the recruiters. At the urging of his grandparents, who had raised him after his mama and daddy were killed in an Indian raid, Ira literally went underground.

As a youngster he'd roamed the black land wilderness surrounding the tiny cotton-farming hamlet of Runnels and was aware of every bend of the river, every peak and valley, even the secluded shelters of the deer and coyotes who roamed the region. High atop a limestone cliff on the river's edge, just over a mile's walk from the Dalton farmhouse, he'd discovered the cave whose entrance was hidden by the tangled growth of mesquites and sagebrush. It was there he'd played countless childhood games and later it became his full-time hiding place.

By day he wouldn't venture outside. Only when nightfall arrived would he fish the river for perch and carp and set traps for the rabbits and squirrels he would cook on a small fire in the deepest corner of his hideaway. He bathed in the river by moonlight. He was alone with nothing but his thoughts and the constant concern he would be found, recording the passage of each day with a mark on the wall of the cave.

Ira Dalton became a prisoner of his own fear.

Small wonder he didn't go crazy as an outhouse rat. I don't intend that observation in a mean-spirited way, you understand. As I've said, I liked him from the first day I met him in a livery stable in Phantom Hill where he was cleaning stalls and tending horses in exchange for room and board. He'd left his hiding place and gone there as soon as his grandpa alerted him that the Confederates had surrendered and the war was over. The only thing he owned was a mule named Bell that he'd left home on. His dog, whose name I can't recall, followed along.

By then he was twenty going on twenty-one, tall and skinny as a rail. The thing that struck me the first time I met him was that he had the saddest eyes I'd ever seen.

I'll tell you more about him later. But for now what I want you to know before you go reading any further is this: Ira Dalton was no coward. Not by a long shot. If not for him, I'd not be around to tell this story.

He saved my life.

Part One

Chapter 1

Coy Jennings was limping almost as badly as his horse when, in the distance, he saw chimney smoke lazily climbing into the clear morning sky. From a small rise he could see a couple of clapboard buildings, a few small houses, and a lengthy row of tents. The wind carried the sounds of people as they hurried about, dogs barking, a rooster crowing, and a steady clanging of a blacksmith's hammer.

Phantom Hill didn't look like much of a town.

"I reckon if we don't fall flat on our faces," he said to the hobbling bay, "we're gonna make it."

The trip took far longer than Jennings had planned. What he had figured would be a two-day ride turned into more than a week after his horse had startled a rattlesnake, which then had bitten him just above the hoof on his back leg. Coy hadn't even bothered to kill the snake, instead dismounting immediately and cutting away a length of rein to tie above the small marks left by the rattler's fangs. He'd quickly tethered his mount to a mesquite tree, taken out his knife, and begun cutting small *X*'s above the wound. Kneeling in front of the animal, he'd sucked the bloody poison from the leg. Once that was done, he'd made a small fire and boiled water to bathe the cuts. He'd then made a mushy plaster of tobacco and placed it on the leg, wrapping it tightly with a strip of cloth ripped from his shirt.

But it still swelled, and soon became feverish. Through the remainder of the day and into the night, Jennings had tended the bay, a gentle animal that his pa had given him when he was still in his teens. He'd ridden him to the schoolhouse and town dances, then during his days as a Confederate soldier. He was the only horse Jennings had ever owned and he refused to consider the idea that it might become his responsibility to put the animal down and relieve him of his misery.

The only time he'd left the horse's side was to walk to a nearby spring for water and to whisper a prayer. *Lord, you know I'm not one for asking favors. Likely as not, I'm not deserving of any. Last time I recall reaching out to you was when that Union soldier shot me in the leg and you saw to it I didn't die. What I'm asking this time is if you could see your way clear to do the same for my horse. Rodeo's his name and he's lived a good and honorable life. More than me, that's for sure. I'd thank you kindly for anything you can do to help him get better.*

On the third morning he awoke long before sunup to find Rodeo standing, chewing on mesquite beans. Though he wasn't putting weight on the affected leg, the swelling had gone down. The horse's eyes were clear as he looked down at his owner.

"Appears you're feeling better," Coy said, climbing to his feet to stroke Rodeo's flank. He filled his hat with water from his canteen and held it for the horse to drink. "Let's rest for another day or so, then see if you can walk the rest of the way. Maybe we'll find someone who can provide you proper doctoring."

The going was difficult, Rodeo slowly trailing his owner, who carried his saddle over his shoulder. Neither could travel more than a mile before stopping to rest. It was well past noon before they reached Phantom Hill and located the livery.

The blacksmith, shirtless with tobacco juice caked in his graying beard, eyed them as they approached. "Can't rightfully figure out which of you two looks worse," he said before bursting into a thundering laugh. "Name's Giles Weatherby. Welcome to Phantom Hill, Texas, such as it is. I call it the Gateway to No Place."

Jennings said, "Y'all got a doctor in this town?"

"You ailing?"

"My horse is."

Weatherby glanced at the Colt holstered on the visitor's hip. "You wouldn't be some outlaw come to stir up trouble, would you?"

"Nope."

"Didn't really think so. If you've got fifty cents you can board him inside. There's hay and oats and a watering trough. Looks like you could do with some time out of the sun yourself. Get settled while I go see if I can fetch Doc Matthews. He tends man, beast, and babies . . . when he's sober enough."

He was chuckling to himself as he turned to hurry down the only street in the dusty little settlement.

In the cool darkness of the stable, Jennings filled a bucket with oats as Rodeo drank from the trough. Every muscle in his body ached as he let the saddle slip from his shoulder onto a bale of hay. Pushing his hat high on his head, he sat against the wall as the horse ate and was asleep and snoring loudly when the doctor arrived half an hour later.

"Much louder and the rafters of this fine establishment would be falling in," Doc Matthews said. One hand was on Jennings's shoulder, shaking him awake. In the other he held a small leather bag.

Coy rubbed his eyes and shook his head. "My apologies. You a doctor?"

"Son, I'm *the* doctor. Only one for miles around. It's my understanding that you've got a horse needing some manner of attention."

He was already peeling away the bloodstained wrap as Jennings explained about the snakebite and what he'd done in an attempt to halt the spread of the venom. "I'd say you've done a good job," the doctor said. "Aside from a bit of infection in a couple of the places where you took a knife to him, I'd say he's doing as well as could be expected. 'Bout all I can do is clean the leg, do a little sewing up, and put some salve on the wounds. Then we give him time to rest and see how things look."

"He going to be okay?"

"Yes, sir, that's my professional judgment." The doctor rose and looked at Jennings. "You, on the other hand, are another matter. Seems to me if you don't get yourself a hot bath, some food, and a considerable amount of rest, you're not gonna be worth shooting." He sniffed. "Wouldn't hurt to have those clothes you're wearing laundered either."

Standing nearby, the blacksmith broke into another of his booming laughs.

"Tell you what," the doctor said. "You go get cleaned up and something to eat, and I'll take care of what needs to be done here. I 'spect Mr. Weatherby or his stableboy can give me a hand, if needed.

"Oh, and I'll be requiring a dollar in payment before you go."

For the first time in days, Coy Jennings smiled as he reached into his pocket and pulled out a coin.

After a pat to Rodeo's muzzle, he took the short walk past a small general store and a saloon that appeared to have been so hastily built that it still had stitched-together tent canvases serving as a roof toward Miss Mindy's Fine Eatery and Bathhouse. A small hand-painted sign near the entrance displayed a sparse menu that included venison stew, cold-water corn bread, and collard greens.

A small dog lying in the doorway lifted its head only slightly, apparently too tired or disinterested to bother to growl or bark. Jennings stepped over him and entered a room where there were four empty tables.

"Lemme guess, mister. You'll first be needing something to eat, then considerable time in a tub to wash all that trail grime away." The small woman stood less than five feet, with red hair that was a tangle of curls. She wore overalls and a flannel shirt and was smoking a cigar. "I'm Mindy. The stew's still hot on the stove and has plenty of potatoes and beans mixed into it. I've got corn bread, but all the greens are gone. Does that tempt your appetite?"

"Ma'am, just about anything that don't bite back does," Jennings said.

"Then take yourself a seat next to the window and enjoy the view—what there is of it—and I'll be off to the kitchen."

She soon returned with his food and a tin cup filled

with coffee, pulled up a chair across the table from him, and took a seat without asking for an invitation. "Not that I'm the nosy sort," she said, "but it isn't often we get strangers visiting. What brings you to this godforsaken part of Texas?"

"Looking for work," Jennings replied as he dipped a slice of corn bread into the sweet-smelling stew. "I heard there was a ranch hereabouts that's hiring."

"That, I suppose, would be Lester Sinclair's spread," she said, "being as it's the only ranch we've got. Just about everybody else—them not employed by Sinclair—tries to farm."

"And what can you tell me about Mr. Sinclair?"

"Not much aside from the fact that he's not one of my favorite people. Truth is, I also work for him. He's the actual owner of this place despite the fact that it bears my name. The saloon down the street is his as well."

With that she rose and wiped her hands on her apron. "This ain't a hotel, mind you, but I do have a couple of rooms out back if you're needing a place."

"I reckon I'll be staying down at the livery," he said, "but I could do with that hot bath you mentioned."

"In that case, I'll go out back and start heating up the water. While you're waiting, feel free to help yourself to the coffee. No charge, since it's likely getting a bit bitter. You'll find the pot on the stove behind that door. I s'pose you'll be wanting your clothes washed as well."

Jennings nodded.

"Then plan to soak in your bath for a considerable time."

Sitting in the tub of hot water did wonders for his tired and aching muscles, and he took another nap. The clean smell of his sunshine-dried clothes lifted his spirits almost as much as the doctor's having said that Rodeo was going to be fine. He was hardly limping as he left Miss Mindy's and decided on a walk through the town before returning to the livery.

There's wasn't much to see and only a few people were moving about. A couple of wagons slowly passed, loaded with provisions, and one driver waved. When Jennings tipped his hat in return he realized that Miss Mindy had dusted it clean while he bathed.

He briefly considered visiting the saloon for a beer but decided his dwindling finances spoke against such an indulgence. Instead he stopped in the general store and purchased a small pouch of tobacco to replace that he'd used doctoring his horse.

The blacksmith was waving as he approached. "My, my, don't you look a sight better? You could go courtin', all cleaned up as you appear to be. Did Miss Mindy offer you some of that sweet-smelling lilac water to put in with your bath? If so, I'd better put out a warning to the womenfolk."

Coy responded with a slight smile.

"Your horse is in the far stall, all mended and doing well," Weatherby said. "I hung your saddle on the wall next to him."

"Appreciate it."

"Just part of the friendly service. Course, I must inform you that if you're gonna be bedding down here tonight it'll cost you another twenty-five cents."

Jennings paid him and walked inside to check on Rodeo.

As he entered the dimly lit stable, he was aware of someone speaking in a low voice near his horse. He approached to find a young man combing burrs from Rodeo's mane, talking gently as he did so.

Jennings stood watching and listening awhile before he spoke. "Who might you be?"

The young man jumped, then turned to face him. "My . . . my name's Ira. Ira Dalton. I help Mr. Weatherby some. I been talking with your horse."

Jennings nodded. "And what is it you two have been talking about?"

"Just things, you know. Gettin'-acquainted talk. Best I can figure, he's right proud you doctored his leg and brung him to shelter. I'm of a mind that 'cause you treat him so kindly he must admire you greatly."

"He told you that, did he?"

"In his way, yeah, he did. He's a mighty handsome animal."

"His name's Rodeo."

"Seems a fine name to me. Did I tell you I'm Ira . . . Ira Dalton?"

Jennings extended his hand. "That you did," he said. "Pleased to know you, Ira Dalton. My name's Coy . . . Coy Jennings."

As they shook, Dalton smiled. "That seems a fine name too. I'm gonna be sure to remember it. *Mr. Coy Jennin's . . . Coy Jennin's . . .*"

"Just Coy will do."

At the sound of his owner's name, Rodeo lifted his head and placed his nuzzle beside Jennings's face, causing his freshly cleaned hat to fall to the hay-strewn floor.

"Yes, sir, Mr. Coy Jennin's," the young man said, "I'd say he likes you a lot."

Chapter 2

Well before sunup, Ira Dalton rose from his cot in the livery loft and groomed Rodeo. He then fed the horse and slowly walked him in a pasture out back. Jennings had just awakened and was shaking straw from his hair when they returned.

"He's doing better. Limp's not nearly as bad," Dalton said. "Gonna be good as new in a few days, though I'd suggest keeping the saddle off him for a bit."

It was the same advice Doc Matthews later gave when he stopped in. "Been helping Clara Beasley to birth her second boy most of the night," he said as he gently removed the bandages to inspect Rodeo's leg. "We'll leave the stitches in a few days longer, but looks to me the infection's clearing nicely. I suggest some exercise—but not too much, mind you. And see to it he gets a good dose of sunshine daily. You'll not find it in the medical books, but it's my opinion that there's a good deal of healing power that comes from the warmth of the sun."

Ira nodded, as if the physician were speaking to

him instead of the horse's owner. "I'll gladly see to it," he said.

The doctor smiled, patted Dalton on the shoulder, then turned to Jennings. "Got yourself a fine helper here," he said.

"Reckon so."

And with that a routine developed. Ira gently tended the healing horse while Jennings mostly watched. He saw that the responsibility seemed to please the young man and didn't interfere with his regular chores of mucking stalls, seeing that the watering trough was kept filled, or stoking the fire when Weatherby was preparing to shoe a farmer's horse or mend a broken wagon wheel. He even soaped and polished Jennings's saddle. "You'll be needing it soon," Ira said.

As the aching of his own leg eased, Coy began accompanying Rodeo and Ira on their short, slow walk each morning. On most occasions, the young man holding the rope loosely in front of the horse said not a word. It was as if he was so concentrating on his task that talking would only be a distraction. Even when they stopped to sit in the sun, Rodeo tethered to a post, the two men remained silent. It seemed to satisfy them both.

Then, in the early evenings, after his work was done and Rodeo was settled in his stall, Ira would climb onto his mule and ride in the direction of a distant stand of mesquites on the edge of town. One day, Jennings watched from the doorway of the livery as the strange young man bounced away to the gait of his lumbering mount.

"I'd say he ain't got the most comfortable ride a man can find, especially traveling bareback." Jennings turned to see Giles Weatherby standing next to him. "He takes that ol' mule for a ride every evenin'. Treats him with the same kindness he's been showing your horse.

"Most days I give him a penny and he goes down to the general store and buys one of them sticks of peppermint candy. Whenever they get to where it is they're heading, I 'spect he'll give it to the mule."

The two men stood silently for a time, looking toward the horizon as the sky began to turn gray. Then the blacksmith said, "He just showed up here almost a year ago, riding that mule with a mangy ol' black dog he called Rip trailing along. I told him I'd give 'em boarding for a time in exchange for doing chores. That's the arrangement we've had ever since."

"He don't talk much."

"Never has, though he seems to have had a good deal of conversation with you lately."

"You don't know his history?"

"Not where he's from or where he might be headed. If he's got family, he's not mentioned it."

"Where is it he rides off to of an evening?"

"I ain't real sure and never asked. All I can tell you is his dog fell ill and died not long after they came. If I was to guess I'd say he most likely buried him somewhere out yonder and is inclined to pay him a visit at the end of the day."

"How'd the dog die?"

"It's my recollection he also got himself bit by a rattlesnake."

Coy nodded. He had a good idea what it was Ira Dalton had spoken about to his horse.

Weatherby continued to talk as the two men moved inside to put tools away. "Now that we're sharing

ourselves a conversation," he said, "I understand from
the gossiping down at the eatery that it's your plan to
try hiring on with Lester Sinclair's crew."

Jennings nodded. "Once my horse is healthy, I'm
gonna pay a visit out to his ranch."

"Could be you won't be needing to wait until your
horse is able." Weatherby explained that Sinclair and
several of his hands regularly came into town on Saturday to socialize at the Phantom Hill Saloon. "Late
of a night, things tend to get a bit rowdy, but if you was
to stop in before everyone's drunk and looking to fight,
you might get a word with the old man."

"Am I likely to find him cordial?"

"Mister," Weatherby replied, "Lester Sinclair ain't
never cordial." There was no laughter in his voice.

"I was wondering how this town got the name it has,"
Jennings said, "since I see nothing around I'd call a
hill."

"Nor is it likely you'll be seeing any phantoms,"
Weatherby said. "Here's the story that got started long
before there was even a town: Some trappers was ridin'
near here and apparently one was certain he seen an
Indian in the distance, sitting on a pony atop what he
later described as a hill. He fired off a shot, and then him
and his fellow trappers rode to see if he'd hit anything.
"They never found hide nor hair of any Indian. So the
story goes that this man's friends took to chidin' him for
shootin' at a ghost, a phantom.

"Truth is, it ain't much of a story. But you asked. That's
how we come to be Phantom Hill—without having us a
real phantom or even a respectable hill."

A near-full moon was peeking over the horizon by the
time Ira returned. He was grooming his mule when

Jennings approached. "Mighty fine evening for a ride," he said.

It was as if the young man didn't hear him. Latching the door to the stall, he turned and silently climbed the ladder toward the loft.

Jennings shook his head. "Reckon Lester Sinclair ain't alone when it comes to not being cordial," he said.

Before bedding down himself, he checked on Rodeo and was pleased to find him resting peacefully. Only then did he hear a voice softly call out from the loft.

"G'night, Coy Jennin's."

Chapter 3

Lester Sinclair sat alone at a corner table in the back of the dimly lit saloon, puffing on a pipe as his eyes roamed the crowded room. A half-full bottle of whiskey was at arm's reach. Occasionally a man would nod in recognition, but none approached for conversation or so much as a handshake. Even his two sons, Pete and Repete, leaning against the bar, kept their distance.

Lester Sinclair was a short, portly man with a coal black beard that was neatly kept. There was nothing about his appearance to suggest he was the region's wealthiest landowner. Everyone knew of his success, but few had any real idea how it had been achieved. All most knew was he was to be avoided lest they found themselves pressured into selling their small farms so they might be added to his ever-expanding Bend of the River Ranch.

In years past he had managed to avoid Indian raids and survive the War Between the States—which he viewed as a foolish exercise—by befriending all who might threaten his growing empire. To the roaming

Kiowas and Comanches, he made a pact allowing them to occasionally cut a few cattle from his herd when food was scarce. Same with the soldiers, regardless of the uniforms they wore. To some soldiers his offer of employment was often viewed as an appealing alternative to fighting winless battles. In exchange for shelter and regular meals, they cleared pasture brush, dug his wells, helped tend his herd, and rode sentry to protect his land against those they'd once ridden alongside.

Lester Sinclair viewed it as a small price to pay for not having his house and barns burned, his cattle stampeded, or physical harm coming to him and his family. He was a businessman, a survivor, and if it occasionally meant making a pact with the Devil, so be it.

Once the Indians were mostly gone, driven onto reservations up North, and the war had ended, the peace should have made him more at ease, a happier man who could relax and enjoy his good fortune. That never happened, and at times it troubled him that he'd not achieved any real degree of contentment. In truth, the answer he never considered was simple: The demon that constantly whispered to the wealthy rancher, relentlessly urging him on, was his insatiable greed.

Jennings waited until nightfall to make the short walk down to the saloon. He'd assisted Weatherby with a few end-of-the-day chores and stacked wood for the next morning's fire before Ira returned from his ride. Then he washed at the horse trough, smoothed his dampened hair, and brushed straw from his hat. He unbuckled his belt and removed his Colt and the holster that still bore the faint letters *CSA* on its flap and hung it next to his saddle.

He was ready to go speak to a man about a job.

Even before reaching the open doorway, he could

hear sounds of boisterous laughter and loud talk. Someone was playing a banjo. As he made his way into the crowd, it was not difficult to spot the man he'd come to see. Lester Sinclair was the only man in the place without a smile on his face.

As Coy approached the corner table, several eyes followed him and much of the laughter subsided. Pete and Repete moved from the bar toward their father's table.

Sinclair waited until the stranger was standing in front of him to speak. "You ain't drinking?"

"I was hoping I might have a word with you before partaking," Jennings said. He removed his hat and held it at his side before taking a seat. The man with the banjo quit playing.

"And what is it we might have to talk about?"

"Name's Coy Jennings. I just come from down South on account I got word that you might be hiring. Should that be the case, I can make you a good hand. I've got ranch work experience, everything from rounding up to branding. I've helped raise barns, mended fences, even slopped hogs. And working long days don't bother me." He explained that the only reason he hadn't already visited the ranch was the problem with his horse.

"What was it that caused you to travel up this way? You on the run from some kind of trouble?"

Jennings explained that his former boss's wife had passed away suddenly, causing him to sell his small spread and return to his home somewhere back East.

Coy added, "It's my opinion he decided he wasn't all that taken with the notion of being a rancher."

Sinclair pointed toward the chair across from him. "Sit." He lifted his glass, signaling one of his boys to bring another to the table.

The whiskey was better than any Coy had ever tasted as it warmed his throat, then his stomach. He rose. "I thank you for your time and the drink," he said. "Now I'll be letting you get back to your business."

"When your horse is fit for travel," Sinclair said, "come out to the Bend and we'll see if we might have need for your services."

"That I'll do."

"I wouldn't be rushing out. You ought to stay a bit and get better acquainted with some of the local folk." The slightest hint of a smile crossed his face for the first time all evening. "'Fore long there'll be fighting."

Weatherby was at the bar, drinking beer, as Coy approached. "I see you succeeded in making contact with Sinclair," he said.

Jennings nodded. "We spoke, yes. And now I reckon I'll be gettin' on back to the livery."

"You can't be leaving 'fore the fighting."

"Mr. Sinclair made mention of the same thing. What fighting is it you're talking about?"

Weatherby explained, "Soon now, the ol' man will walk up this way and place a ten-dollar gold piece on the bar. That means it's time everybody takes their places along the sidewalk outside. Sinclair's older boy, the big one they call Pete, will take on anyone who's dumb enough or drunk enough to step forward and try to win the coin on the bar. All they got to do is still be standing after two minutes have passed on the old man's pocket watch."

"How often is it someone wins the money?"

"Never seen it happen. Closest anyone ever came was his own brother, Repete, and that was only after he fetched a branding iron from his wagon. He got in one pretty good blow before Pete grabbed the iron away, bent it double, and tossed it into the street. That done, he continued pounding on his own kin. A few weeks later Repete showed up in town with the LS brand burned into his shoulder."

Jennings shook his head. "I don't recollect seeing that kind of meanness even during the war."

"Mad-dog mean is what he is," Weatherby said.

"Well, I've seen enough fightin' to last me a lifetime." He pulled his hat tight onto his head and walked toward the door.

Weatherby watched him go and wondered if he should have mentioned that Pete Sinclair, now bare-chested and standing in the middle of the street awaiting his first challenger, was the foreman of his father's ranch.

Chapter 4

The troubling memory, which often returned in a dream, was always the same, beginning on a warm blue-sky day in the spring of 1865.

Jennings and a fellow Confederate soldier were standing on the bank of the Rio Grande while their horses drank. Two miles away was the outline of Fort Brown where their Second Texas Cavalry Regiment was headquartered. With rumors that the war was over and a truce declared, there was a sense of relief among the weary troops.

For the past few weeks Jennings had been part of a small party assigned to patrol the river, watching for Mexican banditos who might try to rustle cattle from the nearby Palmito Ranch. Others in the regiment guarded the seaport of Los Brazos de Santiago, seeing to it that bales of Texas cotton were safely loaded and on their way to European markets. The assignments were made more to pass time than because of any real threats.

All that remained of the North-South battle was for the Confederacy to officially surrender.

Throughout the ranks there seemed little, if any, remorse over the defeat. The soldiers, even their leader, Colonel John Salmon Ford, had grown tired of the death and destruction that had played out over the past four years and were ready to lay down their arms and go home.

None was more eager than Coy Jennings. He had long since lost count of the number of friends he'd seen die.

In the dream, he and his companion were talking of their future plans when the first shots rang out.

Only later would the Confederate soldiers learn a Union colonel named Theodore Barrett, recently promoted to his first field command, was frustrated by the idea of the war ending before he could lead his brigade into battle. Claiming the need to replenish his troops' diminishing herd of horses, he ordered a surprise attack on Fort Brown.

By the time Jennings had ridden close enough to see what was taking place, the fort was under full-out siege as hundreds of bluecoats kneeled side by side, firing their rifles in roaring volleys. Several caissons of cannon had been wheeled into place. From behind the barricades the return fire was just as furious, causing a canopy of blue smoke to rise above the angry scene. Not far away, on Palmito Hill, another battle was under way between the Confederates who had just returned from the seaport and the attacking soldiers.

With no way to make it through the gunfire and into the fort, Jennings chose to join those on the hill. As he approached, he could see that several horses had already fallen, wounded or dead, and stopped short before he was in range of the gunfire. He pulled his rifle from its scabbard, then swatted Rodeo on his hindquarter, sending him back in the direction of the river. Whatever fighting there was to be done, Coy would do on foot.

Reaching the meager protection of a stand of scrub brush, he kneeled next to a fellow soldier. "I see the war's not as over as we've been led to believe," he said as he began firing in the direction of the oncoming enemy. The acrid smell of gunpowder filled his nostrils and caused his eyes to burn.

The fighting was fierce and continued through the late afternoon, the outnumbered Confederates managing to hold off the assault. While none around him were hit, he could hear the echo of occasional screams in the distance as Union soldiers fell.

It was dusk before the shooting slowed to an occasional shot. Then a distant bugle blew and the blue shirts began retreating toward a stand of trees.

Those who had fought from the hill began to move about, drenched in sweat and covered with dust. "I reckon that'll be it for the day," someone said, "but they'll return at sunup. Best we make our way inside the fort and see how things are there."

The two dozen soldiers began plotting their route to safety. Only Jennings stayed behind. "I'll be along," he yelled out. "Gotta fetch my horse."

As the others made their way down the sandy hillside, Jennings headed in the opposite direction, eyes focused on the horizon in hopes of seeing Rodeo. Only after walking the few hundred yards down the hillside did he become aware of how exhausted he was.

He didn't hear the rustle in the nearby brush as a Union soldier yelled out. "That'll be far enough, Reb," he said as he pointed his rifle. Blood was oozing from the front of his tattered coat. There was a crazed look in his eyes, and he struggled to stand. "Somebody's got to pay for what's been done to me," he called out, "and I reckon you're gonna be the one."

As the man aimed, Jennings pulled his Colt and fired. Their shots broke the silence simultaneously. A piece of the Union soldier's skull blew away and he was dead before falling to the sand. His shot had buried itself into Jennings's leg, just above the knee. There was a moment of burning pain, then darkness.

Thereafter, the dream always became fuzzy, a series of quick snapshots of what followed. Jennings awoke to the hot breath from Rodeo's nostrils against his face. He managed to climb into the saddle and steer his horse not in the direction of the fort but instead toward the Rio Grande and Mexico. Later, there was a darkened room in a small shack in Matamoros where he lay on a cot, suffering with a high fever, his wound being tended by an elderly woman with no teeth.

In the dream he always heard the woman say, "You're a soldier." And he was aware of his whispered response: "Not no more."

It would be months before Jennings saw a Galveston newspaper that published a story about General Lee's surrender, officially ending the war. Still, his decision to ride away before the war was over began to weigh on him.

The article pointed out that the two-day battle at Fort Brown was the last fought and, ironically, was won by the Confederates. According to the article, the last man to die in the Civil War was a Union private named John J. Williams.

Jennings could still see the wild-eyed look on Williams's face in the moment before he shot him.

Ira Dalton was kneeling over him, gripping a shoulder, as he desperately tried to shake him awake. "Mr. Jennin's . . . Mr. Jennin's . . . Wake up and open your eyes. Everything's okay, Mr. Jennin's. Jes' fine. Wake . . ."

Jennings sat up, briefly unaware of where he was. Sweat was beaded on his forehead.

Dalton smiled. "Seems you was having yourself a night fright."

"Reckon so. I thank you for waking me."

It was still pitch-dark, but both men knew there would be no more sleep. "I'll go put a fire in Mr. Weatherby's pit and make us some coffee," Dalton said.

From a nearby stall, Rodeo poked his head through the doorway and looked toward his owner. Jennings walked over and began gently rubbing his neck. "I'm okay," he said. "Jest had me that bad dream."

The horse tossed his mane, then retreated back into his stall. Jennings was pleased to see that, after two weeks, he was no longer favoring his leg.

"When can you take him ridin'? Seems he's near well. That's what the doctor said, ain't it, Mr. Jennin's?"

Coy nodded. "Mind some company this evening?"

The western sky was a magnificent blush of oranges and reds as the sun disappeared below the horizon. Rodeo pawed the straw-covered floor impatiently as Jennings lifted the saddle onto him and placed the bit gently into his mouth. The animal, like his owner, was anxious to leave the livery and the sounds of town behind.

As they rode away Rodeo flared his nostrils to take in the twilight breeze and easily kept pace with Dalton's

mule. Jennings was pleased that there was no sign of
the limp. "How far is it we'll be going?"

"Most evenings my destination is just a few more
miles ahead," Ira replied, bouncing with each step his
mule took. "But if it happens your horse shows distress
along the way, we can turn back."

"He seems to be doin' fine. You just lead."

Neither rider spoke again as they slowly distanced
themselves from Phantom Hill.

Soon a half moon was on the rise, beginning to cast
long shadows by the time they approached a thick grove
of trees at the base of a small rise. Ira dismounted and
began leading his mule along a narrow trail, Jennings
and Rodeo following.

They reached a clearing with a neatly stacked
mound of limestone rocks in its center. Nearby was a
fallen tree trunk and a small fire pit. "This here's where
I come to visit my dog, Copper, who is dead and buried
under them rocks," Dalton said. "I find it a peaceful
place."

He then reached into his shirt pocket and produced
a peppermint stick, which he offered to his mule.

"It's indeed a nice place you picked," Jennings said.
"Peaceful."

Dalton was smiling as he began gathering dried
branches and soon had a small fire started. "Ain't much
to do 'cept sit for a while and listen at the quiet," he said.
"I've always liked nighttime better'n days."

The two men sat in silence for some time as their
mounts lazily chewed leaves from nearby branches.

Such was the quiet that Jennings was startled when
Dalton finally spoke again. "It was my impression when
you was dreaming," he said, "that you was recollectin'

on your time in the war. Am I guessing right that you was once a soldier?"

Jennings nodded. "For a time."

There was another long silence. "It was my grandpa's thinking that all the fightin' and killin' was of no good purpose. He was the one told me to hide when the recruitin' men came to our place. That's what I done—hide, me 'n' Copper—until the fighting was ended."

With that Ira Dalton shared his secret. In a halting voice he told of hiding away in the cave, of fishing and checking traps by night, and living in constant fear he would be discovered.

"This is something I've never spoke about to another soul," he concluded, "not even Mr. Weatherby. Sometimes when I come here I talk with Copper about it, but I'm doubtful he hears me. But you bein' my new friend, Coy Jennin's, I wanted you should know. I hope you'll consider this talk private and not think me too cowardly for what it was I done."

"As I look back on it now," Jennings said, "I wish I'd found a place for hiding myself. Might be that my sleepin' would be a bit more restful."

The embers of the fire were fading when Rodeo lifted his head, his ears suddenly pointed, listening to sounds neither of the men could yet hear. Soon they became aware of a faint rumbling in the distance. Together they climbed a nearby ledge and squinted in the direction of the sound. At first they saw nothing but then made out half a dozen tiny spots of light moving in their direction.

Only after time were they able to see that the bobbing

lights were torches being carried by riders following a small herd of cattle.

"Seems a mighty strange time to be moving livestock," Jennings said.

"I thought so myself," Dalton said, "the first time I seen it."

Chapter 5

Despite the directions Miss Mindy had provided, Jennings was well onto the Bend of the River Ranch before he became aware he had reached Lester Sinclair's property. There were no fences, no signposts, just a sprawling range of grassland stretching to the horizon. Only when he approached a herd of cattle grazing and saw the distant roof of a barn did he assume he was nearing his destination.

Convinced that Rodco's leg was finally well, he'd risen early, stopped by Miss Mindy's for coffee and a penny slice of bread fresh from her oven, then set out in hopes of finding employment. His meager bankroll was seriously depleted by the pay for lodging and care for his horse, and if Sinclair didn't offer him work, he wasn't sure what his future would hold.

He'd awakened from a dreamless sleep, thinking of his conversation with Ira and the sighting of the torch-bearing wranglers and the cattle they'd been herding, but those matters were quickly replaced by the anticipation of speaking with Sinclair and his foreman.

As he neared the herd of longhorns, he could see two riders headed toward him at a gallop.

"You got some purpose for being here?" The man's tone was far from welcoming. Despite the spring weather he wore buckskins and his shoulder-length hair was partially hidden by a bandanna tied tightly against his head. He leaned to the side of his horse and spat a stream of tobacco juice into the dust. A young Mexican riding with him said nothing.

"I was recently invited by Mr. Sinclair, who indicated he might be in need of an additional hand."

"You got a name?"

"Coy Jennings."

"I've heard nothing of you being asked to visit."

"You the foreman of this spread?"

"That would be Pete Sinclair, the owner's older son."

"Then I reckon this talk is a waste of my time."

The man reined his horse to the side, blocking Jennings's way, and pointed at his sidearm. "I'll be needing to take that 'fore you travel any further. Boss don't appreciate strangers arriving with pistols on their hip."

Jennings hesitated, then slowly lifted his Colt from its holster. Gripping it by the barrel, he extended it toward the man. "Careful you don't shoot yourself," he said.

"You'll be gettin' it back once you're takin' your leave . . . which ain't likely to be long from now."

Jennings doffed his hat in a mocking manner and rode on.

After another mile he reached a sudden end to the flatlands and found himself looking down into a small valley. In the distance he could see the river, bordered by cottonwood trees, as it lazily flowed past a series of outbuildings and corrals. Not far away there was the huge barn whose roof he'd seen earlier. An L-shaped building nearby, he assumed, was the bunkhouse. There was an orchard, a garden, and a smokehouse. And in the middle of it all was a magnificent two-story house, whitewashed and gleaming in the morning sun.

Lester Sinclair had done quite well for himself.

"I'd 'bout decided you'd forgot to come around," Sinclair said as Jennings approached the front porch. The ranch owner puffed on his pipe while holding a coffee cup with both hands. "Glad to see you made it."

"Almost didn't. One of your hands seemed worried I might be coming here to shoot you. He relieved me of my Colt 'fore he'd allow me to pass."

Sinclair smiled. "You met ol' Poppy, did you? I admit he's not too friendly and can be a tad protective at times—which, mind you, I don't discourage. I'll see to it your gun is promptly returned if you promise not to go shooting the place up." He rose from his chair and placed his cup on the railing. "Climb off your horse—which I assume is now back in good health—and come have a sit so we can talk."

As he spoke a young woman appeared at the front door with another cup of coffee.

"The work's not pleasant," Sinclair said, "but I offer a fair wage. Start-up pay is half a dollar a day. The comfort of the bunkhouse is passable and the cook will see to it you don't go hungry. You'll be allowed one day a week to take your leave and get in your socializing if you're of a mind."

"When is it you'd be wanting me to start?"

"Today's good as any. My boy Pete, he's the foreman. He'll want to make your acquaintance. He's down at the brandin' pen at the moment, seeing to it that a small herd I just acquired from a rancher up north is properly marked before sent out to pasture."

There was a scent of burning flesh as they approached the pen. A steer was hobbled, lying on its side, as a wrangler removed the branding iron from a barrel filled with coals. Soon there was smoke, a faint sizzling sound, then the bellow of the animal. The tethers were removed and he clumsily rose and hurried toward an open gate. "Bring the next one," the brander yelled out.

Pete Sinclair was sitting on the top rail, watching the assembly line activity. His hat was pulled low on his head and he didn't speak as his father and Jennings approached.

"This here's Coy Jennings," the elder Sinclair said. "You seen him when we was in town a while back. He's hired on and ready to go to work."

The foreman didn't so much as nod an acknowledgment. "Repete's got a crew down by the river, clearing and burning brush," he said. "I 'spect they could use some help."

Jennings turned to Lester Sinclair. "Point the way," he said.

The work was hard, but it felt good to be using muscles he hadn't used in some time. Digging out the roots of thornbushes and cacti caused his back to ache, and the heat from the bonfire where they were being burned drenched him in sweat.

He was more than ready when Repete Sinclair finally announced the day was done. As Jennings walked toward a grove of trees to retrieve his horse, the younger Sinclair approached him. "Some of the men'll be jumping into the river to cool and bathe," he said, "but there's a rainwater cistern out back of the bunk-house that you might prefer. If you want to ride along, I'll see to it we find you a bed you can call your own and show you where you'll be keeping your horse. Dinner gets served in an hour or so."

Jennings was pleased to finally hear a friendly voice. "I just hope I can keep my eyes open long enough to not fall facedown into my plate," he said.

Repete smiled. "I reckon you'll get used to it soon enough."

Once he'd washed, seen to it that Rodeo was settled, and had his fill of the stew, corn bread, and peach cobbler delivered from the main house, Jennings felt better. Some of the hands lingered at the dinner table, swapping stories, while others prepared to play poker. Neither interested Jennings, so he stepped outside into the twilight.

Wishing to stretch his aching leg, he walked toward the corral where a mare and her newborn seemed to be celebrating the end of the day. Jennings watched as they pranced along the fence line.

A woman's voice startled him. "Was tonight's supper to your satisfaction?"

He squinted toward the shadow of a nearby shed and made out the silhouette of two people: a woman—the one who had brought him coffee on the front porch earlier in the day—and a young girl.

"It was mighty tasty," he said as they approached. "Am I to guess it was you who prepared it?"

She smiled as the girl bashfully hid behind her skirt. "It's part of the work Mr. Sinclair hires me to do," she said. Even in the near darkness Jennings could see that she was a pretty woman, her auburn hair falling against her shoulders, her skin almond brown. She was slim

and almost as tall as he was and even in the darkness
he could see a hint of sadness in her eyes. "I'm April
McLean," she said, "and this is my daughter."

The youngster stepped from behind her mother to
finish the sentence. "I'm Penelope and I'm almost eight
years old. What's your name?"

"Coy Jennings, Miss Penelope, and it is indeed a
pleasure to meet you and your mama."

April hugged her child. "She likes to come down here
and say good night to the new colt before bedtime. Me,
I enjoy the quiet and watching the stars come out."

As she turned to walk back to the house, she called
out, "I'll be cooking chili and red beans tomorrow.
There'll be biscuits and coffee ready for your breakfast."

"I'll be looking forward to it."

"Very nice to meet you, Mr. Jennings," she said. Her
daughter waved as they reached the front porch.

It was the first conversation with a woman his own
age that Coy Jennings had experienced in some time.

The smells and night noises of the bunkhouse made
sleep impossible. The stale odors of sweat and tobacco
hung in the darkness, and a serenade of snoring filled
the room. Jennings found himself wishing for the gentler
sounds and sweet smell of hay in the livery back in Phantom Hill. He closed his eyes and attempted to call to
mind the image of the woman he'd just met. And in time,
his busy thoughts drifted to Ira Dalton and the story he'd
told of spending his younger years in hiding. Coy was
surprised to realize that he missed his company.

It was past midnight when he heard a low drum of
hoofbeats in the distance. As the sound grew closer he
rose, found his boots in the darkness, and slipped quietly out the front door of the bunkhouse. With no moon
it was at first difficult to see what was taking place. Only

when the flickering of torches came into view did he realize it was a replay of the event he and Ira had witnessed from a distance a few nights earlier. He stood watching as half a dozen horsemen herded cattle into the corral adjacent to the branding pen.

Hidden in the darkness, he watched as they completed their task, then heard a single voice call out, *"Andante, rapidamente."* And with that the riders quickly rode away, their torches no longer lit.

When they were gone, Jennings approached the corral, where the restless cattle moved about. He counted two dozen cows and six calves. As he stood in the darkness, puzzled by what he'd just witnessed, he wondered if he would be told to help with the branding once the sun came up.

Instead he mucked out stalls.

He was spreading fresh hay when Pete Sinclair entered the barn. The foreman said nothing, just watched Jennings at work for a time. Even when Coy stopped to say good morning, Sinclair remained mute.

Coy leaned his pitchfork against the wall. "Is there something you need of me?"

Sinclair shook his head. "Just wanted to see if you're getting settled in okay. Finding everything to your satisfaction?"

"Got no complaints."

"I'm guessing you likely had some trouble sleeping last night, being as it's difficult getting used to bunking with a roomful of strangers."

"Nope, I slept just fine." Even as Sinclair turned to walk away, Jennings was sure Sinclair had seen the arrival of the cattle in the middle of the night. And wasn't pleased.

The remainder of the week passed quickly. There was more brush to clear and trees were cut down and bark stripped to make fence railings for a new corral. Jennings and a young hand named Dallas Frazier spent a day loading hay onto a wagon and hauling it to outlying pastureland where there was more rock than grass.

"How large you figure Sinclair's property to be?" Jennings asked as he steered the wagon toward a jagged hillside.

Dallas shrugged his bony shoulders. "They say you could ride the better part of the day in most any direction and still not take leave of the Bend. I doubt even Mr. Sinclair himself knows the exact acreage he owns. And it seems to continue spreadin'."

"And how is it he manages that?"

"What I hear is he buys out those with small farms, sending the owners on their way with enough money to allow them to travel west and start up somewhere else."

Jennings waited until they had reached their destination before continuing the conversation. "Do these farmers you spoke of generally take leave of their own choosing?"

"It's none of my business, but my impression is that Lester Sinclair—or his boy Pete—ain't folks to take no for an answer once they've set their mind to something."

Dallas looked off into the distance. Coy sensed he was growing uncomfortable with the conversation, so he pressed the matter no further. He stopped short of asking the main thing on his mind: Where did Sinclair's steady arrival of new cattle come from? And why did they arrive in the cover of night?

Instead he said, "When is it we get our pay?"

"That'll be on Saturday morning. Mr. Sinclair himself comes to the bunkhouse to pass out wages. He'll then say who is free to rest or make their visit to town. Most will lie about until day's end, then head in to the saloon. A few will be told to remain to tend chores and keep watch over the place, then have Sunday as their day off. I 'spect you being new, you'll have to wait for Sunday to kick up your heels or whatever it is that suits you."

"Makes no matter to me, though I would like to visit Phantom Hill to purchase some tobacco and pay a visit to a friend."

Early on Sunday morning Jennings was on the trail to town, urging Rodeo into a quick gait, then a brief gallop to test his leg. Satisfied that all was well, he reined the horse in and allowed him to settle into an easy walk.

Soon he saw a buggy up ahead and hurried Rodeo into a trot to catch up with it. Even before reaching it he could tell that a woman was at the reins with a young girl, wearing a bonnet, at her side.

"Morning, ladies," Jennings said as he reached them and tipped his hat.

April McLean smiled. "Morning to you, Mr. Jennings. Wouldn't be you're also headed to town for gospel singing, would it?"

"'Fraid I'm not much for any kind of singing."

She laughed. "I doubt anyone would notice. Truth is, Phantom Hill lacks a proper church. There's not even a preacher in town. We gather in the shade of a big tree down near the livery on Sundays just to sing hymns and say a prayer for those in need of comfort. Sometimes Mr. Weatherby reads us a bit of Scripture."

"I know the spot well. We resided at his livery for a time before I was hired on at the ranch." He didn't mention that he was surprised to learn that the black-smith was a religious man.

Penelope leaned forward to face Jennings. "Wanna come hear Mama sing? Folks say she's got the voice of an angel."

"That," he said, "would be of no surprise to me."

Ira Dalton was already leaning against the trunk of the sprawling oak when they arrived. Seeing Jennings, he hurried toward him, a broad smile on his face. "I was hoping you'd be back," he said. "I been missing you . . . and your fine horse." He placed his face against Rodeo's neck and began scratching behind his ears. "Looks like he's good as new."

"Much of it is due to the good care you provided him."

Dalton blushed. "You come to listen to the singing?"

Jennings stole a glance in the direction of the nearby buggy. "I s'pose I have."

After the hymns were sung, heads bowed for a prayer, and Weatherby read several verses from the Book of Psalms, Jennings said good-bye to April and Penelope. He helped the youngster onto the buggy seat and told her that she had been absolutely right; her mother did sing like an angel. After watching them ride away, he turned to accompany Ira to the livery.

They gave Rodeo a bucket of oats, then sat on a bench, enjoying the warmth of the sun. After a while, Coy spoke. "I was wondering if you can recollect how many times you've witnessed men herding cattle at night."

"Lots. Always with the torches. Lotta times."

"And you have no idea who they are or where they're headed?"

"Nope." A look of concern crossed Dalton's face. "Is it something that worries you?"

"Jes' making conversation," Jennings said. "It's mighty good to see you. Since I was paid my wages yesterday, how 'bout you join me for a meal down at Miss Mindy's?"

Ira smiled and got to his feet. "Most Sundays she has pie."

Several who gathered for the singing stayed in town for lunch at Miss Mindy's, but the dining room was almost empty by the time Coy and Ira entered. The signboard out front advertised corn bread, beans, and fried venison. "Not much left," Mindy said, "but I can scrape together a couple of servings if you're here to eat."

Dalton removed his hat. "Is there a slice of your pear pie remaining?"

"Not to worry, Ira. I had her put a piece aside for you. Was gonna bring it to you." It was the voice of Giles Weatherby. He was sitting alone at a table near the back of the room, an empty plate still in front of him. "I was planning on having me a cup of coffee," he said, "so why don't you fellas come sit and keep me company?"

"I must say you sounded like a preacher with your reading from the Bible," Jennings said.

Weatherby chuckled. "Oh, I gave the calling some consideration in my younger days, but being as I appreciated a strong drink or two on occasion, it seemed I'd be facing too great a conflict. The Devil whiskey won out and I went to blacksmithing."

"Still, you did a fine job with the Scriptures."

Weatherby sipped at his coffee as Coy and Ira ate, then said, "I noticed you paying particular attention to the widow McLean and her daughter earlier. I take it you've made her acquaintance since going to work for Sinclair."

"We've spoke on occasion, but I wasn't aware of her being widowed. Was her husband lost in the war?"

"No, he managed to survive that foolishness and returned here to farm a little place a few miles up the road you came to town on. He was a bit on the ornery side but a good man, and he treated his wife and young'un properly.

"One night the family awoke to find their barn afire and Conley, that was his name, rushed out to try and get his mules and his milk cow to safety. While he was attempting the rescue, the roof of the barn collapsed on him and he died a horrible death. I was called on to build him a casket and speak at his burying. Then . . ."

He fell silent and finished his coffee. "Reckon we'd best be moving on so Mindy can do her cleaning. Let's head on down to the livery."

At the stable Weatherby resumed his story. "It was ol' man Sinclair who came to her and quickly offered his help. There was no way April could keep the farm going, so he offered her a fair price for it along with a job and a place for her and the little one to stay. That's how she come to be working out at the Bend."

"So he got himself additional land and a fine cook and housekeeper," Jennings said.

"That's about the size of it. But there's more I think you need knowing."

"And that is?"

Weatherby waited until Ira had left to check on his mule. "Phantom Hill is a place where gossip is whispered on a regular basis. Word I hear is that April was hired at the urging of the older Sinclair boy, Pete. The one who enjoys his Saturday night fighting. I hear he fancies having her around despite the fact that she's shown no interest in his attention."

He looked at Jennings for several seconds. "I'm telling you this as a warning," he said, getting to his feet. "Come take a walk with me over to Doc Matthews's place."

Chapter 6

The doctor's wife had died years earlier, but his house still retained a feminine touch. The floor of the living room was swept and every table surface carefully dusted. Each piece of aging furniture, hauled by wagon from back East long ago, was spotless. On one wall hung a framed tintype of a young man and woman, handsome and beautiful, posed for a wedding photograph.

Doc Matthews met his visitors at the front door.

"Wanted to come by and check on the Burton boy," Weatherby said. "You remember Coy Jennings here. You doctored his horse a while back."

The doctor shook both men's hands and signaled them to follow him into the back room. In the bed lay a local farmer named Buck Burton.

His face was badly swollen, both eyelids purple and closed. His lips were puffy, cuts so deep that his remaining teeth were visible. Bandages were wrapped along one arm and around both hands. He was unconscious, drugged by the doctor into a deep sleep.

"He's pretty busted up. Near as I can tell he's got

broken ribs, but since he seems to be breathing normally I don't think his lungs were punctured. So that's the good news. The arm's broke. So is one of his hands. Not sure how many teeth he lost. I'll need the swelling to go down considerably before I can stitch up his mouth. For now what worries me most is if he'll retain his sight. I've done about all I can to relieve his discomfort and clean his wounds. I hear there was praying on his behalf down at the meeting tree this morning. I'm just sitting here hoping the prayers are answered."

Jennings felt bile rising in his throat as he looked down on the young man. "What caused him to be in this condition?"

"He consumed himself a bit too much courage last night and took on Pete Sinclair out front of the saloon. Those who brought him to me in the middle of the night said the pounding and stomping went on until Pete just finally wore himself out and walked away."

As they left the doctor's house, Jennings's jaw tightened as he felt an anger he hadn't experienced since his days as a soldier.

"That boy," said Weatherby, "had no business fighting with Pete Sinclair. My guess, he don't weigh no more than a hundred and fifty pounds. He's just a boy, trying to grow up and be a good farmer. Ain't a mean streak in his body." He paused as he stepped from the front porch and kicked at the dirt.

"I'm in need of a drink of something stronger than Miss Mindy's coffee," he said.

By day's end, Weatherby was drunk, gently swaying back and forth on the bench in front of his livery.

"It's no business of mine where a fella goes to earn hisself a living," he said, "but you need to know that there's a heap of meanness in the folks paying your wages. You get yourself crossways with the Sinclairs and you're inviting trouble. I've taken a liking to you, just as young Ira has, and I'd be sorely disappointed if something was to cause you to wind up in the same condition as that Burton boy. I'm speaking out for your well-being when I tell you that they're no-good people."

His smile turned slightly crooked and his speech was slurred by the whiskey as he continued drinking from the bottle he'd retrieved from the tack room. "If I wasn't too drunk to know better, I'd not be telling you these things," he said. "Folks around here have learned not to speak unkindly about what goes on out at that godforsaken Bend of the River Ranch.

"Those Sinclairs . . ." He shook his head and grimaced. "You've seen our poor excuse for a town. Once there were plans for it to prosper and grow. None of that ever happened. We got us no law, we got no church, no town government, nothing that encourages folks to come and settle here. Why? 'Cause Lester Sinclair don't want it."

Jennings only nodded occasionally, allowing Weatherby to continue his rant.

"Sad thing is," the blacksmith said, "we was once friends."

He was six, almost seven, accompanying his parents on a wagon train crossing Kansas, when the Comanches attacked. Weatherby was the lone survivor, hiding in an empty barrel in the back of the wagon until the raiders completed their savagery, stole guns and provisions, and finally rode away.

Several days passed before hands working for Henderson Sinclair happened upon the young boy, stumbling aimlessly, hungry, parched, and near collapse. They took him to the ranch, where Mrs. Sinclair fed and bathed him and nursed him back to health. A gentle and caring woman, she informed her husband that the proper thing to do was to take the orphaned child into their family.

"So I grew up with Lester. We played together, we hunted and fished together, even shared the same room. We became good friends, then like brothers. And as we got older, we helped work the ranch. They were good times."

Weatherby sipped from the bottle before he continued. "Lester had a bit of a wild streak about him even then—fun-loving, you'd say—but he wasn't what I'd call mean-spirited. That developed later, sometime after we arrived in Texas. Fact is, I've often wondered if it's this land, with its dust and wind and open spaces, that gives cause to a man's meanness."

He closed his eyes, as if reliving his youth. "Back when we was in our teens, Lester got it in his mind that it was time to strike out on his own. He wanted me to go with him. So we drove a small herd his pa give him as a birthday gift down this way so he could lay claim to a parcel of land. I can't rightly recall what it was that caused us to settle here. Could be we was just weary of the trail and too tired to go any farther. Whatever the reason, Lester staked his claim up by the river—several hundred acres—and called it home.

"And this town? It was nothing more'n a way station with a cabin that passed for a store and a barn to shelter passing horses."

He rose to stretch his legs but quickly lost his balance and sat back down.

Jennings knew if Weatherby's story wasn't soon

finished, he wasn't likely to hear its ending. "How is it he was able to grow his spread to what it is today?"

"That's where the meanness came into play. That and pure greed. He started resentin' the small farmers who began arrivin'. Every time a new house was built, a barn erected or a well dug, he got madder. Seems he'd made up his mind that all the land as far as one could see rightfully belonged to him—and he set about making it happen. With money his pa had provided him, he hired on a few unsavory characters—Mexicans mostly, who I suspicion were on the run from the law. He had them set about tormenting folks until they were convinced to sell out and move on.

"Lester, he was making himself no friends and didn't care. His ranch was expanding, and so was his herd. And that's all he worried hisself about. And the more he had, the more he wanted. 'I don't want it all,' he used to say. 'I just want my land and that next to it.' Then he'd smile. That was his idea of a good joke.

"In time I realized it wasn't something I wanted to be a party to. Our arrangement when we took leave of Kansas was that he'd give me a few cows from the herd we drove down here. Thanks to a few good spring birthings, it had grown, so I sold what stock was mine to him for a cheap price and moved into Phantom Hill, figurin' it was in need of a livery and blacksmith.

"That was the ending of our friendship. Now we speak only when he has need of my services. Same with him and the doc. If Lester Sinclair don't see you as being useful, you're of no concern to him."

Jennings had a number of questions he wished to ask but knew the conversation would soon end. It was getting dark and Weatherby's head had begun to sink toward his chest. "I take it his boys are cut from much the same cloth," Coy said.

"Pretty much. 'Specially Pete. Truth is, he's mean just for the sake of it. Not so much with Repete, who I think just does what his daddy and brother tell him. They got no real ma, you understand. Lester never married, just had himself a fling now and then and wound up with the two boys."

Coy took the bottle from Weatherby's hand as it was slipping away. "Best we get you to bed," he said.

The blacksmith looped one arm over Jennings's shoulder. "You jes' be careful," he said, "and mind what I've told you."

From the loft of the livery, Ira Dalton had listened to the two men talking. "That's right, Mr. Jennin's," he whispered to himself. "You need to be sure you take care."

Only after he climbed down the ladder and stepped outside did he realize it was too late for his evening ride. Too, Mr. Weatherby had forgotten to give him a penny, and he had no peppermint stick for his mule.

Chapter 7

Coy stepped from the doorway of the bunkhouse and saw the Sinclairs seated on the front porch of the big house. Pete was next to his father, his scuffed boots resting atop the railing, his hat tilted back, while Repete stood nearby drinking coffee and munching on a biscuit. On a table was an iron skillet filled with scrambled eggs and bacon.

As Coy headed toward the barn, Pete said, "Jennings, I'm needin' to speak with you."

He was approaching when April McLean appeared on the porch with a coffeepot in hand, glanced his way, and smiled. Coy removed his hat and nodded, then faced Pete. "Yeah?"

Sinclair cast a displeased glance in April's direction, and she quickly retreated into the house. "I hear there was a mighty lifting of voices in town yesterday," he said.

"'Fraid mine wasn't among them," Jennings said. "I was just there to listen." *Just letting me know he's keeping an eye on me,* thought Coy.

"Poppy'll be needing your help herding some cows up from the south pasture today," Pete said. "Reckon you can do that?"

"I 'spect so." Before turning away Coy noticed that the knuckles of Pete Sinclair's right hand were scraped and swollen. The tightness he'd felt in his chest at Doc Matthews's house returned.

"In addition to the singin'," he said, "there was a bit of praying done as well."

"Well, praise the Lord."

"For a young fella name of Burton."

He could still hear Pete Sinclair's deep-throated laughter as he walked toward the barn to find Poppy.

"I see you was given your pistol back." It was the first thing Poppy said since they'd begun their ride almost an hour earlier.

"Only after I promised not to go shootin' the place up."

"Humph." It wasn't close to a laugh, but it did indicate that the old cowhand might be in a bit better mood than he was when they first met—maybe even amenable to carrying on a conversation.

Such wasn't the case.

Coy said, "How long is it you been working for the Sinclairs?"

"Long enough."

"You among those who went into town Saturday night?"

"Ain't saying."

Jennings laughed. "Reckon it might rain?"

"Rarely does."

"Don't really talk much, do you?"

"Nope."

It was noon when they found the small herd. At a grove of trees Poppy reined his horse in and dismounted.

He reached into his saddlebags and pulled out a bandanna wrapped around biscuits and fried bacon. "Miss April didn't want us going hungry," he said.

"Seems she's a nice lady. And pretty."

Poppy chewed on a piece of bacon as he stared at Jennings. "Best you're aware Pete Sinclair claims her as his lady friend," he said.

"You stating a fact or giving me warning?"

"Jes' saying."

As they mounted their horses a few minutes later, Jennings noticed a lazy plume of smoke in the far distance. "What's that over yonder?"

Poppy squinted in the direction Coy was pointing. "That would be a place called Blue Flats."

Assuming the smoke was rising from land that was part of the ranch, Jennings asked, "There folks living out there?"

"Ask no more about it," Poppy said. "And that *is* a warning."

Herding the cattle was easy work, and the job was done well before day's end. Upon their return Jennings removed Rodeo's saddle and led him to the river's edge, allowing him to drink and graze while he sat on the bank, trying to sort things out. Questions raced through his mind as he contemplated the strange events he'd witnessed, the drunken observations of Weatherby and the subtle warnings from Poppy. Why were cattle herded in the dark of night? What manner of anger could cause Pete Sinclair to almost kill a man for no good reason? Was his pa really so greedy as to make all around him fearful? What was this place called Blue Flats that he wasn't to ask about?

And finally, if the ranch foreman did have romantic

feelings for April McLean, was it possible she welcomed them?

Despite the warmth of the evening the fireplace glowed, flames causing shadows to dance around the dimly lit room. Lester Sinclair was puffing on his pipe, eyes fixed on his elder son.

"Now, what is it you're of a mind we should talk about?" he said.

"I got some concerns about that new hand you hired."

Lester smiled. "'Cause he sassed you this morning about what took place in town Saturday night?"

Pete ignored his father's sarcasm. "Seems to me he's inclined to show interest in too many things that are none of his business. He was prowling about late the other night when Ignacio and his men brought in the new herd. And Poppy tells me he was asking questions today about the Flats."

"And what is it you're thinking he's of a mind to do? Ride into town and tell the law? Need I remind you that there *ain't no law* in Phantom Hill or, for that matter, for miles around? I've made sure to see to that. All I've witnessed in the days since he arrived is a tired-lookin' drifter in need of earning hisself a payday. From what I've seen he ain't been picking fights, has remained sober, and seems to tend whatever chores he's given."

"I still plan on keeping an eye on him."

Lester nodded, then broke into a quiet laugh. "And I'm thinking you won't be the only one. Don't think I didn't see how Miss April smiled on him this morning."

Pete glowered and stared into the fire. "When is it

you think we should approach Buck Burton with an offer to buy his farm?"

"I'd say there's no need for rushing the matter. Last I seen of him—after you gave him that whupping—he was being carried off to Doc Matthews's place. It's likely he's gonna be laid up for a good while. It'll give him time to do some hard thinking about his future plans. I don't want to give the appearance of being unkind and impatient." He rose from his chair and tapped his pipe against the edge of the fireplace. "Now, if we've discussed all that's worrying you, I'll excuse myself to bed."

Pete Sinclair sat alone long after his father had disappeared up the staircase, gazing into the dying fire. In time he smiled. Neither patience nor kindness, he knew, were virtues his daddy embraced. Nor did he.

Poppy was loading supplies into a wagon as Jennings approached him the next morning and said, "Be needing some help?"

Pete Sinclair appeared in the doorway of the shed. "I got this handled," he said, his tone gruff and dismissive. "You'll be needed helping mend the fences of the pigpens down by the river."

When Jennings headed toward the river he turned and watched as Poppy's wagon slowly disappeared in the same direction they had traveled the previous day. Riding alongside on horseback was Sinclair.

Pete's brother was watching over the men working on the fence. A bandanna covered his face, a futile effort to avoid the acrid smell of the pig wallows. "I was to see if you've got enough help," Coy said. "If I'm not needed, I think it would be a better use of my time to take a ride out toward the south pasture. Me 'n'

Poppy spotted a couple of wolves on our way back yesterday and I'm thinking they should be put down 'fore they start attacking the calves."

Repete seemed disinterested, both in the work being done on the pens and in Jennings's suggestion. "If you ain't got nothing to shoot with 'cept that Colt, best you fetch a rifle from the bunkhouse 'fore you head out."

Chapter 8

Blue Flats was on the far southern edge of the Sinclair property, nothing more than an old adobe building, a shallow well, and a corral. A limestone ridge rose on its back side, and a tangle of mesquite trees hid the entrance. The smell of venison roasting over an open fire wafted through the air as the wagon approached.

"Hola, hola, hola . . . Hola, amigos," Poppy shouted out as they neared. Though the voice was familiar, the half dozen men quickly unholstered their pistols until the approaching men cleared the last stand of trees and came into sight.

When Pete dismounted they gathered around him. "Payday and provisions, boys," he said.

Speaking in Spanish, Ignacio Garza instructed the others to unload the wagon and moved to greet Sinclair. He was a short man, his paunch spilling over his gun belt. He wore boots that covered his legs almost to the knees and a sombrero shaded his weathered face. Though his mustache remained coal black, Pete guessed he was near the age of his father.

"It is a pleasure to see you, *mi amigo.* I hope you bring news that your papa *esta bien*," Garza said as he extended his hand.

Aside from the money that Sinclair distributed, the men seemed most anxious to make use of the pouches of tobacco and tins of coffee they unloaded. A cheer erupted when Poppy handed down a wooden box that contained bottles of beer and whiskey.

"We have been without our small pleasures for several days," Garza said. "Your presence is most *bienvenido*."

Pete offered no apology for the late arrival. Despite his awareness of their purpose, he hated dealing with the Mexicans and generally delayed visits to the Flats until his father insisted their pay and provisions be delivered. He thought it foolish that Lester Sinclair would go to such extremes to separate the image of his ranch from the banditos who had been on his payroll for so many years. It was fine for them to rustle cattle for him, even occasionally burn down the barn of a settler reluctant to sell his farm, but the elder Sinclair made it clear they were never to appear anywhere near the ranch headquarters during daylight hours. And they were forbidden to show their faces in Phantom Hill.

Sinclair wished them to be invisible, not so much because of their unsavory ways but the damage he felt would be done to his reputation should anyone learn of his association with them.

It had been years since he and Garza even spoke. Whatever orders Sinclair needed to deliver were done by his son.

"We have something you will wish to report to Mr. Sinclair," Garza said. "If you will ride with me I can show you. Then we will return for *una bebida y comida* before you begin your journey home."

While Poppy remained at the camp, waiting for coffee to be brewed, Pete and Ignacio rode along a dried creek bed for a couple of miles before arriving at the mouth of a box canyon whose entrance was blocked by a fence made of cedar posts.

"From here we must walk," Garza said.

Inside the canyon, a herd of longhorns milled about, grazing on sparse patches of grass and leaves from the mesquite brush.

Pete nodded his approval. "How many this time?"

"By my count," Garza said, "there are almost fifty, mostly cows. There were a few more, but *que lastima*, we lost them on the way. We traveled from *el norte*, a long, hard ride. Still, I think your papa will be pleased, no?"

"I 'spect he will. Was there any trouble?"

Ignacio smiled and shook his head. "No, *mi amigo*, there is no trouble when you steal from a man while he sleeps. It is necessary we get the herd to the ranch *rapidamente*—there is little for them to eat here. I do not wish to bring Mr. Sinclair starving cattle. Is *mañana por la noche* a good time? I would suggest tonight, but I fear my men will enjoy too much of the whiskey *y cerveza* you brought and be in no condition to ride this evening."

"Tomorrow will be time enough. Sometime after midnight."

Jennings followed the tracks of Poppy's wagon at a slow pace, wanting to give him and Sinclair time to get far ahead. He was sure he knew where they were heading. As he neared the south pasture, he again saw rising smoke on the horizon and instead of continuing along the route taken by the wagon, he turned Rodeo off the trail and headed west. He would make a wide circle and approach his destination from the opposite side.

The day had turned hot as he reached the crest of a small mesa. Coy dismounted and poured water from his canteen into his hat, allowing Rodeo to drink before tethering him in the shade of a tree. The smoke was much closer and Coy chose to walk the remainder of the way.

Soon he could hear voices, low at first, then louder as he positioned himself behind a large rock formation. From his vantage point he could look down on Poppy's wagon, now emptied of its freight. Shielding his eyes from the sun, he counted five men, not including Poppy, and the wind carried their excited voices. All were speaking rapidly in Spanish as they mingled about, passing a bottle among themselves.

Jennings watched the celebration for some time before he finally saw Pete Sinclair as he and a man wearing a sombrero emerged from the creek bed and rode into the camp. Pete nodded toward Poppy. "Best we get on our way," he said.

The Mexican turned to Pete. "First," he said, "you must have something to eat. You are our guests. The deer meat is cooked and you have brought drink. And as you have seen, there is reason to celebrate, if only for a short time."

Sinclair dismounted. "Let's make it quick."

Jennings watched as the men carved slices of venison and dipped a ladle into a pot of beans that sat on the coals. The Mexicans opened more bottles.

Even from a distance it was easy to see that Pete was growing impatient.

Lying prone while watching the strange gathering caused Coy's leg to stiffen. He was slowly getting to his feet when he heard a loud exchange. One of the youngest of the Flats residents, obviously drunk, was rocking back and forth, his head bobbing, as he angrily spoke in Spanish to the man who had ridden in with Sinclair.

Ignacio tried unsuccessfully to calm the boy, grabbing him by the shoulders and shaking him until he lost his balance and fell to his knees. He was quickly back on his feet, however, eyes flaming with rage and ready to fight.

Sinclair put down his plate and approached. "What's this about?"

"Jorge, he is young—only seventeen—and *muy* restless," Ignacio said. "*Lo siento, por favor.* I will tend to it."

"What is it needs tending?"

"He is saying that he is tired of being here. He says he feels like a prisoner and wishes to go into town now that he has *dinero* in his pocket. He thinks he should enjoy some fun, that there are senoritas—"

"You know the rules," Sinclair said. He faced the drunken youngster. "No town, no senoritas. *Comprende*, amigo?" He then shoved him in the chest, knocking him back to the ground.

Pete looked at Poppy. "Time we was on our way."

While Sinclair's back was turned, Jorge got to his feet and attempted to balance himself as he drew his gun.

Someone yelled, *"Pistola!"* as he aimed at Sinclair but shot wildly into the side of the wagon.

Ignacio shouted, "Jorge, *baja la arma*!" and the boy lowered his gun.

Pete drew his Colt, swore, and walked toward the youth. He took careful aim and fired a single shot that created a blossom of red on the boy's forehead. Blood streamed into his eyes and life left his body even before he crumpled to the ground.

The others stood their ground, suddenly sobered, their scared eyes moving from Jorge's body to the towering figure of Pete Sinclair. No one spoke, not even Ignacio.

It was Sinclair who finally broke the silence. "I reckon y'all can divide up his wages," he said. "Look on it as a bonus . . . and a lesson."

Jennings watched as Pete calmly mounted his horse and rode away, Poppy driving the wagon behind him.

Though he knew he would need to return to the Bend ahead of Pete and Poppy, Jennings was curious to see where Sinclair and the older Mexican had been before his arrival. He waited until the wagon was well on its way, scanned the course of the creek bed, then returned to where he'd left Rodeo.

He rode along the mesa and soon made his way to the nearby canyon. As he arrived at the wooden fence, he knew what he would find. He dismounted and walked among the cattle. He could see the brand they bore was not the LS burned into the hind sides of the Sinclair herd.

Coy knew that would soon change.

He had unsaddled and fed Rodeo and was having dinner when he heard the clatter of the returning wagon. When Poppy entered the bunkhouse, he made eye contact with no one as he walked directly to his bunk. Trail dust still covered his face and he didn't even bother removing his boots before he lay down. In short order he was asleep and snoring despite the noise from the nearby poker game.

Outside, the air had turned cool and a few stars were already visible in the rust-colored sky. Walking made Jennings's leg feel better and gave him the opportunity to contemplate the events of the day. He was not particularly surprised to learn that rustled cattle were being delivered to the Sinclair ranch, but Pete's dispassionate killing of the young Mexican was something else. In a short period of time Coy had seen the results of the beating given a young man in town, then watched as a man whose only sin was drinking too much and using poor judgment was shot dead. Pete Sinclair was not just mean, as he'd been warned. He was cold-blooded evil.

"Evenin', Mr. Jennings."

He was nearing the corral where the mare and her foal were penned when he heard young Penelope's voice. "And how are you, young lady?"

"I'm fine, thank you. My mother 'n' me have come to tell the horses good night."

April McLean stood near her child but didn't acknowledge his presence.

"Nice to see you as well," Coy said.

The smile she'd previously shown him was absent. Her lips were pursed as she pulled her daughter to her side and glanced back in the direction of the house.

"You seem troubled," he said.

"I've been told by Mr. Sinclair I'm not to talk with you," she said.

"Pete, you mean?"

She nodded. "Pete, yes." With no further explanation she turned and headed toward the house, holding her daughter's hand tightly.

Poppy, awake from his brief nap and sipping from a cup of coffee, was standing in the doorway of the bunkhouse when Jennings returned. There was a crooked smile on his face. "And how's pretty Miss April doin'?" Jennings pushed past him without replying.

Chapter 9

For the remainder of the week, Jennings went about his chores, avoiding Pete Sinclair as much as possible. As he expected, the cattle were herded in the night after his visit to Blue Flats, though he was not asked to help with the branding. Nor did he take any more evening walks that might result in problems for April McLean.

Signing on with the Bend of the River Ranch had been a mistake. The simple answer was to just ride away. *This ain't your fight,* he told himself. *You're a lowly deserter just needing a job, not additional troubles.* Still, he couldn't put aside the fact that bad things were happening and no one seemed interested in doing anything about it.

Coy needed to talk with Giles Weatherby.

When he prepared to ride into Phantom Hill on Sunday, he was careful to make certain Miss April's buggy was still in the barn when he left.

It was still an hour before singing was to begin and the livery owner sat outside, enjoying the sun as he wiped dirt and dung from his boots. He wore a clean shirt and his hair and beard were trimmed and combed.

"Almost didn't recognize you," Jennings said as he looped Rodeo's reins over the hitch rail.

"I make an effort to be presentable on the Sabbath."

From inside the livery came a shout. "That you, Mr. Jennin's?" Ira peeked from the doorway, a smile on his face. "I was hoping you might come."

"He's been warting me plumb to death, asking how long before Sunday," Weatherby said.

Coy placed his arm across Dalton's shoulders. "I been lookin' forward to seein' you too."

"Reckon we'll be getting us pie later in the day?"

"Wouldn't surprise me none."

Weatherby reached into his pocket and withdrew a penny. Handing it to Ira, he said, "You might want to go purchase Bell's candy stick 'fore you forget. Me 'n' Mr. Jennings got us some visiting to do."

Coy took a seat on the bench and watched Dalton hurry off in the direction of the general store. "How's the Burton boy?"

"Doc tells me he's mending slowly. It now appears he's going to be able to retain his sight, which is something we'll soon be giving up a prayer of thanks for."

"How long before he'll be up and about?"

"That's what I'm wanting to speak with you about."

Despite his condition the last time they'd talked, Weatherby remembered most of what he'd told Jennings about the Sinclairs and the warning he'd given. "How are you getting on with your job at the Bend?"

On the ride into town Coy decided to tell the blacksmith what he'd seen and learned since they last talked. Weatherby silently stared at the ground as Jennings told of his ride to Blue Flats, of Pete Sinclair's shooting the young Mexican, and seeing cattle he was sure were stolen.

Weatherby nodded. "Ol' Lester's had those outlaws—or men like them—doing his thieving and dirty work for the longest time. Seems he has the belief that it will keep his own hands clean and his conscience clear."

"There's another thing worrying me," Coy said. "I'm afraid I might have caused someone unneeded trouble without intending to." He told of his brief conversations with April McLean and her daughter and of being informed that Pete Sinclair had warned her not to talk further with him.

Weatherby shook his head slowly. "Mean *and* jealous. I'd suggest that's a highly dangerous combination." There was a lengthy silence before he continued. "I got no proof of what I'm about to tell you, but . . ."

Before he could complete his sentence, Ira returned, still smiling. "Folks are beginnin' to arrive over by the tree," he said. "Time for singing."

Weatherby gave his boots one last swipe, then rose and cradled his Bible under one arm. "Will you be joining us?"

"I reckon I'll be able to hear from here," Coy said.

"We'll continue our talk later, then."

The sound of the hymns being sung lifted Jennings's spirit. He closed his eyes, letting the voices of the community sweep away the concerns he'd wrestled with over the past few days.

His eyes were still closed when he heard his name called. When he opened them April McLean was standing in front of him.

"Mr. Jennings," she said, "I saw you sitting here and came to offer an apology for my behavior the other evening."

He stood and doffed his hat. "None's needed."

She shook her head. "Nice folks need to be treated nice," she said, "and I failed in my Christian responsibility. You did nothing that merited my turning away without a better explanation."

"You told me what it was Pete Sinclair said."

"He may be my boss, but all I owe him and his family is an honest day's work and meals on the table. I'm not owned by Pete Sinclair, and I have a right to speak to anyone I choose."

Jennings said, "My worry is any problem me being friendly might cause you . . . and your daughter. It's my impression that Pete's not a person given to understanding ways."

"Leave me to worry about that," she said. "Good day to you, Mr. Jennings."

"I'd prefer you call me by my given name. Coy."

She smiled, then turned and walked away to join those waiting to hear Weatherby's reading from the book of St. Luke.

"We'll soon be needin' to include you in our prayers for healing if a certain person's wishes continue to get ignored," the livery owner said as he approached. There was an attempt to lend a tone of jesting to his observation, but Coy knew he was serious.

"You think her working for the Sinclairs puts her in any danger?"

Weatherby shrugged. "So long as Pete's got an eye for her, it's not likely. At least until he finally comes to realize she's got no interest in his affections. For now, though, I 'spect he's hardheaded enough—and full enough of hisself—to think he can persuade her if he keeps working at it. Meanwhile, I'd suggest that the best favor you can do for her is to keep your distance and not give anybody cause to be riled up again."

"Again?"

"That's what I was gonna speak with you about 'fore we was interrupted. You recall me telling you what caused the widow McLean to be out to the Bend was her husband losing his life when his barn caught fire?"

Coy nodded.

"Understand, I got no proof for what I'm sayin', but it was my suspicion at the time that the fire was most likely set by Lester Sinclair's henchmen. Like I told you, he'd been attempting to convince April's husband to sell his farm for some time with no success. It wasn't long after his unfortunate passing when the widow agreed to sell to Lester. Then she and the little girl moved out to the Bend at the old man's offering, doubtless thinking what a kind and generous man he was."

Jennings felt his stomach tighten as he listened to Weatherby's story.

Later, after taking Ira to Miss Mindy's for pie, Coy returned to the livery, where he found Weatherby still dressed in his singing clothes. "I wouldn't advise doing blacksmithin' in that outfit," he said.

"Thought maybe you'd like to join me lookin' in on Buck Burton 'fore you head back to the ranch."

The young man was still in Doc Matthews's back room, though now seated in a chair instead of lying on the bed. Much of the swelling on his face was gone and there were stitches on his lips. The red and purple bruises were turning yellow. There was a splint on his hand, and bandages were wrapped around his abdomen. One eye remained closed, but he could see his visitors through the narrow slit of the other.

"He's considerably weakened, but I think once he can do more than take sips of broth and tea and resumes eating regular, that will change," the doctor said. "He's improved to a point where he now feels only terrible instead of like he's about to die."

Burton winced in pain as he attempted a smile.

The doctor placed a hand gently on his shoulder. "It is my professional opinion that this young man is strong and will properly mend, given time. For now, rest is what he needs, and we should leave him to it."

The visitors walked onto the front porch, where Matthews joined them. "He had a visitor last night. In walks Lester Sinclair himself, hat in hand and all sincere-looking, making apologies for what his boy did. Told Buck not to fret over my fee—said he'd be paying it."

Weatherby swore. "I didn't see Pete at his regular place at the saloon last night."

"Sinclair said he was punishing the boy by forbidding him to come into town."

"That won't last long," Weatherby said as he shook his head. "My guess is that ol' Lester's got himself a plan in the making."

As they slowly walked back to the livery, Jennings spoke. "You're figurin' that Sinclair is planning to try and claim Burton's farm, right?"

"Were I a gamblin' man, I'd say that's a good bet."

"If a man can't physically tend his property, he ain't got many options to consider."

"That's the other thing I was planning to speak with you about," Weatherby said.

He explained he had been riding out to Burton's farm daily, milking his cow, and seeing that his livestock were fed. "It's about all I can do, what with folks needing my services here in town. But the fruit in that small orchard he's got is fallin' to the ground to rot or be eaten by crows and raccoons. And his garden's badly in need of tending. And I worry that thieves might soon determine that there ain't no one livin' there, and help themselves to his belongings." He looked over at Jennings.

"I took a liking to you the day you arrived with your injured horse," he said. "And when you told of your plan to seek work out at the Bend, I didn't see it my responsibility to urge you to think twice 'fore doing so. Now, though, I think you've seen what goes on there. And, being honest, I have genuine concern for your safety should you stay. Clearly Pete don't like you, and that can only make for future problems if you don't consider moving on soon. "

Jennings smiled. "Can't say as I disagree."

"While there would be no pay involved," the blacksmith said, "what I was wondering is this: At least until Burton gets back to good health, would you consider moving into his cabin and caring for his place? You wouldn't go hungry, since he's got himself a half-decent smokehouse, and with proper care his garden will provide ample vegetables. And I could spare Ira to give you a hand if the notion suits you. I'm sure Buck would be agreeable."

Coy stopped and looked at Weatherby. "Your thinking is, it might be a way of keeping Sinclair from gettin' his hands on the farm."

"At the moment I've got no other plan."

Jennings sighed and looked off into the distance for a moment. "It seems a good idea to me," he said. "First, I'll need to inform someone at the Bend that I'll be taking my leave."

Weatherby smiled. "Yes," he said, "I reckon she'll be needing to know."

Chapter 10

A mother hen and her chicks scattered as Jennings and Dalton arrived at the dirt yard in front of the cabin. Ira and Bell had taken the lead, having previously made trips to the Burton Farm with Weatherby.

"This here's it," Ira said. "This is where Mr. Burton was livin' 'fore he had to go stay with the doctor."

Coy let his eyes roam from the small cabin to the corral shed from where Buck's cow bellowed her urging to be milked. There was a hog pen located upwind, and beyond that, the small orchard of pear and apple trees. Potatoes, tomatoes, and beans grew in the garden, with a well and the smokehouse nearby. He saw that firewood was neatly stacked and protected with a tattered piece of canvas that had no doubt once covered the wagon in which Burton arrived two years earlier. In the distance, rows of corn waved gently in the morning breeze. Beyond the field was a tree line that marked the eastern edge of the small claim.

Buck Burton had worked hard to make something of his forty acres. It was the kind of place Jennings hoped to one day own. That, however, was unlikely to happen any time soon now that there would be no more pay from the Bend of the River Ranch.

He worked a full day before approaching the ranch house after dinner. When Lester Sinclair met him on the porch, Jennings offered no explanation for his decision beyond the fact that he'd wished to move on. He considered a more elaborate story—suggesting he might join an old army friend working cattle up near Tascosa—but decided against it.

Sinclair shook Jennings's hand and wished him well, but made no offer to pay him for his final day's work. Nor did he suggest that Coy could spend a last night at the ranch before leaving.

Pete, sitting nearby with his brother, glared but said nothing. Repete seemed to pay no attention to the brief conversation.

"Then I'll gather my belongings and be on my way," Coy said.

"You take care," the elder Sinclair said. He struck a match to light his pipe, then disappeared back into the house.

It was dark by the time Jennings returned to the bunkhouse and retrieved his saddlebag from beneath his bunk. None of the cardplayers noticed when he neared the doorway and picked up one of the rifles that leaned against the wall. Nor did they see him dip his hand into a nearby bucket filled with ammunition and put the cartridges in his pocket.

Why not? he thought. Stealing from a thief wasn't really stealing.

After saddling Rodeo he walked him toward the corral, where he hoped to find April McLean and her daughter. As he approached he could see that the girl was holding a carrot out to the colt.

There was a look of surprise on April's face as she realized he was preparing to leave.

"I just wished to say good-bye," Coy said. "And to tell you if you ever need my help with anything, you can see Giles Weatherby at his livery. He'll know where I can be found."

He smiled down at the girl as he climbed aboard Rodeo.

Penelope was still waving good-bye when Pete Sinclair emerged from the shadows to glare at Jennings. April quickly moved between the men as the foreman yelled, "Good riddance."

The days passed quickly as summer soon faded to cooler weather. Jennings enjoyed working the farm, doing repairs that Burton hadn't gotten around to before his injuries, hoeing and harvesting in the cornfield and garden, tending the livestock, cleaning the well. They were chores he and his two sisters had often done on the family farm back in Arkansas. Briefly, he allowed himself to fantasize that Burton's place was his, that he was living his own dream.

Ira Dalton liked being away from the livery and in Coy's company. Only occasionally would he leave for evening rides. He found some traps hanging against the side of the smokehouse and began setting them down near the tree line, always returning with rabbits and squirrels that Jennings would prepare for their dinner. "Trappin' reminds me of a long time ago," Ira said one evening as they sat at the small table. "Only this time it seems more an enjoyment. And you cook a lot better, Mr. Jennin's, 'specially when you add dumplin's."

Coy wondered about his new friend's tortured life in hiding but never raised the subject. He felt certain he'd been told all Ira wished him to know.

"I'm thinking," he said, "that with the evenings now gettin' cooler, it might be time we build a proper pen for the chickens. Seems it would better protect them from varmints, and locating their eggs would be a sight easier if we provided them layin' nests. We should fix it so they can roost somewhere other than in the trees."

Dalton nodded with his usual enthusiasm. "You're the boss." It was his reply to virtually anything Jennings suggested. "Yessir, Mr. Jennin's, you're the boss."

Giles Weatherby would occasionally visit, bringing a bag of peppermint sticks for Dalton and fresh-baked bread he purchased from Miss Mindy. "Man ought not to live by corn bread alone," he would say. Sometimes he would stay until nightfall, once even helping Jennings butcher a hog and hang the meat in the smokehouse.

"It's a good thing you're doin' here," he said to Coy as they were finishing.

Though Jennings never asked, Weatherby always made it a point to mention seeing April McLean in town at Sunday singings.

In time, Buck Burton began to accompany the blacksmith. He still moved slowly and his blurred eyesight continued to cause him problems, headaches mostly, but it was obvious that he enjoyed being back on his farm. He would walk haltingly from one place to another, as if reacquainting himself with what was his, then sit on the cabin porch to rest and breathe in the smells of home.

"If the doctor will allow it," Jennings said one afternoon as Burton watched him hoe weeds from the garden, "maybe it's time you think about moving back. I reckon you're not yet up to daily chores, but me 'n' Ira could stay on for a time and tend them for you. You can always tell us to be on our way whenever you're of a mind."

Burton's smile exposed the empty spaces where teeth were missing. "I'm guessing the doctor would be pleased to be shed of me," he said. "He's done told me there's not much more he can do."

He reached out and shook Jennings's hand. "You know I got no way to repay you for what it is you've done."

Coy shrugged. "We've been eating your food, sleeping in your bed, and warming ourselves nightly by your fireplace. Seems to me it's been a fair exchange."

On Sunday morning Lester Sinclair entered the barn to find his elder son soaping a saddle. "Seeing as how you again made a drunk-staggering fool of yourself in town last night, I'm surprised to see you already engaged in something constructive," the father said.

Since there had been no takers to fight the previous evening, Pete had drunk so much that it was necessary for Poppy and his brother to tie him to his saddle for the late-night ride back to the ranch. At the elder Sinclair's request, they left him to sleep off his stupor in the barn.

Yet it was not his son's behavior in the Phantom Hill Saloon that prompted Sinclair's visit. He found him asleep in a back stall, snoring loudly. He gave him a kick in the behind, and Pete sat up, moaning and holding his head. "Am I correct," he said, "in recalling that you said you were gonna keep an eye on that Jennings fella?"

His mind was fuzzy and his head throbbed. "You mean the one who quit us a while back?"

"The same."

"What of him?"

"While I was in town, I stopped by Doc Matthews's house to see if Burton might be ready to talk about selling his farm. "He wasn't there. Seems he was feeling well enough to return home."

Pete was silent for a while, a puzzled look on his face. Finally he said, "Even if Burton's back to his place, it ain't likely he'll be able to do the work necessary to keep it up."

"That ain't a problem he has to concern himself with. Poppy informed me that he overheard Giles Weatherby telling how this man Jennings—who told me he was ready to move on—rode straight to town and volunteered to take care of things for Burton until he was again fit. As we speak, he's living out there, him and that half-wit who works for Weatherby, doing Burton's chores for him."

Pete rubbed a hand across a bearded face that was turning red with anger. Then he bellowed a loud curse. "That's no business of his. Why is it you suppose he'd do such a thing?"

"Because, you idiot, he wishes to see to it that young Burton isn't put in a position of needing to abandon his farm."

Pete stood up and began pacing, his jaw clenched. "I'll tend to it," he said.

Lester Sinclair shook his head. "No, you won't. What you *will* do is ride down to the Flats and see Ignacio. "Tell him he and his men have a job to do."

Outside, near the tack room, one of the hands finished hitching up the buggy April McLean would take into town to attend the morning singing. As she and her daughter waited in the shade of the barn, she overheard the conversation between Lester and Pete.

The purpose of her trip into Phantom Hill had suddenly changed.

Chapter 11

Pete Sinclair's arrival at Blue Flats was not warmly welcomed. The Mexicans glared at him as he approached, and Ignacio Garza didn't even bother to get up from his place near the cooking fire. Instead he stared into the flames and pulled a blanket tight around his shoulders.

Finally he spoke. "My men have been talking of returning to Mexico," he said as Pete kneeled next to him. "They are no longer happy working for your papa. The travel to find cattle has become longer and will be more difficult as winter approaches. They are growing restless and I can no longer reason with them."

Pete removed his hat and wiped his forehead with the sleeve of his jacket. "Is it me you've got a problem with?"

"I have worked for Mr. Sinclair for *muchos anos*," Garza said, "and he has treated me and my men with nothing but respect and gratitude. But you come to our camp and kill one of our compadres. Perhaps Antonio was not so good. Young and hotheaded. Maybe he was asking for a fight, but what you did was not necessary."

"He fired his pistol first."

"*Sí*, but wildly and with no harm to you. It would have been easy to disarm him. I would then have insisted that he apologize for his drunken behavior. But you chose to take his life. It was an evil thing you did. My men are not pleased, nor am I."

Sinclair stood and looked angrily toward those standing by silently, then down at Garza. "I got no cause to apologize or be regretful. I'd do it again if the situation was the same."

The men backed away, staring into the dirt.

"Ain't nothin' in Mexico for you and your boys 'cept jail. They're gettin' good money here, and plenty of food and whiskey. They got nothing to complain about."

Ignacio got to his feet, his look of defiance fading. "What is it you have come to see us about?"

"A job that'll pay you well," Sinclair said.

Ira sat on the cabin porch, whittling, as Weatherby talked with Burton and Jennings about the warning April McLean had delivered.

"She has no idea what they have in mind to do," the livery owner said, "but she's convinced that you're in danger. I share her concern."

"Do you have a guess as to what their plan might be?" Burton said.

Weatherby shook his head. "Something of a violent nature to convince you farming's no longer a safe occupation. Lester wants this place turned into more grazin' land for his cattle. And believe me when I tell you he's a man who gets what he wants."

Jennings looked at Burton's battered face. For the first time since meeting him, he saw fear in his eyes. He realized it was more than Buck Burton's body that had been broken. So was his spirit.

"Maybe it's time things get changed," Jennings said.

"That, my friend, is the kind of thinking that's apt to get a man killed."

Even as Weatherby spoke, Jennings was attempting to devise a plan. It would, he knew, be the Mexicans he'd seen on his ride out to Blue Flats who would carry out Pete Sinclair's wishes, whatever they were. Most likely, they would come at night, all five of them. The odds weren't good, but knowing they were coming might give him some advantage.

He would need to prepare quickly.

"Take Burton and Ira back to town with you," he told Weatherby.

Only Dalton attempted to argue. Shaking his head, he said, "I'm your helper, Mr. Jennin's. You're the boss. I should stay."

For the first time since they'd met, Jennings's tone was harsh. "Get on your mule and ride outta here. Go back to the livery. I won't be needin' you gettin' in my way."

As he watched their horses disappear, Coy felt a sense of dread he hadn't experienced since his military days. Yet this time it was different. At no time while wearing the uniform of the Confederacy had he ever felt the genuine anger demanded of one fighting for some cause; he had never viewed the Union soldiers as his personal enemy. That confusion ultimately led to his deserting the battle, even though it was all but over.

This fight, for which he had volunteered, was different.

Standing alone in the dusty yard, he surveyed his surroundings. The raiders would likely approach from the direction of the Flats, then ride along a beaten path that cut through the eastern tree line. From that point there would be little but open ground between them and the cabin.

There was no barn to burn, no cattle to stampede. A torn-down chicken coop or hog pen could easily be rebuilt. Same with the corral, where Burton's milk cow and mules—hardly worth the effort to steal—were kept. With the harvesting done, there was little damage that could be done to the cornfield.

What would be their target? Jennings turned toward the cabin. It had been solidly built of sod and live oaks Burton had cut when clearing his field, its chimney made of limestone. Inside, among the handmade table and chairs, the bed and shelves where personal belongings were neatly kept, was Buck Burton's life, his home.

Burning the cabin would be their mission. Rid a man of the roof over his head and he's left with little reason to stay his ground.

As he pondered what was to come, the words of Giles Weatherby returned. *"If what Miss April heard is true, it sounds as if they'd be told to do more than put fear into Burton. It was her worry that Pete was going to tell them he also wanted you left dead."*

It was nearing sundown when Jennings decided that the best vantage point from which to watch for the attackers was the roof. He walked Rodeo a safe distance away, leaving him to graze in a shallow ravine, lingering to stroke the horse's neck and scratch behind his ears. Then he returned to the cabin. He climbed a ladder attached to the back wall, taking the rifle and ammunition he'd stolen from the Sinclair ranch with him.

Leaning against the chimney, he began his wait. It was almost midnight when he saw the distant flickering of the torches.

When the raiders were still a hundred yards away, they dismounted and proceeded, shoulder to shoulder. There was enough moonlight for Jennings to see that three carried rifles. The other two held pistols and torches as they slowly advanced toward the cabin.

Jennings waited until he was sure they were in range and fired. Though he hadn't used a rifle since his army days, his aim was good, the shot hitting one of the torchbearers squarely in the chest. The thud of the bullet's impact was followed by a piercing scream as the man fell. The torch slipped from his grasp, its flame licking at his pants leg.

The others scattered as Coy continued shooting.

Return shots came out of the shadows, one ricocheting off the stone chimney, another slamming into the roof near Jennings's left boot. Squinting to detect movement in the darkness below, he saw that two of the attackers had taken cover behind the smokehouse and one was kneeling in the corral, hiding behind Burton's frightened mules.

He was unable to determine the location of the fourth man until a rapid series of pistol shots from below pierced the roof. One of the attackers had managed to find shelter inside the cabin and was shooting wildly into the ceiling. Coy pressed his body to the chimney as he drew his Colt and returned fire.

A loud stream of Spanish curses came from below before the man staggered onto the front porch, holding both hands to his bloodied face. His legs gave way and he dropped to the ground.

Now there were only three.

As the shooting continued, Coy's throat was getting dry and his leg was beginning to ache. As the night wore on, his mind began playing tricks. He was back on the battlefield, in a desperate fight against a Union attack. Only this time he was alone, with no one to help.

He had to preserve his ammunition, so he assumed the role of sentry, watching for any movement that might suggest Sinclair's men were approaching the cabin. Only an occasional flash came from behind the smokehouse as an impatient shot was fired.

The end, he suspected, would have to wait until daylight. And once the attackers could see that his only protection was the narrow chimney, he would be at a serious disadvantage. He crawled on his stomach to reach the ladder and climbed to the ground. Slowly he made his way through the darkness toward Burton's orchard. From the shelter of the trees he could see the corral and the silhouette of the gunman who had taken shelter there. He was kneeling, his eyes fixed on the cabin.

Jennings moved toward the back of the enclosure, his Colt holstered and replaced by the knife he'd used earlier when slaughtering one of the hogs.

The Mexican was unaware of Jennings's presence until he felt a hand over his mouth and saw the faint glint of the blade. There was no time for him to struggle before his throat was cut, blood and life quickly draining away.

The mules watched the man's dying convulsions without interest.

There were just two left. Jennings worked his way

back to the cabin. As he slipped through the back window, exhaustion swept through him. His head ached and his bad leg throbbed, but he forbade himself to give in to the feelings. He had to finish the job if he wanted to live.

He summoned all the strength he had left and moved Burton's table in front of the open doorway and kneeled behind it, balancing his rifle and pointing it in the direction of the smokehouse. There, in the home of a man he barely knew, he would make his stand.

An hour passed. It was all he could do to stay awake. Then, as a clabber gray dawn appeared, he heard a voice call out.

"Senor, you are being foolish. It was not our plan to come and kill you. But now, because of what you have done to our friends, we must. You have no chance, so why not step out onto the porch so we can be done with this?"

Jennings's reply to Ignacio Garza was a shot that splintered bark from the corner of the smokehouse.

"We will now make your death a slow and painful one," Garza shouted.

When the two Mexicans suddenly abandoned their cover and began running toward the cabin, shouting and rapidly firing their pistols, Jennings was caught by surprise. The attackers made sure they were separated by a considerable distance, forcing him to aim at one at a time.

He fired at one and the man dropped. Then he felt a searing pain in his shoulder and fell backward onto the floor, his rifle skidding away. Before he could get back to his feet, Garza was standing in the doorway, breathing heavily, his eyes aflame, his gun pointed at Jennings.

"It pleases me that my previous shot did not go into your heart," Ignacio said. "Now it will be my pleasure to see that one does."

As he took aim the front wall of the cabin reverberated with a loud boom and the doorway filled with smoke. There was a look of disbelief on Garza's face as he tried to brace himself against the doorframe. He fell forward, his pistol still in his hand. The back of his head had been blown away.

When the smoke began to clear, Jennings was able to make out a familiar form standing over the dead man. Ira Dalton, wide-eyed and shaking, was holding a shotgun.

Jennings tried to stand but fell back to the floor, unconscious.

At first the voice seemed to be from far away, then slowly came closer. "Mr. Jennin's, you gotta wake up. Open your eyes, Mr. Jennin's. Don't be dead. You're the boss. Yes, sir, you're the boss. . . ."

Coy opened his eyes to see Ira kneeling over him. "Seems I owe you an apology for speakin' to you the way I did yesterday," he said.

Dalton had left his side only long enough to get water from the well to wash the wound. He'd retrieved a pillow and placed it beneath Coy's head and covered him with a blanket.

After the dizziness cleared, Jennings braced himself on his good arm, rose to a sitting position, and sipped at the cup of water Dalton offered him.

"How is it you come to be here?" he said.

"When it got dark I sneaked Mr. Weatherby's shotgun from the tack room and left as if taking my evenin' ride. I was worried you might be needin' me," he said, "so I rode here. When I heard shootin' I waited down by where you put your horse. I don't mind tellin' you, Mr. Jennin's, I had terrible thoughts running through my head all night. Then, just before first light, I figured it was time to sneak up this way and see if you was okay. I was just arriving out by the orchard when those men started runnin' and doin' all that yellin' and shootin'. They was bad people, wasn't they, Mr. Jennin's?"

Coy smiled. "Yes, they were. Real bad people."

Dalton tore one of Burton's shirts into strips and attempted to bandage the wounded shoulder. "This ain't likely to help much," he said, "but it'll have to do till we get you to the doctor's house."

Jennings flexed his hand, then slowly lifted his arm and made a circling motion. It was painful, but nothing seemed to be broken and no muscles appeared to be damaged. Most of the bleeding had already stopped. "Appears the bullet went clean through," he said, "in the front and out the back."

"You was lucky, I'd say. But you still need proper doctoring."

"And I'll see to it shortly," Coy said. "First, there's something I need to do while you ride back to town and tell Weatherby and Burton that all's well here at the farm."

Dalton was hesitant to leave but finally stepped over the body that lay in the doorway, averting his eyes as he did so.

"I'll be along in a while," Jennings said. "And if Mr. Weatherby gives you grief about taking his shotgun, tell him I'll be discussing the matter with him once I get there."

"Okay, Mr. Jennin's, okay. You're the boss."

The task took longer than he'd anticipated. Jennings

hitched Burton's mules to a wagon the farmer used for hauling sod and lumber, then began gathering the bodies. Pain shot through his injured shoulder as he struggled to drag each of the dead Mexicans across the yard, then lift them into the wagon.

The sun was peeking over the horizon by the time he slowly steered the mules along the route from which the attackers came. It was almost noon before he reached Blue Flats.

Rats scattered and buzzards took flight as he entered the squalid campsite.

With no one to hear, Jennings allowed himself to cry out in pain as he unloaded the bodies and positioned them side by side near the fire pit.

Chapter 12

"You've been sleeping near a day and a half," the doctor said as Jennings opened his eyes.

Coy was in the bed previously occupied by Buck Burton, a fresh bandage covering his wound.

Ira, dozing in a nearby chair, jumped to his feet when he heard Doc Matthews's voice. Giles Weatherby, on the front porch with his shotgun resting in his lap, rushed into the house.

Coy lifted his head and smiled as the livery owner approached. "I see your shotgun's been returned," he said.

"That we can discuss at a later time. How you feelin'?"

Before Coy could answer, Miss Mindy burst into the room, a wicker basket under her arm. "I got fried bacon sandwiches and a big helping of stew," she said as she gently patted Jennings's arm. "See to it you eat." She turned to Dalton. "I'll not have pie till Sunday. You come by then and I'll have a slice set aside for you."

And with that she hurried out the door, smoke trailing from her cigar.

"That," said Matthews, "is the first time in my recollection she's ever delivered food to anybody—man, woman, or child."

"Makes you right special, I reckon," Ira said. "Yessir, Mr. Jennin's, you're special, okay."

Coy winced as he lifted his arm. "I'm feelin' in a sharin' mood," he said. "Since there's no pie, you want the stew or a sandwich?"

Ira chose one of Miss Mindy's sandwiches. "I'll take it with me," he said, "'cause I've got things Mr. Weatherby's needin' done at the livery. But I'll be back."

Word of what had occurred spread quickly following Dalton's return to town. He had delivered an excited but sketchy account before the wagon pulled up in front of the livery that afternoon with an unconscious Jennings on the seat.

"I wasn't sure you was actually alive until you finally showed up," Weatherby said. "I'd admire to hear more detail of what took place."

Coy's version wasn't much more expansive than Dalton's. It was, he said, the men from Blue Flats who attacked, just as he'd expected. They came with torches, intent on burning Burton's cabin.

"And to see you dead as well, I 'spect," Weatherby said.

Coy swung his legs over the edge of the bed and reached for his britches. "Yep," he said, "I recall one of 'em saying as much. And they would have done so if Ira hadn't shown up when he did. For that reason I'd thank you not to scold him too harshly for taking your shotgun."

"Truth is, after he shared with me what he'd done—I don't recall that boy ever talkin' so much—I went down and bought him a full sack of peppermints. He thinks mighty highly of you, you know. What he done took courage I didn't expect him to have."

The room was silent as Jennings dressed. The doctor was helping Coy with his shirt when Weatherby said, "You know this ain't near over. There's folks who are gonna be highly upset about what took place out at that farm. My advice is you get on that horse of yours and be on your way soon as you feel you can ride. If you're of a mind, you might think on takin' young Ira and his mule with you."

At the Bend of the River Ranch, Lester Sinclair paced furiously, his voice loud and profane. He threw a coffee cup against the fireplace as Pete described the gruesome scene he and the Poppy found at the Flats.

"They're all dead, even Ignacio?" his father asked.

"Buzzards was having themselves a feast."

"It's a message he's sendin'."

"I don't 'spect the farmer would want to get himself crossways with us," Pete said. "I doubt he got the gumption for it."

"Then I suppose it's that Jennings fella," his father said.

Pete grunted. "I suppose, though I find it hard believin' he could stand off five men alone. Unless he was made aware they'd be coming and ambushed 'em."

Lester Sinclair slumped into a chair and shook his head. Who was this man standing up against him, killing his men, and thwarting his plans? Why had this stranger taken on the responsibility of protecting the Burton Farm?

And now what would be *his* answer to the bodies left at the Flats?

Lester shook his head. "This man's a fool who's got himself a death wish."

Pete smiled grimly. "And I'll be happy to see it fulfilled."

His father glared at him. "You idiot, it's been tried once without success," he said. "See that it doesn't happen a second time. I'll not tolerate it. Finish the job or don't come back here."

On Sunday morning Giles Weatherby stood across the street from the big live oak, staring up at its spreading branches. "Soon the leaves will be falling," he said.

For the past few days Jennings had again taken up residence in his livery, and there was no further discussion of his leaving. Instead he rode daily out to Burton's farm, doing what he could to help the owner despite having the full use of but one arm.

As Coy approached, the coffee cup in his hand not hidden by the sling he wore, the blacksmith kept his gaze on the tree. "Bein' as you're hardheaded enough to still be here," he said, "I think it would be advisable if you attended singing this morning."

"You know I ain't one for singin'."

"Won't be none today," Weatherby said. "I've sent out word that it's to be a town meetin' instead. Everybody's been invited, saints and sinners alike."

By midmorning the crowd included almost every resident of Phantom Hill. Children played nearby as their parents talked quietly, wondering why they had been summoned. Coy stood to one side, looking to see if April McLean and Penelope were among those on hand. He was disappointed to see neither.

He did, however, notice Repete Sinclair and another hand from the Bend standing near the back of the gathering. Making his way over to Weatherby, he pointed them out. "Might want to be careful namin' names as you speak your piece," he said.

The blacksmith shook his head. "I've seen 'em, but it makes no matter. I shoulda spoke my piece and named names a long time ago."

When Weatherby asked for quiet and began speaking, it was obvious he had given considerable thought to what he would say.

He talked of the dismal history of Phantom Hill, its lack of progress and ability to attract new residents. He called out the names of several of the community's settlers, asking if things had gone as they expected.

His question was met with silence.

"We've got us no law, no rules for folks to abide by," he said. "Most of you have taken it upon yourselves to tend your business in a proper and Christian way. And that's to be admired. But I needn't tell you that there are those who don't cotton to doing what's right. You know who I'm speaking of."

Heads nodded, and there were low murmurs of agreement.

"We've chosen to ignore bullying and brawling in our street—myself included. And because of it, our friend Buck Burton might not be with us today if it wasn't for the healing efforts of Doc Matthews."

A few "amen"s filtered through the crowd.

He then addressed the recent event at Burton's farm. "It'll surprise no one here to know that the reason for what took place was to convince our neighbor to give up his property and move on. Each one of you knows it ain't the first time. You're likely wonderin' if your homestead might be next, because we've allowed one man to spread fear among us."

From the midst of the crowd someone called out, "Lester Sinclair!"

Weatherby took a breath, then nodded. "Lester Sinclair is right. It's him who wishes to keep us afraid and beholden. Him and those workin' for him."

Jennings watched the crowd as more and more of the residents nodded. The livery owner had their attention.

"To protect our land and provide Phantom Hill with a proper future, it is time we begin watchin' out for one another and not allow anyone to take what we've worked hard to make our own. It's time law is put in place and abided by."

Even before the crowd began to disburse, the two men from the Bend were on their horses.

After watching them ride away, Jennings moved to Weatherby's side. "I reckon your message will soon be delivered."

As they walked back toward the livery, they saw three mounted men waiting near the entrance. Two wore dusty chaps and had bedrolls tied behind their saddles, signs they had been on the trail for some time. The other was an Indian, his black hair shining in the morning sun.

Chapter 13

Weatherby shaded his eyes as he looked up at the riders. "Who might you boys be?"

"Name's Will Bagbee," the man nearest him said as he dismounted and began slapping dust from his hat. He was over six feet, broad-shouldered, and had a faint scar that ran from high on his cheek into his unkempt beard. He nodded toward his fellow travelers. "That there's Clay Taylor. The big Injun I call Tracker, since I can never recollect his proper Comanche name."

"And what brings you to these parts?"

"Lookin' for something that's been stole," Bagbee said. "For now, though, our main concern is getting our horses fed and finding us some coffee. Ran out a couple of days back."

"Both can be seen to here," Weatherby said. "Make yourselves welcome."

While Ira fed and watered the horses, Bagbee and Taylor sat on crates Weatherby had placed around the coffeepot that dangled above a small fire pit. The

Indian sat on the ground, leaning against the wall of the livery. He'd not spoken a word.

"I see you got yourself a lame arm," Bagbee said to Jennings.

"He was shot in the shoulder," Weatherby said. "Bullet went clean through without breaking nothin'."

"Indians?"

"Nope, Mexicans. Banditos, I reckon they'd be called."

"They known to rustle cattle?"

Jennings pushed away from the wall. "Instead of this verbal dancin' around it," he said, "what say you tell us the purpose of you being here? What is it that's been stole and you're hoping to find?"

Bagbee looked at Taylor, who gave a slight nod. "We work on a spread up near the Red River, called Blue Norther," he said, "and a while back some of the boss's cattle was herded away in the middle of the night. Same thing occurred at some neighboring ranches recently. With Tracker's help, we been following their trail. It's led us here."

Jennings poured the remainder of his coffee into the dirt. "You didn't bring enough men," he said.

"That can be taken care of."

Jennings told them what he'd witnessed at the Bend of the River branding corral and Blue Flats canyon. As he finished, Ira approached and tugged at his good arm. Coy smiled.

"I plumb forgot Miss Mindy promised you a slice of pie," he said. "Best we excuse ourselves to go down to the Eatery and see to it."

For the first time since the town meeting, Weatherby's face brightened. "If you boys are hungry, it's likely she's still got some of her Sunday stew—rabbit, most likely—and maybe leftover corn bread," he said.

"We ain't et since yesterday," Bagbee said, and the others got to their feet. Looking toward Tracker, Bagbee asked, "Reckon she'll serve a redskin?"

"Mindy's not what you'd call a real particular kind of hostess. I 'spect she'd be more than happy to feed the Devil himself if he arrived with money to pay. Just be mindful you're likely to discover a few cigar ashes on your plate."

Lester Sinclair's face reddened as he listened to his youngest son tell of what was said at the town meeting. "And my name was used?"

"Yessir," Repete said. "More'n once." He was standing on the far side of the room, distancing himself as much as he could from his father.

"And you're saying it was Giles Weatherby who was doing the talking?"

Repete nodded.

Sinclair swore. "What about Jennings?"

"He was there, but I don't recall him having anything to say. I do recollect he had his arm in a sling. Last I seen, him and Weatherby was walking back toward the livery."

"Go fetch your brother and tell him I need to see him. Now."

Lester was standing in front of a wall safe, putting money in a saddlebag, when his son arrived. "I need you to take a trip," the father said. "Have Poppy ride with you and go down to the border and hire on some new men to replace those we lost at the Flats. Buy 'em outta jail if need be. In fact, that would be my preference. I want men who'll be willing to do as they're told and won't ask any questions about it."

"How many we talking about?"

"As many as this will buy, half a dozen, ten maybe," Sinclair said as he shoved the saddlebag toward his son.

As Ira and Tracker groomed the newly arrived horses, Coy Jennings walked alone into the pasture behind the livery, hoping to sort his thoughts. Weatherby's talk had both impressed and troubled him. It was courageous to openly discuss the problems facing the townspeople—something apparently never before done, at least in public—yet there had been no real plan put forth to deal with the domineering Sinclair.

Weatherby, despite the gumption he'd displayed earlier in the day, was no match for the wealthy landowner. The people of Phantom Hill were farmers, not fighters. Coy knew that word of the meeting would already have reached the ranch and some manner of retaliation, a show of force, was likely to come. Most likely, plans had begun as soon as the dead Mexicans were discovered at the Flats.

When in control, Lester Sinclair could play the part of the gentleman rancher. If, however, that control appeared to be slipping away, his response would demonstrate his true nature.

A phrase from Weatherby's drunken rant weeks earlier came to mind: *"We've got us no law . . ."*

Coy wondered what Sinclair might be thinking. And what effect it would have on the townspeople.

He returned to the livery to find Bagbee sitting on the bench out front, whittling.

"We need to do some more talking," Jennings said.

Bagbee motioned for him to sit. "I could hear some of what was said at that meetin' earlier in the day," he said. "Seems you folks are dealin' with big troubles."

"And they're likely to get bigger."

"Tell me about this fella Sinclair."

"There's no doubt he's the one who's got the cattle you've come looking for. But be assured, getting 'em back to their rightful owner ain't gonna be easy. He's got men working for him who would just as soon fight as whittle on a stick. With all due respect, you and your friends wouldn't have a chance against 'em."

"How many hands he got, you figure?"

"A couple of dozen at least, and I'd guess he could round up more if the need presented itself. It was Mexicans he keeps out on the edge of his ranch who attacked Burton's farm."

Bagbee stared down at the pile of shavings between his feet. "You in the war?"

Jennings nodded.

"Yank or Reb?"

"I wore the gray for a time."

"We whupped you boys good 'n' proper," Bagbee said as he stood and placed his knife in its sheath. "Mostly, I reckon, 'cause we had folks who was better at fightin'." He grinned. "Let me do some thinking on what you've just told me."

An hour later, Jennings saw Tracker leading his horse from a stall. A pouch hung from the Indian's shoulder.

"As best I could, I wrote out a report to my boss, telling him we located his herd and of the situation you've described," Bagbee said. "It'll get delivered in a couple of days. Tracker did a considerable amount of messengerin' in the war and he don't stop much for sleeping. And if things go as I expect, that ol' lady down at the eatery is shortly gonna have herself a number of new customers to feed—all, I might add, who fought proudly for the Union cause."

"Wish to explain that?"

"My boss rode with General Albright at Gettysburg before the war ended and he took up ranching," Bagbee said. "Despite his decision to settle in the South, he'll not hire anybody who wasn't Union."

Jennings laughed. "That'll be fine with me. And I doubt the townsfolk will care either. I'll look forward to their arrival," he said. "One thing, though. I'd suggest you not refer to Miss Mindy as an 'ol' lady' when she's near enough to hear. That might be cause for the war to get started up all over again."

Chapter 14

April McLean had just delivered a pot of chicken and dumplings to the ranch hands and was walking back to the main house when Repete Sinclair approached her.

"Evening," she said without stopping.

Repete hitched his pants and fell into step alongside her. Since her arrival at the Bend, he was the only member of the family she'd really felt comfortable around. He lacked the swagger of his father or the mean spirit of his older brother. Often browbeaten, criticized, and even made fun of—the nickname his father had given him was a show of spiteful disrespect—he seemed as out of place on the ranch as she so often felt.

"I was wondering if I might have a word with you," he said as they neared the kitchen door.

"Of course."

"But not now, not here. Would you be comfortable speaking to me somewhere private?"

April heard the concern in his voice. "Is there something wrong?"

"Yes, ma'am. I fear there might be. And I believe you need to be aware of it."

She knew his father had ordered him to go into town for some reason on Sunday, something she didn't recall him ever doing before. Too, she thought it strange when the elder Sinclair told her an axle on the buggy she usually used was broken and she'd have to forgo her weekly visit into Phantom Hill.

"Is it something to do with what went on at the Sunday singing?"

"There wasn't no singing," he said, "just talk about my pa and how he's making things hard for folks."

April thought back to her earlier conversation with Giles Weatherby and put a hand to her mouth.

"I don't mean to scare you. But we need to talk. Soon." He glanced toward the bunkhouse, then the barn.

"In the evenings my daughter and I sometimes visit the mare and her foal in the corral behind the barn," she said. "Perhaps I could wait until Penelope and everyone else has gone to sleep and meet you there."

Before he could answer, Poppy emerged from the bunkhouse. Repete turned and walked toward the house.

Later, as they stood in the darkness, Repete told her of his father's reaction to the meeting in Phantom Hill. "He won't let something like that pass without a response." He spoke in a whisper and his words came rapidly as he explained what had occurred at the Burton Farm. "Pa 'n' Pete are convinced somebody was warned of what was to take place," he said, "and they'll not likely rest until they find out who's responsible."

Even in the darkness he could see April had begun to shiver, and he resisted the urge to comfort her. "I don't care if you was the one who did it. But I don't think you and your little girl are safe here. I can't rightly say what is gonna happen, but I—"

April reached out and touched his arm. "What of Mr. Jennings? Is he okay?"

"On Sunday he had his arm in a sling for some reason, but he seemed fine. But I can't promise how much longer that'll remain the case. Not only is my pa angry with him for what he done at that farm, but, as you likely know, Pete ain't happy with the fact that you and Jennings have been friendly. It's Pete's temper that worries me most."

April reached through the fence to stroke the colt's neck. "I'll not let any harm come to my daughter," she said. "What do you suggest we do?"

"Leave." There was an urgency in his voice. "Pete's gone for a few days and I think it best you was gone before he returns."

"But your father . . ."

"Ain't likely to be pleased neither. It'll have to be done without his knowin'. So, here's my thinking. It's but two days till Sunday, and Pete ain't likely to have returned by then. You and your girl make plans to head out for slinging like you normally do. I'll accompany you, telling Pa I'm riding into town to see if I can learn more about what might be going on."

"But that's likely to cause you trouble."

"The important thing is you don't return to the ranch. Once we're there, I'll speak with Jennings for his advice on what might best assure your safety." He forced a smile. "I 'spect he'll gladly help."

April moved closer and kissed him lightly on the cheek. "Thank you," she said. "You're a fine man. It worries me to think what might happen to you should your father and brother learn what you're doing."

There was a look of sadness on his face as he turned to go. "Truth is," he whispered, "I really don't much care."

The cantina, located in the center of a dusty village just south of the Rio Grande, was dimly lit and reeked of sweat, tobacco, and warm beer. Though it was the middle of the afternoon, it was filled with solemn-faced patrons. Most were young.

"I reckon ain't much work gettin' done today," Pete said as he looked around the room.

"There is no work," Poppy said, "until it grows dark and they can cross into Texas to search for things to steal."

"How is it you know about this place?"

"Long ago, before I went to work for your papa, I lived not far from here." He nodded to a table where four men were slumped over their beers. "In another time, I sat in that very place."

"Waiting for nightfall?"

Poppy snorted and strode toward the bar.

It occurred to Pete that he knew little of his traveling companion. For as long as he could remember, the quiet Mexican had worked on his father's ranch. Of all the hands at the Bend, he was the most loyal, ever ready to do whatever Lester Sinclair asked. There were even times when Pete felt a tinge of jealousy over the fact that his father seemed to trust a nonkin more than him.

"*Dos cervezas, por favor,*" Poppy said to the graying and overweight man standing behind the bar.

As they drank the foul-tasting beer, Pete was aware of hushed talk in Spanish from across the room. One of the few words he understood was *gringo*. "What is it they're sayin'?"

Poppy grinned. "They're wondering if you have money and should be robbed."

Only then did Pete fully understand why he'd been told to leave the saddlebag his father gave him hidden on the opposite side of the river. And why Poppy was with him. It was far more than his knowledge of the language.

"You know, it was in this place that I found Ignacio for your papa," Poppy said as he finished his beer and crossed himself.

"I didn't expect you to be a religious man," Pete said.

"Oh yes, amigo, I am *muy* religious. I believe the Bible when it tells us to take 'an eye for an eye.'"

With that he turned toward the room. "Now," he said, "I must speak with these men and learn who their leader is, who the new Ignacio will be."

Pete motioned toward the bartender for another beer. It pleased him that the second one didn't taste as bad as the first.

Giles Weatherby began carrying his shotgun everywhere he went during the day and slept with it propped near his bed at night. Will Bagbee sensed the livery owner's apprehension and, with little to do but wait for Tracker's return, stayed close by.

Meanwhile, Clay Taylor passed his time making regular visits to Burton's farm to see that all was quiet. Dalton resumed his evening rides, always accompanied by Jennings.

"Maybe ain't nothing more's gonna happen," Ira said as he bounced along on his mule. "Could be the bad folks now know you're the boss and want no more trouble."

Jennings was moved by his young friend's innocent

optimism, but he knew such was not the case. He was certain the problems of Phantom Hill were just beginning. Whenever a plan to retrieve the stolen cattle from the Bend was devised and put in motion, no one would be safe.

Later, as they sat by the dog's grave site, Ira stoking a small campfire, Jennings was surprised to realize how attached he'd become to the little town and the people he'd met. His thoughts wandered to Weatherby, Doc, Miss Mindy, and all those who came to lift their voices in song beneath the oak tree on Sundays. They were the kind of people he one day hoped to become.

Closing his eyes, he visualized April McLean and Penelope at the ranch and struggled to think of a way he might keep them safe.

Ira rose and climbed onto the ridge. "No torches, Mr. Jennin's," he yelled back. "Don't see no torches."

The sky was black and sprinkled with stars as they slowly returned to the livery. Ira was quiet for most of the ride, waiting until they neared town before speaking. "You reckon I'll be going to hell 'cause I shot that man?"

"No, son, it's my understandin' a man don't go to hell if he's saved another's life."

"All the same," Dalton said, "I'm thinking maybe I'll start joining in on singing next Sunday."

The sun was barely up when Weatherby entered the livery and shook Jennings awake. "You gotta come and have a look at this," the blacksmith said. "I've seen nothing like it in all my born days."

From outside Jennings could hear the clatter of wagons and a chorus of voices. Several mules bayed.

"Get your britches on and come look," Weatherby said.

In an open space across the street from the livery, a flurry of activity was under way. Farmers were unloading lumber and tools from their wagons while several women carried baskets of food to the shade of the large oak tree.

Buck Burton, accompanied by Clay Taylor, waved from a wagon loaded with large stones and freshly cut firewood.

Miss Mindy stood in the middle of the street, arms folded, as she called out instructions and puffed on her cigar.

Jennings reached her first, with Weatherby a step behind. "What's going on?" he said.

Mindy smiled. "I figured it time we had us a new eatery," she said. "Ain't gonna be quite as fancy as the one you've been frequenting, but it'll do us fine. If, of course, it don't get burned down." She looked at the men standing next to her. "Seein' that don't happen will be your responsibility."

For several days she had been spreading the word of her plan among the townspeople. She'd explained the need of everyone's help to raise a building, build tables and chairs, and lay rocks for a fire pit to cook on. For her plan to succeed, the farmers had to be willing to donate a portion of the crops from their gardens and an occasional hog or calf. A deer on occasion, she'd said, would be nice for making chili. Profits from the new enterprise she outlined would be equally shared by everyone who pitched in. She would run it and see that the earnings were fairly distributed.

"Everybody's been willing to take the gamble," she said. "I'm thinking on calling it the Town Café."

Weatherby watched the activity in amazement. "Being as this was your idea, why not call it Miss Mindy's Town Kitchen?" he said.

She blew cigar smoke into the air. "I'll think on it. Only thing important to me is that I'll no longer be beholden to Lester Sinclair. I've worked my last day for that worthless man."

They watched the workers as they used picks and shovels to level the ground for the building's floor. For the moment, Jennings didn't allow himself to think about what Sinclair's reaction to losing one of his businesses would be. Instead he marveled at the community effort playing out before him.

"There's another thing you need be aware of, Mr. Weatherby," Mindy said. "I know that you admire taking a Saturday-night drink—or more—but thanks mostly to the urgings of the womenfolk, most of their husbands have promised to no longer frequent Lester's saloon. From now on, the Sinclairs and their hired hands will be doin' their drinkin' and fightin' by themselves."

Weatherby shook his head. "Tell you what," he said. "I'm known to brew a passable beer, and I've got a not-too-bad recipe for pear brandy. If you'll allow me as a partner, I'll see to it you have something other than coffee and sweet tea on your menu."

"I suppose that would be nice," she said, "but I'll tolerate no drunkenness and no fightin'."

Jennings was pleased to hear Weatherby laughing as they walked across the street to join the workers.

When the men stopped to have lunch, Coy watched as Mindy circulated among them, thanking each individually.

"She seems a mighty strong woman," he said.

"That she is. Strong . . . and stubborn as any of them mules tethered over yonder. She and her husband, and their two boys, came here from somewhere in Tennessee. Her husband fell ill on the trail and passed before they could find a doctor to tend whatever ailed him. She and her boys buried him somewhere in the Ozark Mountains, then made it this far on their own."

"What became of her boys?"

"They was both lost early in the war, fightin' for the South just like you done. It was after learning they was killed that she began running the Eatery for Sinclair."

A familiar feeling of guilt briefly tugged at Jennings. "You know," he said, "seeing as how she seems to have ample grit and a gift for organizing things, I'd not be surprised if she could be a fine mayor if this town ever decides it's in need of one."

Again Weatherby laughed. "Don't recall ever hearing of a female holding such an office," he said, "'specially one so often foul-tempered and with such a cravin' for cigars." He paused. "But you know what? I think you're right."

Chapter 15

The concerns that weighed on the people of Phantom Hill briefly eased as they focused their efforts on construction of the kitchen. For three days the men worked in shifts from sunup until dark. When some put down their tools and left to tend chores on their farms, others arrived to take up the work.

Several women helped Mindy pack pots, dishes, and silverware from Sinclair's eatery and move them down the street. "He'll not be needing these, nor is he likely to pay what's still owed me," she explained, "so I see it as a fair trade."

The grand opening was scheduled for Sunday, after singing.

On Saturday night, Lester Sinclair and several of his men arrived in town and hitched their horses outside the saloon. They were surprised to find an almost deserted building. Even the banjo picker was absent.

"Ever'body die or somethin'?" one of the Bend's hands asked the elderly man standing behind the bar.

"I reckon folks have been so busy down to the other end of town of late they're too wore out," he said.

Sinclair hurried into the street and walked in the direction of the livery, his ranch hands close behind. When he reached the new building, he stopped, folded his arms to his chest, and silently stared for several seconds.

"Won't be open for business till tomorrow," Giles Weatherby called out. He was sitting in front of the livery with Jennings and two men Sinclair didn't recognize. "As you can see, Miss Mindy's decided to relocate."

The ranch owner glared at Weatherby but said nothing. Only after he turned to walk back toward the saloon did he let out a loud curse.

Bagbee watched as he walked away, then turned to the blacksmith. "I reckon that's the rancher fella Sinclair you've spoke of."

"That's him."

"Didn't look none too happy."

Weatherby stroked the barrel of the shotgun lying across his lap. "Never does. But I'm guessing you ain't seen nothing yet."

Ira Dalton completed his morning chores long before people began gathering for Sunday singing. He'd fed the horses and his mule, then turned them into the pasture for exercise while he made sure the water troughs were cleaned and filled. Coffee was already brewing.

"I'll be listenin' to hear your voice," Jennings said as he watched his friend attempt to smooth his hair, then hurriedly rub a rag across his weathered boots.

"Yessir, Mr. Jennin's, I'll be singing real loud. I sure will."

Long before Giles Weatherby appeared, his shotgun replaced by a Bible, the crowd was larger than any he could remember. Many of those on hand had already spent a considerable amount of time in town, helping build the kitchen.

As the gathering began another hymn, Jennings climbed onto the bench in front of the livery, in hopes of seeing April McLean and her daughter. He finally found them in the shade of the oak tree. He was preparing to walk over when he heard Repete Sinclair's voice.

He had entered the back door of the livery and was standing in the shadows.

Instinctively Coy reached for his Colt.

The young Sinclair raised his hands. "I mean you no harm," he said. "I was just hoping we might talk for a moment—about the McLean woman and her daughter." There was a worried look on his face as he beckoned Jennings inside. "I'd just as soon no one sees us having a conversation."

Jennings followed him into the stable.

"Miss McLean is in danger if she stays out at the Bend," Repete said. "It's not hard to guess that she was the one who told you that Ignacio and his men would be coming to that farm. Once my brother becomes aware of it, I fear what his reaction will be. He and my pa are already angry over what resulted. I've spoken with April and I believe she's now convinced to remain in town. She knows I planned to talk with you."

"What you've done is the right thing," Jennings said.

"What now needs deciding," Repete said, "is how best to keep her from harm's way once my pa learns she won't be returning."

"It's your brother that worries me."

"He won't find out for a while. Him and Poppy rode south to Mexico a few days back and aren't likely to return soon."

Jennings didn't need to ask the reason for their trip. They were, he felt certain, seeking replacements for the men he'd killed at Burton's farm.

From the doorway of the livery, he could see that the singing had ended and Weatherby was reading Scripture in a booming voice. Shortly he would invite everyone to celebrate the opening of Mindy's new kitchen.

Coy looked at the young Sinclair. "What is it that's caused you to come?"

"April McLean is about the only good thing I've seen at the ranch, and it's not right that she should be affected by what goes on. Havin' spent time at the Bend, you know what I'm sayin'."

Jennings nodded. "I'll see to her safety."

As the meeting was breaking up, Coy approached April, a big smile on his face. "It's a pleasure seeing you ladies again," he said, doffing his hat to Penelope.

The girl returned his smile and said, "It's nice seeing you again too, Mr. Jennings. Since you've been gone the colt has grown—a lot."

"I'd admire to see him. But, for the time being, you've likely heard we have us a new eatin' establishment in town. I was wondering if you and your mama would be my guests for the special lunch I hear Miss Mindy and her helpers are preparing."

Penelope tugged at her mother's sleeve. "Can we, Mama? Please."

April still had not smiled but looked directly at Jennings. "I think perhaps we should," she said.

* * *

The crowd waiting to be served the first lunch at Miss Mindy's Town Kitchen was such that the seating inside quickly filled. Others spread blankets and enjoyed their meals of fried pork, turnip greens, potatoes, and corn bread picnic-style. Even with the help of several women volunteers who served, washed dishes, and saw to those who wished second helpings, the scene was frantic. Mindy barked orders in one direction, then another as she checked to see if the pear cobbler was done. "'Fore long, folks'll be licking their plates," she said to Weatherby. "We're 'bout out of everything."

Once the children finished eating, they began playing games, their shouts and laughter echoing throughout the gathering.

"This," said Weatherby, "is how things should be."

April had eaten little and said less before Jennings rose and excused himself. "I'll be back shortly," he said. "I need to have a word with someone." As he spoke he searched the crowd for Doc Matthews.

The doctor nodded as he approached. "I feared I'd be too late," he said, wiping his mouth with his handkerchief. "My attention was needed to extract some festered teeth from Raymond Dobson's cow. The infection was causing her milk to have something of a sour taste."

"You're a dentist as well?"

"Whenever there's a need. What is it I can do for you?"

"Can we speak privately? Maybe you'd take a walk with me over to the livery."

"Only if I can be assured to get back 'fore the cobbler's served," the doctor said as he got to his feet.

Once they were away from the others, Coy said, "I need to speak with you about April McLean."

Matthews nodded. "A mighty attractive woman," he said. "I tended her daughter last winter when she developed a case of the croup."

"They came into town for the singin' this morning," Jennings said, "and they ain't inclined to return to Sinclair's ranch. We can keep a watch on her and the little girl here in town, but they'll be needing a proper place to stay. With Miss Mindy's vacating of the eatery, the rooms she had out back are no longer available. And the livery ain't no place for womenfolk."

"So you're wondering if the back room in my house might be—"

"That's what I was gonna request."

"You tell her it would be my pleasure to have visitors who aren't beat up or shot for a change," Matthews said. "You can assure her that the room where I do my sleeping is up front, so they'll have their privacy."

Jennings shook the doctor's hand. "Payin' you rent might take some time," he said.

"Not to worry. Just warn her and the young'un they're likely to hear some frightful snoring now and again."

Penelope was playing games with the other children when Coy returned and told April of the arrangement he'd made.

She reached out and touched his hand lightly. "Serious things are soon going to happen, aren't they?"

"I'm afraid so," he said. "But I'm gonna see to it that you and Penelope are kept safe."

Ira had approached unnoticed and overheard the

promise. "You can feel assured by what Mr. Jennin's says. He'll watch over you real good, yes, ma'am. He's the boss."

For the first time all day, April McLean smiled. "It seems he is," she said.

Chapter 16

Pete Sinclair was drunk and growing impatient. Poppy's efforts to round up a crew were taking longer than expected. "I eat one more bite of *cabrito*, I'm liable to keel over dead of heart failure. I hate that stinkin' goat meat almost as much as I do the music these people play."

"On the brighter side, it seems you've developed a taste for their *cerveza*," Poppy said.

"How long 'fore we can head home?"

The problem, Poppy explained, was selecting the ideal man to serve as the leader of those they would take back to the Bend. After a few days of observing, Poppy determined that an older man named Armando Blanca was the one most feared and respected. Tall and still muscular despite his age, he immediately received everyone's attention whenever he entered the cantina.

And he was the only one in the village who spoke English.

"As a boy," he told Poppy, "I knew Antonio Lopez de Santa Anna. We were friends back in Xalapa. But his family was rich and mine was poor, so we grew apart. As you know, he became a famous army *caudillo* and *el presidente*, while I could do nothing but steal cattle from the gringos across the river." He spat on the dirt floor. "But I have no regrets." He stroked his drooping mustache and broke into a grin that displayed a mouthful of discolored teeth. "It has paid me well and allowed me more time with the senoritas."

Poppy didn't know how much of what Blanca said was true, nor did he really care. What concerned him was that somewhere along the way, apparently, he'd learned to be a stubborn negotiator. In exchange for convincing the others to accompany them to the Bend, the big Mexican wanted all the money. He would, he said, assume responsibility of distributing it as he saw fit.

"Sounds to me like his plan is to keep most of it for hisself," Pete said. "Reckon the others trust him?"

"We're not here to find men who are trustworthy," Poppy said. "I think we should get the money and make the deal so we can be on our way. Your father will be wondering why we've been delayed."

"I'll fetch it. I'd admire to be away, even for a short while."

"Best I do it," Poppy said.

"No," Pete said, "I'll be the one tending my father's money."

The hiding place they'd chosen was a hollowed tree just a few miles on the other side of the Rio Grande. It was a short ride, yet Sinclair was sweating profusely and his head was throbbing even before he found a shallow spot where he could cross the river.

After some difficulty, he located the rotting tree.

He was retrieving the saddlebag when he heard a rustling in the nearby bushes. Before he could turn he felt the barrel of a pistol pressed against the back of his head.

"*Hola*, amigo," the young man who had followed him from the cantina said as he bent to take Sinclair's gun from his holster.

As his attacker leaned forward, Pete drove his right arm back, the elbow catching the man just below the throat. The Mexican gasped and fell backward, his pistol flying from his hand.

Getting to his feet quickly, Sinclair kicked the fallen man in the face, then picked up his gun. It was already cocked and ready to fire.

"You're a fool." He then placed the barrel against the man's forehead and pulled the trigger. "By wantin' it all, you got yourself nothing," he said, then tossed the gun away.

Poppy was waiting outside the cantina when Sinclair returned, the saddlebag draped over his shoulder and a riderless horse trailing him.

Blanca walked into the sunlight and glared.

"Did you have anything to do with planning to rob me?" Pete asked.

A slight shake of the head was Blanca's only reply.

"If you wish to collect your friend," Sinclair said, "best you hurry. I left his body to float down the river."

"He is of no importance. He was young and stupid."

Poppy breathed a sigh of relief as Pete tossed the saddlebag down to Blanca. "Can I now assume we've got ourselves a deal and can get on our way?" Sinclair said.

Blanca opened the bags to inspect the money. "We will leave tomorrow at first light."

Once April McLean and her daughter had settled in, they busied themselves cleaning Doc Matthews's house. Every night, they saw that his evening meal was ready when he returned from his daily rounds. Since the doctor was a tidy housekeeper, she found little to do besides sweep the already clean floors and dust the photograph of him and his late wife. Most days she took Penelope with her to the kitchen, where they helped Miss Mindy.

The fact that Coy Jennings, often accompanied by Ira, came by for coffee every day assured April that she and her daughter were being looked after.

Mindy, meanwhile, began baking pies more often. "Keep coming here regular," she said to Ira, "and I'll put some meat on them skinny bones."

Dalton's response was a quick burst of laughter and a polite "thank you, ma'am."

"How are you and Penelope taking to town livin'?" Coy said as April brought his coffee one afternoon.

"Folks have been really nice, real friendly. The lady down at the general store came to the house the other day with a change of clothes for us, asking for no payment. I'm guessing the doctor made an arrangement with her. And he seems real taken with Penelope. They're becoming friends. She also enjoys having other children to play with. The only thing she misses about being at the ranch is seeing the colt in the evenings. She asks about him every night as I'm getting her ready for bed."

April pulled out a chair opposite Jennings and sat. "Truth is," she whispered, "I can't help feeling scared, worrying that Mr. Sinclair, or maybe Pete, might come to town and confront me for leaving so abruptly. They're people who aren't used to having anyone go against their wishes. I find myself lying awake nights, worrying that Repete got himself in trouble for helping me . . . it bothers me some that there's no one there to cook for the hands . . . and they'll not be pleased their buggy I borrowed hasn't been returned."

"Sounds as if you're a born worrier," Coy said. "Seems to me the only people you need be concerned about is yourself and your daughter. It ain't likely anybody at the ranch will starve, and I doubt there's any need for the buggy, since you're the only one I ever saw use it."

She smiled. "I suppose you're right. But what about Repete?"

To that question Jennings had no answer.

Giles Weatherby entered Mindy's Kitchen after shoeing Clayton Taylor's horse, nervously wiping his brow as he nodded toward Coy and April. "I need to speak with Miss Mindy," he said.

The urgency in the blacksmith's voice troubled Jennings. "You'll find her out back, adding wood to the fire so she can start her cookin'," he said. "Is there a problem?"

"No problem," Giles said, "I just wish to speak to her on a matter I've now been thinking about for several days. It can wait no longer."

She was hanging a large pot above the fire when he approached. "Stew won't be ready for at least another hour," she said.

"That's not what I've come about. I got something I want you to think on."

Mindy rolled her eyes. "Giles, are you suddenly too blind to see how busy I am?"

He said, "You should be mayor of Phantom Hill. What's your thinking on the matter?"

For a moment, Mindy was silent, letting her cigar droop toward her chin. Her ladle dropped into the pot. Then she began to laugh. "My thinking is you've finally gone plumb crazy, Mr. Weatherby. Where on God's green earth did you come up with such a notion?"

"It was Jennings who first got me to thinking on it," he said. "We watched as you brought folks together to build this kitchen, and how you generated a community spirit I ain't seen here before. This town needs itself a leader if it's to amount to anything. Somebody to look up to, somebody who can makes decisions people will show respect for. You and I both know there's likely to be troubled times ahead and folks are going to be needing somebody strong and forceful to see to their needs. It's my opinion you're that person."

Her laughter faded into a blush. "Need I remind you there's no such thing as a female mayor? Never has been, if I know my history. Last I heard, womenfolk ain't even allowed to vote. It's pure foolishness to even have this conversation."

Weatherby raised his hand. "Just promise me you'll think on it. We've got no rules wrote down that we're obliged to follow. We can do as we please. I'll wait till Sunday for you to decide. Then, if you're willing, I'll ask for a show of hands at singing."

"Would those be hands of men *and* women?"

"Even the children if they're of a mind."

"Let me give it some thought," she said. "In the meantime, would you mind taking your leave so I can finish my cooking?"

* * *

Ira was leading his mule from the livery while Jennings saddled Rodeo, preparing for their evening ride. Seeing they were ready to leave, Miss Mindy waved as she crossed the street. "I need to speak with Giles if he's here," she said, "and I'd like it if you would remain for a minute."

Weatherby appeared in the doorway.

"Foolhardy as your suggestion sounds," she said, "I've decided I'm agreeable to it. I can make no promises, but it occurs to me we do need better organizing if Phantom Hill is ever to amount to a hill of beans. I accept your offer and will do whatever I can to help should the town's residents see clear to vote me mayor."

Giles smiled broadly. "I think you will—"

"Hold up. There one request I'm needin' to make before we shake on this matter."

"And that is?"

"If, as you say, folks are to feel we're a proper town, we need some laws that are abided by. Not that we have that many scalawags among our own, but, as you know, we're occasionally visited by those with a likin' for drunkenness and fightin'. And from time to time, livestock gets stole or a farmer's smokehouse gets raided. It's time we have somebody who sees unlawful deeds don't get ignored. We need us a sheriff."

Weatherby's face went blank. "I agree with what you're sayin', of course, but as you know, we ain't even got us a jail."

"We can see to it one's built, just like we done with the kitchen. Seems to me that's the kinda thing a mayor has a responsibility to make happen."

"But we ain't even got a badge a sheriff might wear. Or money to pay him wages."

"'Fore we headed to Texas, my husband was briefly a sworn deputy back in Tennessee. I've kept his badge and have it somewhere among my memory treasures. It don't say 'sheriff' on it, but seems to me it would suffice. As to payment, you can offer the same you're likely to pay me for bein' mayor, which is nothing—unless you count the misery it'll cause."

She looked at Jennings. "I believe folks would feel good about *you* wearin' a badge," she said.

Dalton let out a whoop and raised his hands into the air. "Yessir, Mr. Jennin's, it's a fine idea. A real fine idea. If I'm allowed, I'll sure be votin' for ya."

Miss Mindy smiled at Ira. "Of course you'll get to vote," she said. "So will April McLean and that pretty young'un of hers."

The following Sunday morning, even before the first hymn was sung, Miss Mindy was elected mayor of Phantom Hill. Her first official act was to nominate Coy Jennings to serve as the town's sheriff.

She was pinning the badge to his shirt even before the last hand was raised.

Chapter 17

Armando Blanca let his eyes roam the Blue Flats encampment. "This," he said, "is a pigsty."

Pete couldn't care less what he thought. "It'll look better once you and your men have done some cleaning up and we've returned with supplies," he said. "I'll see to it you have plenty to eat—beef and pork instead of that foul-tastin' *cabrito*—and whiskey for washing it down. Being as the weather's turning cold, I'll also bring along some blankets."

As he and Poppy rode away, Blanca was still cursing.

They arrived at the ranch house just before sundown and were met on the front porch by Lester Sinclair. "'Bout decided you boys took up residence down south or got yourselves killed," he said.

"There are now a dozen new men waiting at the Flats," Poppy said before heading toward the bunkhouse.

"I'm near starved," Pete said as he walked toward the kitchen. Lester said nothing as he watched his son survey the clutter of unwashed dishes. The room smelled of stale grease.

"I ain't much of a cook," Lester said. "Same can be said for the boys out in the bunkhouse."

"Where's April?"

"Gone." Sinclair waved his son toward the sitting room. "I need to tell you what's been happening in your absence."

Pete paced, veins in his neck bulging. "Gone where? Tell me and I'll go fetch her back."

"What Repete told me," his father said, "was he seen her in town at that singing gathering a couple of Sundays back, but he wasn't aware of her making the return trip. We ain't laid eyes on her since."

"I'll go find her."

Lester raised a hand. "Not till we have ourselves a plan," he said. "I know you got an eye for the woman, but while you've been gone I've done some hard thinking. I fear April McLean has betrayed us. Not just by taking her daughter and leaving, but also by giving warning that the Mexicans would visit Burton's farm. I'm now inclined to blame her for the deaths of Ignacio and the others. It's my guess she must have overheard our discussions on the matter and told someone what we had in mind to do.

"Since then there's been all manner of strange goings-on in town. My eatery has been abandoned and a new one built. And now there seems to be a boycotting of the saloon. When I was last there I also saw a couple of well-armed strangers who didn't look as if they had any interest in farming."

Pete poured himself a drink and slumped into a nearby chair. "Jennings," he muttered. "Nothing but bad things have occurred since he showed up. He's the one turning folks against us."

"I've thought on that as well. It's likely you're right."

"He needs killing," Pete said as he threw his glass into the fireplace. "He needs killing and the whole town of Phantom Hill burned to the ground."

Lester Sinclair stared at his son, seeing himself as a younger man—angry, impulsive, mean. It pleased him.

"Where's Repete?"

"He's taken to sleeping in the barn of late," Lester said. "You'll likely find him there. But I don't want you to go blaming your brother for April's leave-taking."

The last sentence was lost on Pete as he rushed onto the porch and down the steps.

Repete was at the far end of the barn, removing his boots, when his brother appeared in the doorway. The younger Sinclair had been avoiding his father and even the hands for days, fearing that his role in April's leaving might somehow be discovered. He'd also dreaded Pete's return.

"You in here, little brother?" Pete said. There was anger in his voice.

"Fixin' to bed down."

"We need to do some talkin' first," Pete said as he walked past bundles of hay and carefully stacked sacks of grain. "Pa says when you was in town recently you didn't bother to see to it April returned to the ranch." His face was inches away and his foul breath caused Repete to turn his head.

"Ain't none of my business what she chooses to do."

"Where is it she's gone to?"

Repete shrugged. "That's also none of my business, but if I was to speculate, it's as far from you as she can get."

Pete shoved a shoulder into his brother's chest with such force that it knocked him against the wall. He then smashed a fist into Repete's face. "You're worthless and a pitiful excuse for a Sinclair," he said. "It shames me to call you kin." He turned and walked from the barn.

Blood trickled from Repete's nose as he whispered, "That shame runs both ways."

It was midday when Tracker, followed by a wagon and more than a dozen men riding two by two, reached Phantom Hill. The town was far busier than it had been when the Indian left to deliver Bagbee's message. The sounds of hammers and axes filled the air as a new building was being constructed directly across the street from the saloon.

"Looks as if the cavalry's arriving," Jennings said as he joined Bagbee and Clay Tucker in the street to greet the newcomers.

"As you can see, that's what they once were," Tucker said. Several of the men were wearing remnants of Union uniforms. "I've cleared it with Weatherby for them to bivouac in the pasture down behind the livery."

In short order the wagon was unloaded and tents were being pitched. Ira and Weatherby hauled watering troughs and helped unsaddle the newly arrived horses. Dalton greeted each of the strangers personally.

Miss Mindy walked across the street to watch the flurry of activity. "Lordy," she said, "I'm gonna be needin' more help with cooking. Most likely we'll have to start feeding folks in shifts."

Bagbee smiled. "The man drivin' the wagon—his name's Jakie—is also the cook, though I can't say I'd compare what he prepares to what you serve. Still, I think he'd be more'n happy to help out. He does make fair to middlin' coffee, and his biscuits are half passable."

"Then send him over to the café soon as he's settled

and I'll make his acquaintance. I hope he thought to bring some provisions."

As the men watched the campsite take shape, Bagbee placed an arm on Jennings's shoulder. "I was thinking while waiting for them to arrive that in your newly elected job as sheriff, you'll be in need of deputies." He pointed toward the tent village. "Long as they're here, consider 'em deputized."

"I was countin' on it when I took on the job," Coy said.

"One thing you'll need to know. For the time bein', these men are tired and no doubt thirsty. I won't be able to convince them to refrain from visitin' the saloon, no matter who's the owner."

"We can make that exception . . . at least till ol' man Sinclair decides to get stubborn and refuse service."

"And should they get a bit rambunctious?"

Jennings grinned. "Jail's not yet finished."

Bagbee patted the badge on Coy's chest. "Then all we've got to do in the days to come is figure out how we're going to get my boss's cattle returned to him." He paused. "It ain't my intention to involve the town in whatever it is needs to take place."

"I pray things turn out that way," Coy said, "but I'd like to sit in on your planning just in case."

"Seeing as how you know the lay of the land out at Sinclair's place," Bagbee said, "I was countin' on your help."

As he left to walk to the encampment, Weatherby approached Jennings, smiling. "I gotta say I'm right pleased to see these folks here," he said. "You take a look at some of 'em? They appear mean enough to bust an anvil bare-handed. I doubt Sinclair and his hands have met up with the likes of these fellas."

Jennings forced a smile. "Well, you recollect they won one war," he said.

As he arrived at the ranch house, Isaac Hatchett, the saloon-keeper, was sweating profusely despite the fact that the first norther of the season had just hit. It was his first visit to the Bend in longer than he could remember, and arriving without an invitation made him nervous.

Lester Sinclair walked out on the porch. "What brings you here on this chilly morning?"

"There's things going on in town I felt you needed to know of."

Sinclair invited him inside to sit by the fire. "I'm already aware folks have chosen to stay away from the saloon."

"That was far from the case last night," Hatchett said. "The place was filled with men I never seen before. Near as I can tell, they just arrived. At first, I figured they was just passing through. But seems they've camped down behind the livery."

"Did they state their reason for being in town?"

The bartender was hesitant to admit that he'd carefully avoided asking questions of those for whom he'd poured drinks until past midnight. "I found them to be a secretive lot," he said. "Wasn't much talking I could hear. But I can tell you they was all wearing sidearms and looked as if they knew how to use 'em."

"Anything else?"

"I'm told Phantom Hill's now got itself a sheriff," he said.

"And who might that be?"

"That Jennings fella."

* * *

Sinclair sat alone long after his visitor left, pondering Hatchett's news and trying to determine what it all might mean. Something, he knew, had dramatically changed in Phantom Hill since his men failed so miserably in their attempt to drive Buck Burton from his farm. It puzzled him that the townspeople seemed suddenly united and determined to improve the town, even feeling a need for a sheriff. And who were these recently arrived men the saloon-keeper spoke of?

Despite the fire, he felt cold, and his stomach tightened.

He walked into the yard and signaled to one of the hands. He instructed him to locate his younger son and send him to the house. Repete soon arrived with his nose badly swollen and the skin below one eye turning purple.

"Your brother and Poppy took a wagonload of supplies to the Flats this morning," Lester said. "I want you to ride down and catch 'em before they head back." He didn't bother asking about his son's injured face.

Repete showed little response to the urgency in his father's voice. "What is it I'm to tell 'em?"

"Have 'em bring the Mexicans back with them," Lester said. "They'll now be staying in the bunkhouse."

Part Two

Part Two

Chapter 18

For several days most of the hands at the Bend followed morning orders to arm themselves and ride the perimeter of the ranch, watching for any unusual activity. Poppy, accompanied by Blanca and two of his men, took up sentry duty at the ranch's entrance.

All remained quiet, however, testing Lester Sinclair's patience and adding to his concern.

"Could be you've got no call to worry. Might be nothin's gonna happen," Pete said as he leaned against a rail on the front porch. Still, as he'd done every day since hearing the news the saloon-keeper had delivered, he urged his father to allow him to ride into town. "I could set your mind at ease by learning what's going on," he said. He had quit mentioning his desire to determine the whereabouts of April McLean.

"What day is it?" Lester asked.

"Unless I've lost track, it's a Friday."

"That being the case, I'm thinking tomorrow night we should keep to our normal routine by riding into town and having us a drink or two." He poured the remainder of his bitter coffee into the dirt. "If, as I believe, there's some manner of confrontation brewing, it should be us who starts it. Alert some of the boys to ride with us."

"What about the Mexicans?"

Lester shook his head. "We'll leave them here for Poppy and Repete to look after," he said. "They can see to it nothing gets stolen from the house."

Miles away, Coy Jennings was using a stick to draw a map in the dirt as Bagbee watched.

"I wasn't there long enough to get a full understanding of the size of the place," he said. "But I do know that the biggest part of Sinclair's herd is kept here." He pointed to the southern edge of his crude map. "There's a canyon not far, next to a camp where some of his hands once stayed. That's where the stolen cattle are kept until they're brought in for branding."

"Our intent's not to take all his herd," Bagbee said. "We only want what belongs to our boss . . . and perhaps a few more to account for our time and risk."

"Is there any chance what you're plannin' might be carried out peacefully?" There was no real hint of hope in Jennings's voice.

Bagbee shook his head. "You've begun sounding like a sheriff," he said. "Truthfully what you're askin' ain't likely. Not if what you've told me of this Sinclair fella is true. Once he's made aware that his cattle have disappeared back to where they belong, he'll likely want someone to be held accountable and pay. I'd be surprised if he wasn't already in that frame of mind, even before he finds his cattle gone."

Weatherby had told him of the gunfight at the Burton Farm, and how the event had aroused the townspeople. He'd also shared with him the warning that April McLean delivered.

"I hope you've come to realize you're safe here only as long as we're in town," he said.

"That's about how I'm thinkin'," Coy said.

At first, Jennings thought it strange that Bagbee had let so much time pass since the arrival of his men. He hadn't even bothered to ask how many men there would be at the Bend. Coy finally realized he was not planning a cattle rustling so much as preparing for a military action. Bagbee's patience was impressive. Not only was he showing attention to the possibilities that might occur; he was allowing his men—his troops—to be rested and ready.

"Could I persuade you to take a ride with me out to this canyon you've mentioned?" Bagbee said. "Maybe tomorrow night? We could have Tracker accompany us. It would be to our advantage to better know the lay of the land."

"Fine by me."

As the two stood up, Penelope McLean approached, skipping across the dusty street. "Mr. Jennings, my mama said to tell you there's chili left over at the kitchen," she said, "and pie for Mr. Dalton, if he's hungry."

Coy called out toward the livery, "Ira, you've been invited for pie."

For a moment, the appearance of an excited Ira Dalton and the smiling face of a little girl allowed him to forget the troubles he feared were soon to come.

Armando Blanca was invited to accompany the Sinclairs and their ranch hands into Phantom Hill. As the men gathered in front of the ranch house, Lester issued instructions. "It'll not be our intent to confront anyone or do any fightin'. This is only to appear as one of our regular Saturday-night visits—and show our numbers. Our purpose is to look and listen, and determine who these new folks in town might be and their purpose for being there."

Pete stood next to his father, noting that for the first time he could remember, Lester Sinclair would be wearing a pistol to town.

"It will be good to taste some of the whiskey your son promised but failed to deliver," Blanca said. "Will there be senoritas at this place?"

Lester glared at the Mexican, then spoke to him for the first time since his arrival at the Bend. "Just see to it," he said, "you cause no trouble unless you're told. Do I make myself clear?"

"*Sí*, senor," Blanca replied.

By the time they arrived at the saloon, it was almost filled with patrons, and a half moon was on the horizon. A man none of them had seen before sat outside near the doorway, a beer bottle in one hand as he petted a mangy-looking dog with the other. He nodded as Sinclair passed.

Bagbee, Jennings, and Tracker had ridden in the opposite direction to take a southern route to Blue Flats.

When they arrived, Bagbee shook his head as he surveyed the deserted encampment. "People was actually livin' here?"

"Men from Mexico, hired to rustle cattle and other things."

"Like occasionally raidin' somebody's farm?" He pointed to a fresh mound of dirt near the old adobe building. "Don't reckon I need to ask why such a big hole was recently dug over there."

Jennings didn't reply. He led Bagbee and Tracker to a nearby ridge that provided a view of the box canyon, then pointed toward the horizon. "If the moon was a bit brighter you could see there's a trail that heads that way," he said. "It leads to the pasture I spoke of. You'll likely find a large herd of longhorns grazin' there. It's probably the best way to enter the ranch."

With Pete following him, Lester Sinclair made his way to the back of the saloon. Three strangers were seated at his table. "Seems you fellas are in my place," he said. None of the men looked up. Pete pushed past him, but his father held him back.

"Perhaps you'll allow me to have a sit and buy you a drink," Lester said. Only when he introduced himself did one of the men look up.

"Name's Clay Taylor. Boys, let's provide Mr. Sinclair some room," he said.

Sinclair sat and called for whiskey. After the bartender placed a bottle on the table, the ranch owner looked at Taylor. "We don't get many strangers in here," he said. "Certainly not as many as I'm seeing tonight. Where you fellas from?"

"Up north," Taylor said.

"And what is it brings you our way?"

Taylor reached for the bottle and filled his glass. He downed the shot in one swallow, then stood. "Pleasure meetin' you, Mr. Sinclair," he said as he nodded toward his companions. "Time we turned in."

Pete had been standing at the bar. As they walked away, leaving Sinclair alone at the table, he walked over. "They have anything of interest to say?"

"It seems they're not much for talking."

"Same with the others," Pete said. "I never heard

this place so quiet. Could be that'll change once they've had more to drink."

But by the time he returned to the bar, the crowd was already beginning to thin. Blanca sipped at his whiskey as he watched the young Sinclair signal the bartender for another shot. He was well on his way to getting drunk.

"You drink like a man whose heart is heavy," Blanca said.

The young Sinclair stared into his glass. "You ain't been hired to make conversation—or observations. I've got something I need to do, so I'll ask that you to keep a watch on my pa till I return." He downed another drink, then made his way toward the doorway.

He walked in the direction of the livery.

He wondered what the half-completed building across the street was intended to be. When he reached the darkened kitchen, he stopped in front of it to silently curse the strange changes that were taking place.

Across the street, the front door of the livery was partially open. He walked over and stood listening. Only the breathing of horses resting in their stalls broke the silence. "Anybody to home?" he called out.

When there was no reply he made his way into the dark building. He staggered through the livery to the back door that opened onto the pasture where the visitors were camped, stumbling over something that blocked his way. Opening the door slightly to allow in moonlight, he was able to see the dim outline of a buggy.

As he stood staring at it, he heard a faint sound coming from the loft. Someone was humming a hymn.

Pete listened for a moment, then spoke. "Show yourself."

He squinted up into the darkness as a form slowly made its way down the ladder. His pistol was drawn. "You're that feebleminded fella," he said as Ira reached the floor of the livery and stepped into a ray of light.

"I just returned from taking my mule for a ride," Dalton said. "You here to rob Mr. Weatherby? If that's the case it ain't likely you'll find much."

Sinclair looked at the wide-eyed young man standing in his bare feet. "No," he said, "I ain't no robber. What I want to know is where Giles Weatherby is. I need to speak with him."

"Don't know."

"What about that fella Jennings?"

"Sheriff Jennin's?" Ira said. "He rode away before the sun went down and I ain't seen him since."

Pete pointed toward the back corner. "Where's the woman who drove that buggy to town?"

Dalton shook his head vigorously—until Sinclair's backhand knocked him into the ladder.

"Even someone dumb as you ought to know better than to lie to me." Pete reached for a pitchfork leaning against the wall and pressed it to Dalton's chest. "I'm of a mind to burn this place down, with you in it."

"I don't know where they're at."

Pete kneed him in the ribs, and Ira sank to the floor and curled into a ball. He covered his face with his hands, struggling to breathe. Sinclair repeatedly smashed the toe of his boot into Dalton's body. Ira was barely conscious when he felt a gun barrel pressed against his forehead and heard the click of a hammer being pulled back. In a voice that seemed to come from somewhere far in the distance, Sinclair continued to ask where April McLean was hiding.

Pete was still yelling when he felt arms closing around him from behind, pulling him away. He swore and tried to break free.

"I have not come to hurt you," Armando Blanca said calmly, "but if you wish I will see that you're lying in the dirt next to the boy you have just beaten. I am stronger than you, amigo. I am known to be a good fighter. And I am sober. The choice is yours."

"What are you doin' here?"

"Your father feared you had gone seeking trouble and sent me to find you." Blanca loosened his hold.

Pete's shoulders slumped and he shook the Mexican off. He picked up his pistol. He was breathing heavily, and feeling as if he might be sick to his stomach.

Blanca looked down at the battered young man. His breaths were shallow and irregular. Blood trickled from his mouth.

"He is not likely to live," the Mexican said.

Pete grunted. "Let's get outta here."

As they walked from the livery, Armando grasped Sinclair's arm. "I was wrong earlier, senor, when I said you had a heavy heart," he said. "It seems you are a man with no heart at all."

Sinclair pulled away and bent forward. With his hands braced against his knees, he vomited.

The saloon was dark by the time Jennings, Bagbee, and the Indian returned to town. At the livery, several lanterns were lit, and men from the encampment milled around out front. Giles Weatherby sat on the bench, his hands covering his face. He was shaking, and tears leaked through his fingers.

Jennings quickly dismounted and approached the blacksmith. "What's happened?"

"It's Ira." He lifted his eyes toward Coy and slowly shook his head. "It don't look good."

"Where's he at?"

"We took him over to Doc Matthews to be tended."

"What happened?"

"I was over visitin' with Miss Mindy about town business. When I returned I found him inside, near dead. Someone beat him up bad."

Jennings turned and ran toward the doctor's house, Bagbee close behind. Several of the visiting ranch hands stood on the porch, each holding a rifle. They silently moved aside to allow Jennings to enter.

In the back room, Doc Matthews was cleaning Dalton's wounds as April stood nearby, cradling a basin of water. Miss Mindy was at the foot of the bed, wringing her hands as tears ran down her cheeks.

Dalton was unconscious. His face was bruised and badly swollen, his bare chest a mass of ugly welts and cuts.

"He gonna make it?" Jennings said.

The doctor looked at him but didn't reply.

"You can't allow him to die," Jennings said, his voice breaking.

"I'll do all I can," the doctor said, "but it might require help from someone with a power greater than mine."

Even as he spoke, Miss Mindy was quietly praying.

Coy remained at his friend's bedside through the night. It was near dawn when April brought him a cup of coffee and said that Will Bagbee was outside and wished to speak with him.

"This business," Bagbee said, "ain't the doing of none of my men. I want you should be clear on that. They were told they could visit the saloon last night, but weren't to indulge to the point of gettin' themselves drunk. No man sober and right-thinking would have beat up somebody like what was done to that poor boy."

In his hand was a hat, sweat stains rimming the base of its brim. "I was in the livery soon as it got light and found this. It was lying over near where the beatin' took place, part covered in the hay."

"I think I know whose it is. Was there people from the Bend visitin' the saloon last night?"

"That's my understandin'. Clay told me he met Lester Sinclair and spoke with him briefly. I'm told his people rode in with him."

Jennings's jaw clenched. He took a deep breath and reached for the hat. "I'll see it's returned to its proper owner," he said.

"Is it your intent to arrest him?" Bagbee said.

"No," Jennings said. "I'm gonna kill him."

Chapter 19

Poppy saw the cloud of dust being raised by the buggy and the men riding alongside it well before it arrived. He and the two men assigned to stand guard at the ranch's entrance were waiting, guns drawn, as the visitors approached.

"You're not welcome here," he said.

Despite the fact that his arm remained in a sling, Jennings managed to rein the buggy to a stop. "Didn't expect to be. But unless you and your friends make way and let us pass, it'll likely be the last mistake you ever make." Coy nodded toward the three men riding alongside. "These folks carrying rifles are military-trained and ain't had the opportunity to shoot nobody in quite some time. As sheriff of Phantom Hill, I've given them the right to fire their weapons on anyone who looks to cause trouble. Poppy, I know you're a man of few words. I expect now would be a good time for you to remain that way and let us go by. It's not you I've come to see."

The ranch hand glared at Jennings, then swore in

Spanish before he holstered his pistol and signaled the others to do the same.

"Another time," he said as the buggy, followed by Jennings's saddled horse, passed.

Lester Sinclair was walking from the barn when the visitors arrived. His jaw tightened as he recognized several of the men who had been in the saloon on Saturday night. He also saw it was his buggy Jennings was driving.

"What are you doing here?" he said. "How'd you get past—"

"Poppy was gentleman enough to invite us in," Jennings said. "In answer to your first question, I got two purposes for my visit. First off, I wanted to return this fine horse and buggy that belongs to you. Second, I wish to speak with the man who owns this." He sailed Pete Sinclair's hat toward the ranch owner.

Lester let it fall at his feet. "It's not familiar to me. That's what a sheriff's job is nowadays? Returnin' buggies and trying to find the owner of a hat?"

"Where's your boy Pete?"

"You'll not find him here," Sinclair said. "And I resent you coming here with accusations."

Jennings pushed past him. "As long as I'm here," he said, "I'll have a look through the house—in case you might not be tellin' the truth."

Sinclair glared at the sheriff. "You 'n' me ain't gonna get along, are we? You need to know I have little use for people who enjoy acting too big for their britches."

After his search of the house, a crowd of hands gathered as the men accompanying the sheriff looked through the barn and the bunkhouse, only to return shaking their heads.

"He don't appear to be here," Bagbee said. "I'd not recognize his horse, but a fella in the barn told me it and a saddle are gone."

"Could be he's out tending the stolen cattle you're lookin' for," Jennings said.

"I've got no stolen cattle," Sinclair said.

Jennings was untying Rodeo's reins from the back of the buggy. "Not for much longer," he said. As he climbed into the saddle he looked down at Sinclair. "I got one more thing of yours that I've not returned. When I took my leave of this place, I borrowed one of your rifles from the bunkhouse. I'll be needin' to keep it for a while longer." As he spoke he turned his eyes to the hat that still lay at the ranch owner's feet. "I've got use for it."

In the shadows of the barn, Repete Sinclair silently watched as the visitors turned to ride away.

Coy felt better astride Rodeo as they returned to town. Bagbee and Taylor rode alongside him.

"You think it was wise to alert him that we're looking for our boss's livestock?" Bagbee said. "That leaves us without the element of surprise."

"Lester Sinclair's far too smart to be surprised," Jennings said. "His purpose in coming into town Saturday night was to learn what you and your men are here for. I ain't suggesting he was told directly by any of your people, but you can rest assured he figured it out."

What he didn't mention was that he felt by his alerting Sinclair, whatever confrontation was to play out would be at the Bend rather than in town. The ranch owner would most likely be far more interested in defending his own property than doing battle in Phantom Hill.

"My suggestion," said Jennings, "is that you get on with your business in a timely manner, now that he knows you'll be comin'. He'll have his men waitin'."

While Jennings was confronting Sinclair, Bagbee and Taylor had tried to take count of the number of hands working at the ranch. "By what I could tell," Taylor said, "their bunkhouse is apparently filled to overflowing. Appears some are even sleeping in bedrolls on the floor. If my arithmetic is right, they have a considerable numbers advantage."

Coy thought back to his brief time living there. "You seen those two fellas riding with Poppy when he tried to block our way? They couldn't speak a word of English even if a gun was pointed to their heads. Ol' man Sinclair went and got hisself some more Mexicans."

"Ain't like we haven't fought 'em before," Taylor said.

They were nearing town when Bagbee asked Jennings how he planned to find Pete Sinclair.

"I 'spect his daddy, knowing he's acted the fool and cowardly, has sent him away somewhere," Coy said. "Might be I'll need some assisting from your Indian, but I'll find him. I'll not rest till I do. Ain't a place far enough for him to go hide. First, though, it seems my duty as sheriff is to help you steal back your cattle."

Ira remained unconscious but was resting easier when they returned. His breathing, though still shallow, seemed more normal.

"There's been no worsening of his condition," Doc

Matthews said. "I've applied medication to his wounds and, with April's help, have kept damp towels on his face and chest to reduce the swelling. No doubt he has some internal injuries—broken ribs to be sure—but I have no way to know their full extent. I should be able to determine more as he improves."

Weatherby, still grim-faced, entered the room. He still carried his shotgun. "When he wakes, assure him his mule's being cared for." He looked across the bed at the doctor. "You'll take note that I said *when*, not *if*."

"It's the proper attitude to take," April said as she joined them, carrying more towels. Seeing that Jennings had returned, she moved toward him. "I was too busy earlier to express how sorry I am about your friend's condition."

"You've been here since he was brought to the doctor?"

"Yes. Miss Mindy agreed to watch over Penelope at the kitchen." She placed a hand on Coy's arm as she looked down at Dalton. "What kind of person could do such a thing?"

"Somebody you're well acquainted with," Jennings said. "I'm certain it was Pete Sinclair who near killed Ira. I can't say why, 'cept for his bein' pure mean and most likely drunk at the time, but it was him."

"He was looking for me, wasn't he?"

"That seems likely. But don't worry. Will Bagbee has placed two of his men on the front porch to see to your safety. And rest assured, I'll soon find Pete. When I do, I'll make sure he harms no one else."

After sitting with Dalton for the remainder of the day, Jennings walked down to the pasture in the evening. The neatly spaced tents and glowing campfires reminded him of his days as a soldier. He found Bagbee sitting by a fire, leaning against a saddle with a blanket wrapped over his shoulders.

"It's good a wind ain't blowing outta the north," Coy said as he held his hands above the fire. "Soon it'll be too cold for lingering outdoors."

"It's not my plan to be here much longer. Take a sit. Miss Mindy and Jakie brought coffee after they finished serving supper." He passed a tin cup to Jennings. "I'd like to hear your opinion on what we're planning to do." He poured himself more coffee before continuing. "I can't think of any way there won't be shootin'," he said, "and I've seen to it my men are aware of the fact. I told 'em if there was anyone who wished to avoid gunfightin' they could head on back to home with no questions bein' asked. As I figured, not a man saddled his horse. So there's fifteen of us, counting the Indian—"

"Sixteen," Coy said. "I'll be riding with you."

Bagbee wasn't surprised. "Thinkin' on what you've told me about Sinclair," he said, "I've tried to figure what he might do now that he knows our intent. Seems him and his rustlers are inclined to carry out their thievin' at night, so likely he'll expect us to do the same."

Jennings nodded. "Which ain't what I've a mind to do. We'll show up at first light, before they're bright-eyed and bushy-tailed and in a proper frame of mind to fight."

He described his plan. The initial phase of the raid would not occur in the south pasture where the cattle were but instead the headquarters of the ranch. Sinclair, he assumed, would divide his men, having some guard the cattle night and day while others remained on alert at the compound.

"He'll want some of his men protectin' him and his

fancy house," he said. "If we can successfully surprise 'em and take prisoners—or shoot 'em if need be—we'll have an advantage once we head out to the pasture."

Bagbee agreed. "I've instructed Tracker to ride south tomorrow night and see if he can determine how many men are out guarding the herd you spoke of. Once he returns, we'll know better what we're up against there."

Jennings reached for a nearby twig and began drawing a map in the flickering light of the campfire. "The hands at the bunkhouse are less likely to be alerted prematurely if we avoid the way we entered today. Poppy and his friends will probably camp where they tried to stop us this morning. And you can count on shots bein' fired when they see us comin'. Even if they don't kill nobody, they'll be sending a warning signal to folks down the way."

It would take longer, he pointed out, but it would be safer if they approached the house from the back side. "We'd need to ride north to the Brazos River, then follow along its banks back to the Bend," he said.

"Can you could show us the way?" Bagbee said.

"I reckon so."

Coy could see that Bagbee was in his element now—back in a Union uniform, making ready for an attack on enemy troops. "It might reduce our numbers at the ranch house," he said, "but I'm wondering what your thinking would be if we was to send Clay and a few men—three, maybe four—down to the back side of the pasture. They could stand off Sinclair's people there if need be and turn back any cattle that might get stampeded."

"You've been thinking on this for some time," Jennings said. "Don't it concern you that we'll likely be outnumbered? That this might be a losin' battle you're takin' on?"

The suggestion seemed to anger Bagbee. "Bein' outnumbered was never a concern back when we was fightin' you Confederates. Yes, I've been thinkin' on this since we arrived—and it ain't never occurred to me we might lose."

Coy was pleased with the answer. "I see splittin' up as a good idea. One more thing. It's not likely there'll be any trouble in town," he said, "but just to be on the better side of caution, I'd like to alert Weatherby to what you're intending to do. I figure he can find a few farmers who know how to handle a shotgun and wouldn't mind helping him to stand guard in our absence."

For the first time since their discussion began, Bagbee smiled. "That too is a good idea. Wouldn't want no harm comin' to the townsfolk. 'Specially that pretty lady over at the doctor's house."

Soon after Jennings departed, Poppy left his position at the Bend entrance. Lester Sinclair had summoned him to the house for the second time in a matter of days. On the night he had brought Lester's son back from Phantom Hill, drunk, sick, and belligerent, Lester had instructed his most loyal hand to hitch up a wagon and immediately take Pete to the abandoned Mexican encampment. After what Armando Blanca described, Lester was worried his son had killed the young man in the livery and should go into hiding.

"Ride back out to the Flats and alert that idiot boy of mine that he's caused himself a large measure of grief and is now in serious danger," he said.

In his hand was a small leather pouch filled with gold coins. "See he gets this and advise him not to spend it all on whiskey. Tell him I said he should head south and lie low somewhere until things settle."

"Anything else?"

"Take him his hat and see to it he's got ample ammunition. And tell him if he's not of a mind to do as I say, he's likely to wind up dead."

Chapter 20

When Poppy reached the Flats late that afternoon, Pete Sinclair was standing in the doorway of the adobe building, wearing an abandoned serape he'd found. His hair was tossed, his beard in tangles, and traces of dried blood remained on his boots.

"You, senor, are a pathetic sight," Poppy said as he dismounted.

Sinclair spat into the dirt. "I'm ready to be gettin' home."

"Well, that ain't happenin' soon. I've come to deliver a message from your papa," Poppy said as he began gathering wood for a fire. "You are not to return."

Pete cursed. "I'll not have hired help tellin' me what I'm to do."

"Ain't me telling. It's Mr. Sinclair's decision. I'm just the messenger."

As he began building a fire, he told Pete of the arrival of men at the Bend and the likelihood they'd soon attempt to retrieve the stolen cattle. "They got some plan, which I believe will be carried out soon. We're preparin' for a fight."

"More's the reason I need to get back."

"Ain't the men who come for the cattle that should concern you. Jennings ain't happy with what occurred in town. He'll be looking for you, most likely to see you dead. For that reason, your papa says you're to leave as quickly as possible. Ride to the south, he says, and hide until matters are settled."

"Jennings has no call to think it was me in the livery. Wasn't nobody else around 'cept that Mexican who interfered and pulled me away."

Poppy rose, walked to his horse, and took Pete's hat from the saddle horn. "Wasn't Armando who made Jennings aware it was you who gave the beating to the young man." He handed Pete his hat. "This was found there."

Pete took the hat and threw it to the ground. "Where is it I'm supposed to go?"

Poppy placed the pouch of money and the bag of ammunition on the ground next to him. "Senor," he said, "I don't care."

Giles Weatherby couldn't shake the feeling that he was responsible for what had happened to Ira. Troubling thoughts raced through his mind when he was awake and visited his dreams whenever he managed to sleep. *I should not have left Dalton alone at the livery. If I had returned in time . . . What if he dies?*

He was sitting on the steps of Doc Matthews's house when Jennings and Bagbee approached.

"How's he doin'?" Jennings said.

"Doc says no better, no worse. He ain't opened his eyes yet."

"I'll go in and sit with him for a bit," Coy said, "but first, we got something we need to speak with you about."

Bagbee outlined the plan they had discussed the previous evening, saying that his men were already making preparations for the ride to the Bend. "We'll be headin' out well before sunup."

Coy explained the need to have the townspeople prepared in the event of problems in Phantom Hill.

"My druthers would be to ride with you boys," Weatherby said, reaching to touch the stock of his shotgun. "It'd do me good to look into Lester's eyes when he learns somebody's stood up to him and that cowardly son of his."

As he spoke, Miss Mindy approached, carrying a basket under her arm. "Since the doctor has shown no interest in visitin' my kitchen," she said, "it appears I've now taken on the added chore of deliverin' what I've cooked." She removed a towel from the basket and produced a slice of pear pie. Handing the plate to Weatherby, she said, "Till Ira's appetite returns, I 'spect he'd like you to have this. I've seen you eat nothin' in two days."

Giles accepted the pie and took a bite. "Much obliged," he said. "But I wish it was Ira thanking you."

He quickly finished the pie, then got to his feet. "I'll go see if I can round up some folks to stand guard here in town," he said. "First, though, I need to visit the general store. It just occurred to me Dalton's mule has had no peppermint sticks in quite some time."

Miss Mindy called out to Bagbee as Giles walked away, "Not that I was bein' nosy, but I overheard some of what you're plannin.' See to it your men come to the kitchen this evening. Me 'n' Jakie will make certain they're properly fed."

"How you 'n' him gettin' along?" Bagbee said.

Mindy's response was a gruff look followed by a faint blush. "I reckon I'd like him better if he knew somethin' 'bout cooking and had a few more teeth," she said. "But, those matters aside, we're doin' better than I'd expected."

Poppy returned to the Bend late in the afternoon and found Lester Sinclair on the porch, talking with Armando Blanca.

"I don't reckon the boy took kindly to my message," Sinclair said as Poppy walked up the steps. "He wasn't too happy, but I watched him ride out of the Flats before I left."

"And he was headed south?"

"Seemed so."

"Such a fool," Blanca said. "We will be better off with him far away."

Sinclair's jaws clenched. Blanca, he knew, was right—particularly about his son being a fool.

While Poppy was away, they had discussed how best to prepare for whatever the visitors from up north had in mind.

"Some of the hands are already rounding up the cattle, bringing 'em in closer so we can keep a better eye on 'em," Sinclair said. "We'll station men in the pastures and here around the house." He told Poppy to return to his position guarding the entrance. "Everyone's been told to arm himself with a rifle. It's Blanca's idea that we put a man with good eyesight on the roof of the barn to keep watch. Beginning tonight, there'll be little sleep."

As Poppy turned to go to the barn and feed his horse, Blanca walked with him.

When they were far enough away that Sinclair couldn't hear, Blanca said, "My men and I did not come here to get ourselves killed. You lied to us when we were hired."

"Not as I recall," Poppy said. "Tell your men they'll do as they're told, what they're being paid for. And tell 'em if they refuse, they'll never see that little cantina in Mexico again. And that, you can be assured, is *not* a lie."

With the crescent moon hidden behind thick clouds, it was almost pitch-dark when Miss Mindy and Jakie arrived in the pasture with lanterns and large pots of coffee. A chilling fog had settled over the encampment.

Weatherby stood near Jennings, shivering as he watched the activity. "I got me a feeling something of a historic nature is about to get itself played out," he said.

Coy turned to him. "Historic?"

"If things go as I'm hoping, this'll be the day Phantom Hill starts to become the community it has a right to be." He reached out to shake Jennings's hand. "Just don't get yourself shot again to make it happen."

"You just inform Ira I'll be back soon to check on him, and I'd appreciate his being awake when I get there."

With the sheriff and Bagbee leading, the men left, again riding two by two. Those headed to the southern edge of the ranch, led by Tracker and Clay Taylor, had already departed.

They moved through the thick fog, slowly making their way across the prairie to the banks of the Brazos, and turned in the direction of the ranch. The only sound was the occasional squeak of a saddle as a nervous rider adjusted his position.

Though it was still impossible to see the ranch house or outbuildings, Jennings raised his hand to halt the advance after they had ridden another mile. "We're close," he said to Bagbee. "No more 'n a couple of hundred yards, I figure."

Bagbee signaled for his men to dismount and spread out. Once they were in position, sheltered in tall grass and a small gulley near the hog pen, he and Jennings crept closer to the house.

"How is it they haven't yet been alerted to our presence?" Bagbee said. "They may be sizable in numbers, but not all that smart."

"They're ranch workers, not soldiers," Jennings said. "In whatever planning they considered, they must have figured we'd come at the ranch straight-on."

On a clear morning they would have been able to see that the ranch house was ringed by armed ranch hands, squinting into the murky gray in an effort to detect movement.

Lying on their bellies behind a stand of mesquite shrubs a hundred yards away, Bagbee and Jennings were attempting to do the same.

"Don't think we can get much closer without bein' in danger," Bagbee said. "Only thing we can do is bide our time till it's daylight and this fog lifts. Otherwise we'll be in a position of fightin' blind on unfamiliar ground."

They crawled back toward the others.

An hour passed before the fog began lifting and they could finally make out the faint outline of the house and see the men standing around it.

"I reckon it'll be a waste of good breath," Bagbee said, "but it's time we see if this might be settled in a gentlemanly manner."

Cupping his hands to his mouth, he yelled in the direction of the house, "Hello the house . . . Hello, Lester Sinclair." Bagbee called out, "We've come only for our cattle, not to do anybody harm. Have your men put their guns aside and assemble in the yard with their hands raised. Then we'll be about our business and on our way."

The answer was a shot fired wildly from atop the barn. "They're down near the river," a voice yelled.

"So much for gentlemanly behavior," Jennings said as he lifted his rifle to his shoulder. Bagbee signaled the others to begin moving toward the house.

A volley of shots was fired in the direction of the lookout, a cloud of gun smoke suddenly mixing with the fog. The man fell from the roof and lay motionless in the dirt.

The attackers hurried toward the bunkhouse, taking cover behind it as bullets thudded into the walls. At the house, some men kneeled on the porch, their rifles resting on the railing as they took aim, while others retreated inside and fired from windows.

Huddled against the fireplace in the middle room, Lester Sinclair barked orders and oaths. His voice was shrill and panicked. "See to it you kill 'em every one," he said. "I want them all dead. Nobody's going to treat me with this manner of disrespect."

As he spoke, several shots tore away the curtains from one of the windows and another of his men groaned and slumped to the floor. Sinclair swore louder as he crawled on hands and knees to hide behind his padded chair.

* * *

At the first sound of gunfire, Poppy left his post at the entrance to the ranch and rode quickly toward the compound. A full-fledged gun battle was under way as he arrived. He dismounted before his horse came to a halt and took a position at one corner of the barn. He began firing in the direction of the bunkhouse.

No such heroics were being played out in the middle pasture, where Blanca's Mexicans were instructed to watch over the cattle.

Taylor and the men assigned him were surprised to reach the southern pasture and find it deserted. By the time they located the herd, it was unattended, the longhorns grazing quietly.

As the first shots echoed through the thick morning air, the Mexicans had kicked their horses into a gallop and ridden away, headed toward the border. Leading them was Armando Blanca.

At the compound the exchange of gunfire continued through the morning as sunlight finally peeked through the clouds and burned away the fog. From his spot at the corner of the bunkhouse, Jennings could see three bodies lying on Sinclair's porch. Another was slumped over the railing. His rifle had fallen to the ground.

From one of the broken windows, he saw a white kerchief being waved. "No more," someone yelled. "We're finished."

Bagbee eased his way to Jennings's side. "Seems they don't have much taste for fightin'," he said. "But we'll not leave our positions until they've come out into the open. Bein' as you're the sheriff, it should be your pleasure to give that instruction."

Jennings called out to the house, "Leave your weapons behind and show yourselves."

A single-file parade of ranch hands began walking into the sunlight, stepping over one of the bodies as they slowly made their way across the porch. Their hands were raised.

By the time Clay Taylor and his men arrived, the Bend defenders were on their knees, guns pointed toward them from all directions. "Looks as if we've missed somethin'," he said.

"Bein' as you've done little to contribute thus far," Bagbee said, "you can see to it these folks are properly tied up." He ordered the others to begin a search to make sure everyone had surrendered. "We're in particular looking for ol' man Sinclair, who don't seem to be among these who kindly gave up."

"Reckon he's lying dead inside?" Taylor said.

"From your mouth to God's ear."

While the house was being searched and weapons gathered, Jennings walked toward the entrance of the barn. He stopped in the doorway, letting his eyes adjust to the darkness. Pointing his rifle, he said, "If anyone's in here, you might want to join the others who have done give up. We need no more shootin' today."

He was only a few steps inside when he felt the barrel of a pistol against the back of his head. "The shooting is not over," a voice said. "Nor is the killing." Coy heard the click of the gun's hammer and closed his eyes tightly.

There was a deafening sound. It took Jennings a moment to realize it had not come from a handgun. He turned in time to see blood pouring from what remained of Poppy's face as he went to his knees, then pitched forward onto the ground.

Only then did Repete Sinclair emerge from the shadows, smoke still wafting from the barrel of the gun he was holding.

Bagbee was the first to reach the barn after hearing the shot. He looked first at Jennings, then the body, then the young man who was still holding the gun. He had already unholstered his pistol when Jennings grabbed his arm.

"This young fella here has no responsibility for what was going on earlier," he said. "His only fault is to be called a Sinclair. Wasn't for him, I'd be shot dead instead of speakin' to you. Leave him be."

Bagbee was holstering his pistol when they heard Taylor call out, "We found him."

They ran toward the back of the house, past a garden, and through the orchard. Taylor was pointing his rifle toward the ground, a wide grin on his face. On the floor of a dank root cellar, Lester Sinclair lay in the fetal position, his shaking hands covering his face.

"I beg you don't shoot me," he said. His voice was almost childlike.

Bagbee began to laugh. "Pull him outta there," he said, "so the sheriff here can make a proper arrest."

"You know, I ain't never arrested anyone before," Jennings said.

"I 'spect you'll be gettin' used to it. It'll need doin' before we can put all these cattle thieves in that new jail you got."

Bagbee was in the saddle, surveying the aftermath. The clouds had disappeared and the day was warming. He was clearly pleased that none of his men had been killed or injured. He was already planning to allow them time to rest a day, maybe two, before they returned to round up the cattle and begin the drive back toward the

Red River. He would also see that those who died were buried.

"I got no grievance against them," he said to Coy. "They was just doin' what their boss told 'em. Even that hand who near killed you in the barn."

Bagbee looked down at the huddle of men who had their hands tied behind their backs. "How far is it into town?"

"Near five miles, I'm guessin'," Jennings said, "if we take the trail leading from the entrance."

"I reckon a nice walk might do these fellas good."

"Wonder, could I ask a favor?"

"What might that be?"

"It's a far piece for a man of Lester Sinclair's age to be walking," Coy said. "What's your thinkin' on taking him to town, all bound and looking pitiful, ridin' in back of his own buggy? Maybe allowing Tracker to drive. Seems to me there's folks in Phantom Hill who might find that a real amusement."

Bagbee was still chuckling as he told Tracker to hitch up the buggy.

Chapter 21

People lined the windswept street as the strange assemblage made its way into Phantom Hill. Jennings and Bagbee rode out front, followed by the buggy flanked by two armed riders. In it, Lester Sinclair, hands bound and his hat pulled low against his face, attempted to ignore the taunts that were shouted as he passed. Behind him walked ten exhausted ranch hands.

"Got ourselves a parade," Giles Weatherby said as he stepped out to greet Coy. "An honest-to-by-God parade."

Miss Mindy was standing in front of the recently finished jail, a ring of padlock keys in her hand. Lifting them up to Jennings, she said, "You'll be needin' these."

He had not even been inside the building since its completion. He entered and inspected the sturdy log walls and high ceiling, breathing in the clean odor of the earthen floor. Timbers had been deeply buried to discourage any occupant's thought of digging out to freedom. The single, windowless room was barely twelve feet wide and maybe thirty feet deep. The prisoners, he realized, would be shoulder to shoulder once they were marched in.

"They'll be needin' water and somethin' to eat," Jennings told the mayor. "Maybe some leftover corn bread."

"Make it stale as you got," Bagbee said.

While Weatherby waited for Jennings to tend to the prisoners, he heard details of what had occurred at the Bend from Bagbee, including Poppy's attempt on the sheriff's life.

"That's now two close calls," he said to Coy. "Seems you're a man guarded by angels."

"It would seem," Jennings said. "Mostly, though, I think the credit goes to folks like Repete Sinclair and young Ira."

Coy's thoughts turned to Dalton. "Any improvement?"

"The doc appears more optimistic, though the boy remains unconscious. Last I looked in on him, he seemed to be resting easy."

By nightfall a full-fledged celebration was under way. Miss Mindy kept the kitchen open longer than usual, repeatedly filling the plates of the men who made their way from the tent encampment. "I've done cooked everything I've got," she said to Jakie, "and some of 'em's still hungry."

Jakie was mixing the last of the flour for a final pot of dumplings. "If folks want breakfast in the morning, they'll have to look elsewhere," he said. "We'll have nothing to offer but empty plates."

Down the street, the saloon was filled with laughter and banjo music. Townspeople mixed with the visiting ranch hands, thanking them for bringing Lester Sinclair in to be jailed. Even Isaac Hatchett, the bartender, seemed to be enjoying himself.

Jennings, Weatherby, and Bagbee sat outside the livery, watching as people milled about. "Nice seeing folks enjoyin' themselves," Giles said. "What you fellas done out at Sinclair's place today was long overdue—and highly appreciated."

The handshakes and back-slapping that had gone on since their return made Bagbee uncomfortable. "Soon we'll be outta your hair and on our way home," he said.

"When will you be leavin'?" said Weatherby.

"We'll select what seems a proper number of cattle belongin' to our boss and his neighbors and start headin' 'em north. I'd like us to get home before the weather gets too much colder."

He paused for a second. "I've been thinking we might also cut out a few cows and calves, maybe even a steer, and herd 'em into town. If you got room in your pasture after we've removed our tents, we could leave 'em so Miss Mindy'll have a start that will provide additional beef for her kitchen."

"Can't see ol' Lester in a position to do much arguing about that," Weatherby said. He stood to stretch his legs. "If you boys will excuse me, I think I'll pay me a quick visit to the saloon 'fore the whiskey runs out."

Jennings had been quiet since padlocking the jail and looking in on Dalton. He'd been assured by the doctor and April that they would contact him if there was any change.

The activities of the day had drained him of all energy, and his bad leg ached. Even when Miss Mindy had offered to bring him a plate of food, he'd declined.

"Seems you're troubled," Bagbee said.

"Just wondering what'll become of those fellas we brung in. We got no judge to hold 'em accountable. I'm not even sure the badge given me makes me a legal sheriff."

Bagbee chuckled. "You can always just shoot 'em all and be done with it. Be a fine way for Phantom Hill to begin itself a cemetery."

Then he turned serious. "On our way up north we'll pass close to Fort Worth, where there's likely to be a marshal. How 'bout I advise him of the situation so he can come down and take charge? My guess is he'll be pleased to know all the hard work's been done and will gladly take ol' man Sinclair to be tried and locked away in prison. Or, better yet, hanged. As to the others, he'd likely give 'em a swift kick in the behind and a strong suggestion they quickly get themselves as far away from these parts as they can."

"A solution of that nature would suit me fine," Jennings said, "'cause I don't figure to be around much longer. Soon as Ira wakes and I'm told he'll recover, I've got business to tend to."

"You're speakin' of the Sinclair boy who hightailed it?"

"Yep," Jennings said. "He's deserving of far more than a swift kick," he said. "I plan on it bein' me who settles with him."

The following day Bagbee left several of his men to begin breaking camp and loading their wagon while he and the others rode to the Bend to begin rounding up cattle. They were surprised to find Repete Sinclair on horseback, surveying the herd, as they arrived.

"Don't appear they were too disturbed by all the shootin'," Bagbee said.

"This ain't all of 'em," Sinclair said. "There's a

bigger herd down near the river and cows and calves that have returned to the south pasture. I got no idea what rightfully belongs to you—you'll see the Bend's brand has been burned over yours—but I'll take you at your word and help you gather 'em up."

The sad-eyed young man didn't ask about his father. Instead he wanted to know if he might get some help digging graves before the roundup began.

"It was one of the things we'd figured on doin'," Bagbee said.

By midafternoon the dead had been buried near the orchard and Sinclair and Bagbee sat under the bare branches of a peach tree.

"Won't be necessary to bring the other herds up," Bagbee said. "It was my boss's thinkin' that he and the neighborin' ranchers had two hundred or so head stolen. Tomorrow, we'll return and cut that number from the herd and be on our way."

He removed his hat to knock the dust away and looked at the young Sinclair. "That'll still leave you with a sizable number of cattle to look after. They're now yours, I reckon, unless some others like ourselves come seeking what might have been taken from their property. It ain't likely that'll happen."

Repete looked tired and overwhelmed by the events that had played out. "I haven't given much thought to any of that," he said.

"It's also our plan," Bagbee said, "to give Phantom Hill a few head that we was planning to drive into town today. I think it might be a proper gesture if you rode with us and personally gifted the cattle to that woman now acting as town mayor."

"You're speaking of Miss Mindy?" Sinclair said. "The one who smokes cigars and don't mind speaking her piece?"

"That's who."

Sinclair smiled faintly. "Then best we arrive with some stock that has ample meat on their bones," he said, "lest she go on one of her tirades, which I've personally been witness to on occasion."

By late afternoon a dozen range cattle and a milk cow were herded into the pasture behind the livery. Sinclair tipped his hat to Miss Mindy and told her that pigs would also be delivered once a pen to hold them was built. "Seems some layin' hens might be useful as well, if you're of a mind," he said.

Mindy removed her cigar from her mouth and reached up to shake Sinclair's hand. "This," she said, "is a mighty fine thing for you to do, Repete."

"It'd be my preference that you and everyone else refer to me as Peter from now on. It's my true given name. My brother was born Pete, me Peter."

"Then Peter it is," she said. "It's far better-soundin' for a gentleman such as yourself."

Standing nearby, Jennings smiled. "I'm told that fixin's are a bit in short supply over at the kitchen," he said to Sinclair, "but if she can see fit to scrape us somethin' up, I'd admire to buy you supper and do some talkin' 'fore you head back."

"All I got is sweet potatoes and stew made from rabbits that one of the hungover farmers brought in today," Mindy said as she set two steaming bowls on the table. "I sent Jakie over to the saloon to see if there might be a couple of bottles of beer left from last night's carryin'-on. He'll be servin' Mr. Bagbee and his men their dinner, picnic-style, out by the Sunday singin' tree. I figured you two might like some privacy."

She put a hand on Sinclair's shoulder and leaned down. "I also heard what you done for our sheriff," she whispered. "I'm mighty grateful."

Long after they finished their meal, the two men sat alone in the kitchen. Only when Mindy brought a lantern and placed it on the edge of their table did they realize it had grown dark.

"I'd be interested in knowin' your plans now that you'll be runnin' the ranch," Jennings said.

"Truth be known, I'd like to be shed of the whole worrisome mess. But as that ain't possible, I guess I'll be looking to hire some new hands." Sinclair stared into his empty glass, then said, "You know, most of the men you brought in to be jailed had no part in my daddy's wrongdoin's. They'd just hired on to work and make themselves a livin'. They had no choice but to do as they were told. I'm not saying they didn't know about the rustling, mind you, but it was the Mexicans you encountered out at Burton's farm who were responsible for the stealin' and whatnot."

"I figured as much," Jennings said. "Which of those now over in the jail might you trust?"

Sinclair thought for a moment. "Dallas, he's a good man. Don't say much, but he knows a good deal about ranching. Noah and Luke Joslyn, they're brothers, and was with us only for a short while. But I came to like their cuttin' up in the evenings after work was done. And ol' Jen, he's good at doctoring livestock. The others I can't say much good about."

"Would you be willing to take those you've mentioned back on, at least for the time bein'?"

Sinclair gave Jennings a surprised look. "You sayin' you'd consider releasin' 'em?"

"Them and maybe a few others if their behavior warrants it. But only if they agree to go back to the Bend and continue workin'. At this point I can't see any other way you're going to manage things."

"What about my brother, Pete, should he return? He'll be layin' claim to the ranch soon as he learns Daddy's no longer around."

"Peter," Jennings said, "your brother *ain't* coming back. I'm making it my business to see to that."

Jakie appeared from the kitchen after returning the plates used by Bagbee's men. He was rubbing his hands on an apron as he approached Sinclair. "I couldn't help overhearing some of your conversation," he said. "What I was wishin' to ask is what your plans are for hirin' a cook. Men working cattle got to eat, even if it ain't nothing more'n red beans and biscuits."

"Truthfully it ain't somethin' I've thought on," Sinclair said.

"Once you get around to it, I'm of a mind to apply for the job. If, of course, Mr. Bagbee says it's okay for me to remain behind."

Jennings was amused. "And what'll Miss Mindy do without your helping her here at the kitchen?"

Jakie blushed. "Likely as not, she'd be right pleased to get me out of her way."

Though the night was clear, the wind was colder and howling as Peter Sinclair mounted his horse for the ride back to the Bend. He promised to return in the morning to learn whether Jennings had convinced his father's jailed hands to return to work.

Coy pulled his jacket tight against his neck as he

walked toward the livery, trying to remember when he'd ever felt so weary. He was in the middle of the street, swirling dirt lashing against his legs, when he heard his named called. It was April McLean.

"Mr. Jennings, Mr. Jennings," she yelled from the front porch of the doctor's house. "Come quick. There's somebody inside who is awake and wishing to see you."

Running toward her, he suddenly didn't feel nearly so tired.

Ira Dalton's voice was weak and his eyes had no sparkle. He looked as if he'd aged ten years. Still, he was smiling as Coy stood over his bed.

"Hey, Mr. Jennin's," he said. "I been sleepin'."

"And I'm proud you finally decided to wake up," Coy said as he reached for Ira's hand. As they talked it became obvious that the young man had no memory of what had happened to him. When he asked, Jennings replied only that he'd been hurt. "But now you're gettin' well. You'll soon be good as new and ready to resume our evenin' rides."

After being assured his mule was being cared for, Ira went back to sleep, the smile still on his face.

"Could be that he'll eventually recollect what occurred," Doc Matthews said, "though I must say I'd just as soon he didn't. What's most important is that he seems to be on his way to recoverin'. I think he's gonna be all right."

April stood nearby, wiping tears from her cheeks. Jennings, overcome with joy, reached out and hugged her, then shook the doctor's hand. "This day," he said, "has come to a fine end."

"And you should now get yourself some rest," Matthews said.

Jennings moved to a nearby chair. "If this spot ain't taken," he said, "I'll do my sleepin' here tonight."

April left to find him a blanket. When she returned, he was already asleep. She gently removed his hat and placed it on the end of the bed, then blew out the lamp.

Even as the room darkened, Coy Jennings was having a pleasant dream.

Dawn was just breaking as Peter Sinclair stopped his wagon in front of the jail. Jennings stood near the front door, a cup of coffee in his hand.

"I've spoken to the fellas you mentioned," he said, "and they all seem anxious to be freed from this place and headed back to the Bend. They're yours if you want 'em."

"Lemme load 'em up and I'll see to it they don't bother you again," Peter said. "They'll not even be comin' into town to do their drinkin'." There was a sound of authority in his voice that Jennings hadn't heard before.

As the men stepped into the crisp gray morning one by one, each nodded in the direction of the young Sinclair before climbing into the back of the wagon.

Jennings moved to stand next to the new Bend of the River Ranch boss as the procession was ending. "While you're here," Coy said, "do you have a mind to look in on your pa?"

Sinclair shook his head. "I reckon not," he said. "We've got nothing to talk about." As he climbed onto the wagon he said, "Tell that Bagbee fella me an' these boys will be ready to help him round up his herd soon as he gets out to the Bend."

Jennings shook his hand. "Best of luck to you, Peter," he said. "And don't be a stranger. Seems you've begun makin' yourself some friends here in Phantom Hill."

Sinclair hesitated before unlocking the brake and looked toward the doctor's house. "How's that Dalton boy doin'?"

"Doc says he's gonna be fine." He could tell Sinclair was still not quite ready to leave.

"When you catch up with my brother, Pete," he said, "be careful you don't let him get the drop on you."

Soon after Sinclair left, Bagbee was organizing his men to ride in the same direction. Before leaving he stopped into the livery, where Jennings was grooming Rodeo.

"We'll be headin' the herd due north from the ranch, so I'll not be seein' you once we leave town," Bagbee said. "I just wanted to stop and say I've admired knowin' you and to remind you I'll be looking for that marshal to send this way. I also wanted to tell you . . . well, I'm of a mind you're gonna make Phantom Hill a fine sheriff."

"Thanks. And thanks for your help." Jennings smiled. "Peter Sinclair's got men waiting at the Bend to help you boys out," he said. "Gonna be a bit lonesome with you folks no longer around."

It wasn't until after they were gone that Coy walked to the back of the livery to look out at what had, just a day earlier, been a tent city. Now cattle were leisurely grazing. He smiled when he saw that Jakie's tent remained. Either Miss Mindy had a new helper or Peter Sinclair would soon have a full-time cook at the Bend.

What surprised him was a second canvas hut at the back of the pasture. A small campfire burned in front of it.

Coy was walking toward it when Tracker emerged and folded his arms.

"What is it you're still doin' here?" Jennings said.

"I was told you will need help finding the man who hurt your friend," the Indian said. "I am to stay and assist you with your search."

They were the first words Jennings had ever heard Tracker speak. "Will Bagbee told you to do this? And you're okay with such a plan?"

Tracker nodded. Jennings thought he detected a faint smile.

"Well, if that's the case, I reckon the thing you should do is move out of this cold and into the livery. There's a cot up in the loft that ain't being used at present."

Chapter 22

The first snowfall of the season came earlier than usual.

"Ain't exactly fit weather for travelin'," Giles Weatherby said as he watched Jennings pack his saddlebags.

In the two weeks since Bagbee and his men had left on their homeward trail drive, Coy had busied himself preparing to go in search of Pete Sinclair. He deputized Weatherby and Buck Burton and told them to expect a marshal to arrive shortly to take Lester Sinclair into custody. In the meantime, he asked Doc Matthews to look in on the prisoner and make sure his health remained good. Though she didn't particularly care for the idea, Miss Mindy promised she would see that he was delivered food and water daily.

Despite the fact that Sinclair wore an iron ankle cuff crafted by the blacksmith and was chained to a post buried in the jail floor, she adamantly refused to bring him his meals personally. Nor did she have any intention of daily removing the refuse bucket.

"That would be man's work," she said. The responsibility fell to Weatherby.

The loud demands and profanity from the prisoner had finally ceased, and he now passed his time sitting mutely in a corner, a blanket wrapped around his shoulders.

The only conversation Jennings had with him after the Bend hands were released was a single attempt to learn the whereabouts of his elder son. Lester spat in his face.

What gave Coy comfort was the fact that Ira Dalton had improved to the point where he was spending several hours a day sitting in a chair instead of lying in bed. His appetite, as well as his color, had returned, and though his ribs still pained him, his breathing was again normal. With the help of Weatherby and the doctor, he'd even slowly walked over to the livery to give his mule a peppermint stick.

"I've got business to tend," Jennings said to him one afternoon, "but I'll be returnin' soon. I hope to see you good as new by the time I get back."

"When'll that be, Mr. Jennin's?"

Standing nearby, April McLean listened for the answer.

"Soon as I'm done," he said.

Ira seemed satisfied. April wasn't.

Neither was Weatherby. As Coy and Tracker were leading their horses out of the livery, he stood in the doorway. "I'm not seein' much in the way of supplies," he said. "Don't you reckon it would be a good idea to take a packhorse along?"

"Tracker tells me his preference is to travel light," Coy said.

As he spoke, Penelope McLean ran toward them. She held a kerchief filled with freshly baked muffins up to Jennings, then one to Tracker. "Mama said to give y'all these," she said, "and tell you to be safe. She'll be praying for you, Mr. Jennings. So will I." She looked up at the Indian. "You too, Mr. Tracker."

Coy looked toward the doctor's house where April stood in the doorway, her arms folded across her chest. He tipped his hat. "Tell your mama we'll be returning soon."

There had been little discussion of any specific plan to track down Pete Sinclair. "I never made a trip before where I didn't know where I was goin'," Coy said to the Indian. "All I've got is what I'm thinkin' is a starting place. That and a hunch."

At midday they arrived at Blue Flats. The deserted encampment looked more dismal than it had the last time Jennings saw it. A portion of the sod roof of the old adobe building had collapsed and even with the cover of fresh snow, the stench of the place remained.

Tracker dismounted first and walked slowly among the ruins, circling what was once a fire pit, then kicking at a pile of discarded food cans. He ducked his head at the doorway of the building and walked into the darkened room as Jennings followed. The foul smell was even worse inside and he removed a bandanna from his neck and put it to his face.

In one corner he saw more empty cans and a broken whiskey bottle. There was evidence that a small fire had been built, its smoke leaving a black trace on the crumbling wall. When something shiny caught his eye, he crouched to examine it. It was a small penknife that had been used to cut the top from the fruit cans.

"He was here," Tracker said.

"That's what I figured. Most likely his old man sent him here to hide after he near killed Ira. I'm jes' guessin', mind you, but sometime soon after he likely headed south."

Jennings felt certain that it had been Pete Sinclair's responsibility to recruit the Mexicans who worked for his father. In doing so, he was most likely familiar with the routes that led to the dusty villages south of the Rio Grande.

As they walked outside, Coy pulled a tattered map from his pocket that Doc Matthews had long ago used to find his way to Texas. Snow fell onto it as he held it for Tracker to see. With a gloved finger, Coy traced the most direct route to the border. "You'll see there are no towns indicated, just open space until one gets much farther to the south," he said.

"Too much time has passed for tracking," the Indian said. "We can only head in that direction and hope to find signs of a camp along the way, or meet someone who may have seen your man pass. It will not be easy. Now I think we should move away from this foul place." Tracker turned to look toward the snow-covered mound where he knew bodies had been buried. "There is evil here," he said. "I can feel it."

Over the course of the next two days, the weather gradually improved. The snow decreased, then ended, leaving only a gray and weeping sky in its place. The terrain was flat, making travel easy. With no sign of creeks or ponds, they stopped occasionally to allow their horses to nibble at the remaining patches of snow.

It was nearing dusk on the third day when they reached a wash that promised some shelter from the cold wind that was certain to blow once night fell. Tracker kicked his horse into a trot as he went ahead to look for a possible spot to camp for the night. He was

standing beneath a limestone overhang, gathering wood
to start a fire, when Coy and Rodeo arrived.

"Tomorrow," Tracker said, "the land will change.
We will see trees and water and hills. And there will
be people who may know of the Sinclair man you
seek."

"You know these parts?"

"When I was a young boy my tribe hunted in the
place I speak of. We lived in peace until the white settlers began to arrive and the soldiers forced us to move
to the north."

Jennings detected bitterness in his companion's
voice, and he asked no more questions.

Soon the campfire was blazing, and Coy warmed his
hands above the flames. "If Doc's map is to be believed,
there should be a town we're likely to see sometime
after noon tomorrow. With luck we'll soon be eatin'
food a bit more tasty than jerky and hard biscuits."

As Tracker spread his bedroll next to the fire, he
offered no response.

Jennings shook his head as he walked away to gather
more wood. "Might even find someone who's of a mind
to have a conversation," he muttered.

The Indian's description had not done the landscape justice. As they rode in silence the following
day, the stark flatlands abruptly turned to rolling hills
and stands of towering cedars. They forded several
clear streams that had been fed by the snowfall and
rode past occasional cabins sitting on the edges of
plowed fields. Once they even passed close enough to
a homestead for playing children to wave and a dog
to bark.

That afternoon, as they reached the crest of a hill
and emerged from the shadows of a cedar break, they

saw the town in the distance. Jennings squinted toward the horizon and counted several buildings. Smoke was rising lazily from chimneys. "If Sinclair traveled this way," he said, "it's likely he took himself a brief rest in a place like this one we're approachin'."

Tracker nodded. "And if it's got itself a saloon, that's the first place he would have headed."

Despite the fact that the snow and rains had left the main street muddy and almost impassable, the town was impressive. It was clean, its buildings whitewashed, the wooden sidewalks swept clean. As they rode in, they passed a town square with a marketplace, a bandstand, and a slow-flowing fountain sculpted from limestone. Despite the cold, children were playing in front of a small schoolhouse. There was a church, a general store, and a livery far more impressive than Giles Weatherby's. In the middle of town was a building with a signboard above its door welcoming customers to the Encina Saloon.

It was a town, Jennings thought, like what Phantom Hill aspired to be.

"We'll tend first things first," Coy said as they tethered their horses to the hitch rail. "I've got money enough for us to have a hot meal, then one drink."

Inside, they were greeted by a stout man wearing a white apron. His hair was white, as was his beard. He spoke with a thick German accent. "You fellas passing through?"

"And mighty hungry," Coy said.

"Then you've arrived at the right place. Today I have been roasting venison and have an ample supply of boiled vegetables. And there's corn bread on top of the stove. The weather seems to have kept some of my customers away, so I'll be serving sizable portions."

"And do you have coffee?" Coy said.

"Boiling as we speak."

Jennings reached into his pocket for one of his few remaining gold pieces. "In that case, we'll enjoy your hospitality while having our meal."

The old German briefly cast a wary eye toward Tracker. "Well . . . ain't many customers in here. Guess he can come in. Make yourselves at home," he said. "Warm by the fireplace and I'll return with your coffee. Will that be two cups you're needing?"

Tracker removed his hat and held up two fingers.

Steam was still rising from the cups as their host set them on the table a minute later.

"What's this town called?" Jennings said.

"You saw it displayed on the sign outside. We're known as Encina, though lately there's been some talk of changing the name to Uvalde, to do honor to some Mexican general whose claim to fame I can't at the moment recall."

He launched into a brief history of the town. "After the war, a man known as Reading Wood Black, a person of some wealth and forward thinking, came to greatly admire this region and filed claim to the land on which the town now sits. He hired a surveyor from San Antonio—a man of German background, I'm told—to plot the settlement and, with the help of some well-financed investors, commenced to build. Soon German immigrants like myself were arriving in Galveston and being told this place would remind them of home. You'll find that most who live here are of German heritage. Some never even bothered to learn English.

"Should you plan to remain for a while, I think you'll see it's a fine town. I'm told we'll even soon have a stagecoach stopping through. Then, perhaps, a post office."

"We'd admire to learn more about your fine town," Jennings said, "but for now something out in your kitchen smells mighty good."

"Of course, of course. My apologies for going on so. I'll bring your plates right away."

He didn't say another word until they had finished their meals and had more coffee.

"Would you also be the tender of the bar?" Jennings said.

"That I would. What is your pleasure?"

When he returned with two whiskies, Jennings invited him to sit with them. The proprietor again began extolling the virtues of Encina. He talked of the goats and cattle being raised on small nearby ranches, of the plentiful pecan orchards and a special brand of honey called *huajillo* that bee-keeping locals produced. The nearby Leona River, he said, yielded catfish, bass, and sunfish to even the worst fishermen.

"But I must apologize," he said. "I sound like a salesman trying to convince you to purchase land and settle here. Truth is, I tend to ramble at times." He extended a meaty hand across the table. "Name's Frog Penny, by the way."

Jennings introduced himself, then Tracker. "Our purpose for bein' here," he said, "is to find someone who might recently have passed this way. A big fella with a lot of thick black hair. I doubt you would recall him as a pleasant individual. Name's Pete Sinclair."

Penny leaned back. "If it's the man who passed through a few weeks back, maybe a bit longer—I'm terrible at remembering times; it comes with growing old—the word *pleasant* most certainly would not be proper to describe him. He was here for only a few days and it's my memory that he never drew a sober breath.

Sat at this exact same table most of the time, bragging about how a ranch he owned up north was larger than this entire county. I'll not repeat the unsavory words he used to describe our town. And he tried to pick a fight with just about everyone who walked through the door. I figure he was about as mean a man as I've seen in some time."

"Was there fightin'?" Coy asked.

"No, none I was aware of. Not in here, at least. The people of Encina are peace-loving. They were even against the war, particularly what the Confederates were attempting. If you were to ask around, you would find that most people here felt sympathy for the Union."

Jennings shrugged. "Tell me more about this fella I'm thinkin' was Sinclair."

"I'm being God's honest truthful," Penny said, "when I say he struck me as a bit touched in the head. So I finally alerted our sheriff to his presence. He came and firmly informed the man it was time he was on his way."

"You don't recall him givin' his name?"

"No. And last I saw of him he was on his horse, drunk as a papa skunk, riding out of town. And all I could say was good riddance and don't come back."

"Which way was he headed?"

"Probably toward the border," Penny said. "Just like that rowdy bunch of Mexicans who passed through not long after he did."

Jennings shot a glance in Tracker's direction. The Indian gave a slight nod.

"And what's your recollection of them?"

"Oh, they were a rough-looking bunch. Smelled as if they hadn't bathed in ages. There was half a dozen of them and only one spoke any English so far as I could tell. Had they stayed much longer, I'd have likely been obliged to notify the sheriff about them as well. Fortunately they had little money, so they were on their way after a single glass of beer each."

"The one who spoke English," Jennings said. "What was his name called?"

Penny rubbed his hands to his beard, thinking. "It was unusual, not the sort of name one would expect of a Mexican." He began to laugh. "But, then, whoever heard of someone being named Uvalde before? Or Penny, for that matter."

He was rambling again, and Jennings's patience was reaching an end. He took a long breath before speaking. "Could it be his name was Blanca? Armando Blanca?"

"That sounds about right," Penny said. "Yes, sir, I think that's what it was. And before you ask, I don't recall him being the pleasant sort either."

An hour later, as they rode from town, Jennings chuckled. "That man greatly admires the sound of his own voice," he said. "And his town."

He was surprised when Tracker responded, "Your Phantom Hill could have used the wisdom of the man he called Reading Black," he said.

Coy laughed. "More important than that, it wouldn't hurt none for Phantom Hill to have this kind of scenery. Seems the Good Lord paid special attention when he set about creatin' this part of Texas."

Late the following day the landscape had changed back to flat grassland. There were few trees except for bushy mesquites. They rode past large patches of cacti and through dry, rocky creek beds.

"My fathers tell of a time when many buffalo roamed this land," Tracker said. "They provided the tribe with food and their skins were used for teepees and coats to be worn in weather like this. Their dung made hot campfires, and their bones were valuable for making tools and weapons. But then the white hunters came with their rifles. . . ."

Jennings had heard the stories of the white hunters who killed off huge herds, skinning their hides to be sold, leaving the carcasses to rot and be scavenged by wolves, coyotes, and buzzards. In time, the only remaining buffalo had migrated far to the northern plains, leaving this part of Texas barren of the food tribes had depended on for generations.

"It was a highly unfair thing my people did," Jennings said.

Tracker turned to Coy, surprised by the observation. "Yes," he said. "Yes, it was."

Though the subject was unpleasant, Jennings was glad that Tracker was finally talking. He wanted to know more about this man who had remained behind to accompany him.

"Ain't none of my business," he said, "but I figure it unlikely your real name's Tracker."

"It is the name given me by Will Bagbee and I accept it."

"But . . ."

Tracker continued. "As a young man, I was called Windrunner. I was the swiftest in our tribe. I never lost a footrace, not even to the fastest ponies. I once chased a deer for almost a mile before catching him. I intended to slit his throat and return him to the village for a feast. But because he ran so swiftly and with such grace, I chose to set him free.

"But that was long ago, before my youth was gone. Today, I am an old man and can only chase slowly, with my eyes and my ears."

"How is it you speak better English than me? And what caused you to become a tracker for Bagbee and his crew?"

"Tracking is something I have always done well," he said. "I did not wish to spend my life on a reservation in the Indian Territory, so I accepted Bagbee's offer of a job. It was his boss, a man called Colonel Swindle, who sent me to a white man's school to learn your language."

For several miles the two rode in silence.

With a full moon high in a cloudless sky, they broke camp well before dawn. As they rode, they chewed on the last of the biscuits they'd purchased before leaving Frog Penny's eatery. Both agreed that the German's cooking didn't compare to Miss Mindy's.

"It ain't likely Blanca knows Sinclair's whereabouts," Coy said, "but if we can speak with him he might have a notion where we should be lookin'."

Armando Blanca was not easy to find. After crossing the Rio Grande into Mexico, Jennings and Tracker visited several downtrodden villages along the border, asking if anyone might know the man they were seeking. They were met by silence, menacing stares, and the unspoken message that neither gringos nor Indians were welcome.

It was a young goatherd, watching his animals drink at the river's edge, who pointed them in the right direction. He spoke no English and Jennings's Spanish was limited to only a few words. *"Donde esta Senor Blanca?"* he said.

The youngster smiled and nodded. *"Sí, Senor Blanca,"* he said. *"Muy malo hombre."* He spoke with obvious admiration. Then he pointed south, toward yet another village.

Jennings pulled a coin from his coat pocket and flipped it toward the boy. *"Mucho gracias, amigo,"* he said.

Chapter 23

It was not difficult to pick Armando Blanca from the men drinking in the cantina. He was almost a foot taller than any of the others, his shoulders broad and his weathered face hidden beneath a tattered sombrero. He looked toward the gringo as he entered, then at the Indian who remained in the doorway. A hush fell over the smoke-filled room.

"You are lost, no?" he said as Jennings approached.

"In a manner of speakin'. You're a hard man to find."

"And why is it you are looking for me, amigo?"

"Ain't you I'm looking for, but I was hopin' you might be of help. You'll recall a man name of Pete Sinclair."

Blanca's jaw tightened; then he swore. "The loco gringo who came here with promises that were only lies," he said. "He and a man calling himself Poppy came to us, offering work and money. Instead they only wished us to risk our lives. So we returned home."

"It's a smart thing you did," Jennings said. "Others got themselves killed a while back, including Poppy."

"That news pleases me greatly. I hope his death was

slow and caused him great pain." Blanca took a long drink from his beer and belched. "Why is it you seek Sinclair?"

"Among other things, he near beat a friend of mine to death and I'll not tolerate him gettin' away with such behavior." He lifted his coat to display his badge.

"Was it in a barn in the town near Sinclair's ranch that this occurred?"

"In the Phantom Hill Livery, yes."

Blanca motioned for Jennings to sit with him at a nearby table and signaled for more beer. "I must agree with you," he said. "Pete Sinclair is an evil man. A coward, but also evil. If I knew of his whereabouts, I would gladly put a knife to his throat myself."

Though Tracker had not moved from his position in the doorway, Blanca motioned for the man standing behind the bar to take him a glass of beer.

With the tension eased, Jennings explained his theory that Pete's father had sent him away after the incident at the livery. "Seein' as how he knows this territory, it seemed to me he would likely head this way. A fella up in Encina recalled seein' him shortly before you and your men rode through. According to him, Pete left town headin' south."

"He would be a fool to show his face here," Blanca said. "But there are many villages along the border. If a man has money to pay, he can easily hide. Not from me, however. If he is in Mexico I can learn where."

"How?"

"I know many people," Blanca said. "And even those I do not, know me. I will send some men to ask questions. For now, I suggest you and the Indian remain here. Rest your horses, drink some beer, sleep out of the cold, and be patient. It is not my nature to give aid to a lawman, but I will help you find your Pete Sinclair. Maybe then we can see who gets to kill him."

Jennings scanned the room. Everyone in the cantina was staring at him, none with the slightest hint of warmth.

Blanca smiled as he reached across the table and placed a hand on Coy's shoulder. "Do not worry, my friend. You and the Indian will be safe here," he said. "I will order it."

By the time Pete Sinclair reached the border, he had sobered. Still, his head pounded, his stomach ached, and the bitter cold caused him to ride in a slumped position with a blanket wrapped around his shoulders. It provided him little comfort. Nor did the fact that he was so far from home, wandering aimlessly only because his father and Poppy had demanded he do so. He cursed them both and vowed he would take no more orders from either. After a few more days he would return to the Bend and warm by the fireplace, drink his father's whiskey, and rest in his own bed.

He would also find April McLean.

Meanwhile, he kept riding. Had the sheriff in Encina not threatened to put him in jail unless he left, he could have spent his time hiding there. It would have been far more comfortable, despite the endless chatter of the German innkeeper. The old man's whiskey was good and fairly priced, and he could have tolerated the town's unfriendly people in exchange for being out of the cold.

He found shelter where he could. He slept in the open for a few nights, catching a fever that caused dizziness when he tried to ride. For two dollars, he stayed two days and nights in the drafty barn of a farmer before being told to leave after making what the farmer considered ungentlemanly advances toward his wife. Pete doubted the man would have actually fired the shotgun he'd pointed at him, but he chose to leave just the same.

When he reached the border he camped near the river and tried to think of a plan. It would be a mistake, he decided, to go near the village where he and Poppy had hired the Mexicans. Even though he'd arrived with money and the offer of work, the men there had been unfriendly, even hostile. It was a place to be avoided, even with Blanca away. Still, Sinclair wouldn't mind meeting up with him one day soon and putting a bullet between his eyes. But since he was still in Texas, rustling cattle for his father, settling with him would have to wait.

Alone, Pete found his thoughts clouded by self-pity, and he could only escape the depression by turning his mind to other things. Each time he settled on revenge, and Blanca always was the first who came to mind. Had the Mexican not dragged him away from the half-wit that night in the livery and told his daddy what occurred, none of this would have happened. And there was Coy Jennings back in Phantom Hill, the man who was trying to steal away April's affections. He hated him as well. Too, he owed that smart-mouthed sheriff in Encina a good whipping, maybe worse. His anger spread to Poppy and even his father. What right did they have telling him what to do?

Truth was, Sinclair decided, he didn't like much of anybody.

It also concerned him that he'd lost track of time. How long had it been since Poppy arrived at the Flats to tell him to be on his way? Two weeks? Three? Maybe more. Drunkenness and the fever had caused him to lose track. No matter. Soon he'd be headed home, the cold and loneliness and senseless wandering behind him. Then things would be good again.

* * *

Sleet was peppering the tin roof of the cantina as he approached. He'd followed the bank of the river for miles, past several grim-looking villages, before deciding he'd reached a place where he would not be recognized. There was a lean-to attached to one side of the building that sheltered a water trough and a few bales of hay and he tethered and tended his horse before entering.

He knew he needed to be careful, and not draw attention to himself. He asked the first man he encountered who he needed to pay for sheltering and feeding his animal. The man spoke no English, but after Pete pointed through the doorway to the shed, the Mexican held out his hand. Sinclair gave him a silver dollar and moved toward the bar. *"Dos cervezas,"* he said, then added, *"Por favor."* He'd already used up his manners and most of the Spanish he knew.

The small room was dimly lit, but a potbellied stove gave it warmth. Except for two old men who had sought shelter from the foul weather, the place was almost empty. Sinclair walked past them, nodding in their direction, and sat at a table in back.

Hidden in the shadows and warmed by the stove, he set about to get drunk.

In time he nodded off and was dreaming of April McLean, unaware that two men carrying rifles had pushed their way through the canvas that covered the entrance. He was awakened by their high-pitched voices and lifted his head to look in their direction. They spoke in rapid Spanish to the man behind the bar and the only word Sinclair understood was *gringo.*

Even before the bartender pointed in his direction, Pete reached under the table and unholstered his Colt.

He didn't wait for the men to approach. He jumped to his feet and fired a shot that struck one in the chest. The man screamed and gripped the bar in an unsuccessful attempt to remain on his feet, blood pouring from his wound. As the other man raised his rifle, Pete fired a second shot that struck him in the shoulder, causing his weapon to fall to the floor.

His right arm was dangling limply as he staggered out the door and into the stinging sleet. By the time Sinclair could follow, the Mexican was already on his horse, riding away at a gallop.

Pete was in a rage when he reentered the cantina. Stepping over the body of the man he'd killed, he pointed his pistol at the bartender. "Who were they? What was it they wanted?"

Sweat dotted the man's brow as he lifted his shoulders in a shrug. *"No hablo inglés,"* he said.

Sinclair shot him in the face.

He spared the two frightened old men who were huddled beneath a table, eyes closed, their hands covering their heads. One of them had soiled himself. They could still hear his curses as he rode away in the opposite direction the wounded Mexican had taken.

Pete whipped his horse unmercifully, riding west with no real destination. His only thought was that he needed to quickly distance himself from where he'd been found. He was near a small pig farm when his exhausted animal collapsed, its knees buckling and pitching the rider forward onto the icy ground.

Sinclair got to his feet and approached the cabin. He banged on the door and demanded a new mount from the frightened farmer who greeted him. At gunpoint, the man removed the saddle from Sinclair's fallen horse and placed it on a sorrel he'd led from the barn.

Pete gestured toward the panting animal that was now lying on its side. "I'd relieve him of his misery," he said, "but it could be he'll survive. If he does, he's yours. Consider we're making us a trade."

As he left, the farmer felt his own knees give way, the fear he could have been killed causing him to be sick to his stomach.

The wounded Mexican arrived at the cantina the following day, slumped in his saddle and delirious from the loss of blood. Tracker saw him first and rushed to help him dismount.

"We have a badly hurt man here," the Indian yelled toward Blanca and Jennings. They hurried outside to find Tracker seated on the ground, the young rider cradled in his arms.

Blanca went to his knees and gently placed a hand to the wounded man's face. He leaned forward and spoke in Spanish. The man pointed in the direction from which he'd come and gasped a single word before he fainted: "Gringo."

After they carried his limp body into the cantina and laid it across a table, Tracker heated his knife over the fire. "The bullet must be removed so his blood will not be poisoned," he said.

Blanca and Jennings held the unconscious man down as the Indian dug his blade into the damaged shoulder. As he looked across the table at Blanca, Coy was surprised to see he was crying.

"Now there is no question who will kill Pete Sinclair once he is found," Blanca said.

"Why's that?" Coy said.

"Because this is my son."

Chapter 24

Giles Weatherby watched as Ira stood in front of a stall, gently scratching the ears of his mule and speaking to it in whispers. "He's been missin' you," the blacksmith said.

Dalton smiled. "I know. That's what he told me. He's wantin' to go for a ride, but the doctor says we'll have to wait a little longer. Till I'm well. When's that gonna be?"

"Soon," Giles said. "Doc says you're doin' fine. Just show a bit more patience."

"Wish Mr. Jennin's was here."

"For that you'll also have to be patient."

"I'm missin' seein' him."

"Me too."

"Okay if I go look at the new cows?"

"Please do. Soon you'll be helping me feed 'em."

"You're the boss, Mr. Weatherby . . . till Mr. Jennin's returns."

A few minutes after Dalton left, a booming voice came from the doorway of the livery. "Anybody to home?"

Weatherby turned toward the silhouette of the largest man he'd ever seen. "Lordy, I hope to learn you're fully grown," he said as he approached the stranger, extending his hand. "For a second there I was thinkin' you was two people."

"I'm Sloan Singletary, marshal outta Fort Worth. A fella came to me a while back with information that you're holdin' a known cattle rustler in your jail."

"That would be Lester Sinclair, and, yes, he's stole his share of livestock. Among other things that I 'spect the law don't allow. Our sheriff is away for the time bein', but since he swore me to be a deputy, I'm happy to assist in any way. I could start by offerin' you some coffee. And if you're hungry, we can walk across the street to the kitchen. I reckon Miss Mindy will be amazed to see a man of your stature—and, no doubt, appetite—enter her establishment."

"I'd first like to see your prisoner," the marshal said, "so I can show him papers that allow me to take him into custody."

Weatherby reached for the key ring that hung near the entrance of the livery.

Sinclair squinted into the small shaft of light that appeared as the jail door opened but did not bother to get to his feet. His hair was matted and his beard, once so carefully groomed, was in tangles. His body odor mixed with the smell from the refuse bucket Weatherby hadn't yet removed.

"Pitiful-lookin' fella for a cattle rustler," Singletary said. He walked closer to Sinclair, showing his badge and a sheet of paper. "This," he said, "allows me the right to escort you to the judge whose signature you see on this warrant. If you've got any questions, let me hear 'em now."

When the prisoner refused to respond, the marshal turned to Weatherby. "I'm ready for that coffee you offered," he said. "After that, we'll be on our way."

At the Bend, Peter Sinclair tried to dismiss all thought of his father. On the few trips he'd made into town since the raid, he'd turned his head away whenever he rode past the jail.

His focus was on running the ranch. The hands, glad to be free, resumed their work and even offered their new boss helpful advice at times. They responded well to his quiet, even-tempered manner, and their complaints were few. Jakie's cooking was certainly no match for April McLean's, and they missed weekend visits to the Phantom Hill Saloon. In an attempt to appease them, Peter had begun a habit of sharing his father's ample supply of liquor with them on Saturday nights.

He was unaware when the marshal and his father left on their trip toward Fort Worth. Even had he known, he would not have made the ride into town to say good-bye.

The only thing that really troubled him was the whereabouts of his older brother—and that Pete might one day show up and insist the ranch was his.

Returning to the Bend was exactly what Pete Sinclair wanted to do.

Cold, hungry, and exhausted, he found shelter beneath a rock overhang on the river's edge and built a small fire. He considered trying to shoot a rabbit or maybe a couple of squirrels to cook but thought better of it. A gunshot would alert anyone who might be on his trail.

He had difficulty concentrating as his mind raced from one thought to another. He knew that if the young Mexican he'd wounded was able to survive and report what had occurred, he could count on someone coming to look for him. How far behind were they? Who were they? *Gotta think. Gotta make a plan.* Why was everyone so determined to make his life miserable?

He considered his options. He could continue riding, hoping that whoever might be trailing him would finally grow weary of the chase and give it up. He could find the right place and wait to ambush them once they caught up with him. Or he could change his course and ride north, back toward home.

It was the third choice he finally settled on, and the decision briefly calmed him. He would allow his new horse to rest—no sense running him into the ground too—and maybe get some sleep. At first light he would head for home. It was, he thought, high time. Once there, he would be safe. His father—and his father's loyal men—would protect him.

Miles away in the cantina, Armando Blanca waited for his injured son to awake and a woman from the village to come watch over him. He paced the earthen floor, alternately muttering prayers and curses. After digging the bullet from the young man's shoulder, Tracker had cleaned the wound with a mixture of warm water and whiskey, then covered it with a poultice of herbs and sulfur he took from his saddlebag.

Jennings carried in firewood to keep the stove burning. He tried to convince Blanca to stay behind but knew it was of no use.

"There is nothing more I can do here," Blanca said. "The old woman will care for him. I must help you find the man who did this. I know the way he is going."

He leaned over his boy and lightly kissed him on the forehead, then looked up at Coy. "I now understand your feelings," he said. "Sinclair almost killed your young friend. Now he has tried to take the life of my son. We both have reason to deal with this man."

The sun was just over the horizon when the three men rode away. By noon they reached the dead horse lying in the farmer's field. At the house, the farmer answered the door with his shotgun pointed at them. They finally calmed him enough to recount the event that had played out the previous day. "His eyes were like fire," he said. "He was crazed as nothing I've ever seen. Before he took my horse, I was sure he was gonna kill me just for the pure meanness of doin' so."

"Which way was he headed?" Jennings said.

Blanca had already turned his horse westward before the farmer replied.

A few hours later, Tracker kneeled over the remnants of a burned-out campfire. Silently he walked along the overhang, then down toward the river where Sinclair's horse had been tethered. On his knees, he examined the rocky ground, then rose and walked back toward Jennings and Blanca. He pointed northward.

"He is no longer following the river," he said.

Sinclair settled his horse into a steady gait as he left the Rio Grande behind. The sudden flatness of the terrain was interrupted only by an occasional sand hill. Each time he reached one, he spurred his horse to its crest and scanned the horizon to see if he was being followed.

By midday the cold wind began to gust, swirling the sand into tiny funnels. With the reins in one hand, he used the other to pull his hat low against his face and hold the collar of his jacket tight against his neck. He was in unfamiliar territory. The only thing he was sure of was that he was traveling north. Somewhere in the distance, he told himself, there would be a recognizable landmark that would point him homeward.

With the snow melted away and the sky clear, tracking him was no longer difficult.

Blanca was amazed that Tracker could so quickly recognize signs that their prey had passed. The Indian would halt his horse, dismount, and carefully inspect a twig broken from a mesquite bush or examine rocks that had been disturbed. Though the wind had destroyed many of the hoofprints left in the sand, the Indian found enough to indicate the speed at which Sinclair was traveling.

"He is a day's ride ahead, maybe a little more," Tracker said. "But his horse is in no condition for such a long ride. He is only a farm animal and tiring quickly. We will soon gain ground."

"What if we rode on through the night?" Blanca said. "He must stop to rest."

"Even if there are no clouds and the moon gives us light," Tracker said, "it is too dangerous. There are many burrows made by small animals—the prairie dogs and rabbits and armadillos. If a horse steps into one, his leg will be broken."

He looked at Jennings. "You must be patient." Then back to Blanca. "And you as well."

"Where you figure he's headed?" Coy said.

"I cannot say. For now it appears he himself does not know."

* * *

Resigned to waiting, the three huddled by a campfire as darkness fell. As it turned out, there was too much cloud cover for the moonlight to have helped them travel farther even if Tracker hadn't warned against it.

They ate cold tamales and *cabrito* wrapped in tortillas that Blanca had brought from the village.

"Tell me of this ranch where you come from," he said to Tracker.

"Why? So you can visit at night and steal from it?"

Blanca laughed. "But, amigo, it is what I do."

Jennings shook his head. As he listened to the exchange, he considered the irony—a gringo lawman and a Mexican cattle rustler following a loaned-out Indian, all riding for the same cause. "Let's try to get some sleep," he said.

Somewhere to the north, Pete Sinclair had neither food nor anyone to talk with. And sleep continued to elude him.

Chapter 25

High on the list of duties Marshal Singletary had sworn to carry out yet disliked greatly was retrieving prisoners. Especially when the task required him to travel long distances. There was plenty of hell-raising and lawbreaking in Fort Worth to keep him occupied. During his career—if he was to be believed—he had chased bank robbers, solved murders, broken up more saloon fights than he could recall, and seen nineteen horse thieves he'd tracked down dangle at the end of a hanging rope.

Before he wore a badge he'd earned a reputation as an Indian fighter. He'd been shot, stabbed, and once set afire by a jealous lady friend, but had always survived and returned to his duties with renewed vigor.

Yet here he was, with an old and angry ranch owner riding beside him, a cowardly man who ordered others to rustle cattle for his benefit. He didn't even sit a horse well, making the going much slower than Singletary preferred.

"I'm of a mind to just go ahead and shoot you and be done with it," the marshal said.

Lester Sinclair stared down at his saddle horn and did not respond. He hadn't uttered a word since being led from the Phantom Hill jail in handcuffs.

At dusk they could see a small farmhouse in the distance, smoke rising from its chimney. "Hope these folks have themselves a barn," the marshal said. "It would provide us far better shelter for the night than camping in the open."

A lantern glowed through one window and chickens, not yet gone to roost, pecked away in the hard dirt out front. They scattered, wings flapping, as the riders neared.

"You fellas needing help?" the farmer said as he appeared on the porch. Two children peeked from the doorway before their mother shooed them back into the cabin.

Singletary doffed his hat. "Marshal Sloan Singletary. We're travelin' to the northeast," he said, "and looking for a place to bunk down for the night. Reckon there's a chance we might sleep in your barn? I got money to pay."

"You bein' the law," the farmer said, "there'll be no charge. Proud to have the company. We'll soon be sittin' down for supper if you're hungry." He noticed the shackles on Sinclair's wrists. "That some desperado you've got with you?"

Singletary laughed. "Nope, just an old man who'll not do you or your family any harm. You needn't worry."

The marshal joined them inside after tying Sinclair to a corner post in the barn and taking the saddles from their horses.

"Won't the man riding with you be needing some supper?" the wife said as they sat down. "I've got hot biscuits and redeye gravy and what's left of the greens I put up at the end of the summer."

Singletary was already reaching for a biscuit. "I suggest we wait to see if there's anything left once everybody's had their fill," he said. "If you got somethin' to spare, I'll take him a plate directly." He smiled across the table at the children, who were unable to keep their eyes off the two pearl-handled Colts on his hips.

"He'll also be needing a blanket," she said, "as will you."

The visitor seemed in no hurry to feed his prisoner. Long after the meal ended and the dishes were cleared, he remained at the table, entertaining the farmer and the children with stories of his past exploits.

He told them of the thief he'd chased all the way up to the Palo Duro Canyon and the daylong gunfight that had ensued. Of running the famous Doc Holliday out of a gambling establishment in Fort Worth after proving he'd been cheating. And of range wars he'd helped settle and Indian raids he'd fought against.

There was, he told them, even some talk that a writer from back East named Ned Buntline might soon be doing a book about his life.

Outside the cabin, the darkness and howling wind hid the approach of a mounted man. He left his horse a way back and crept up to the window, where he kneeled, listening as the marshal spun his tall tales.

Except to those who visited his saloon, Isaac Hatchett was an invisible man in Phantom Hill. He had no real friends, never attended Sunday singing, and rarely ventured into Miss Mindy's kitchen, the old one or the new. He rarely mingled with the townspeople. Few even knew his last name or how he'd come to run Lester Sinclair's drinking establishment. No one really cared.

Nor had anyone in town noticed when he locked the front door of the saloon and disappeared shortly after the marshal rode away with his prisoner.

In the days after Sinclair was brought into town and placed in the jail, Hatchett had been the only one other than Weatherby to visit him. At night, after the last customer left, the bartender would sneak across the deserted street and speak with his boss through a small space on the back wall.

There was a purpose for his nocturnal visit—to offer whatever show of support and encouragement he could. He'd spent his entire time as the man's employee trying to curry favor, and he saw no reason to stop simply because his boss was chained inside a jail.

"It saddens me to see you being held this way," the gaunt old man would whisper through the crack. "If there was somethin' I could do to provide you a measure of comfort, I'd quickly do it."

Sinclair's angry reply was always the same. "Get me outta here. Ride out to the ranch and tell my idiot boy that his duty is to see me set free."

Hatchett didn't have the heart to tell him that he'd spoken with Peter when he recently came into town, and was told by the youngest Sinclair that he had no intention of getting involved in the matter. The boy had even hinted that he intended to soon offer the saloon for sale or, worse, shut it down. That would leave Hatchett without a job, the only one his poor health would allow him to keep.

He was amazed by the difference in the Sinclair offspring. Pete, he was certain, would have ridden into town and killed anyone necessary to free his father.

Then he'd probably have a few drinks and maybe pick a fight before leaving. But the saloon-keeper had no idea what had become of him.

Without success, Hatchett had tried to think of a plan whereby he could fulfill Sinclair's demand. But there was no way he would risk trying to break him out with so many people nearby. Too many eyes that might be watching, too many ears listening. In the first place, he knew that Weatherby had the only keys, and he wasn't about to attempt to steal them, lest he be shot or thrown in the jail himself.

But when he learned that a marshal had arrived to take his boss away, he began considering a way to not only demonstrate his loyalty but perhaps be rewarded for it.

He would take the shotgun he kept under the bar, saddle his mare, fill a canteen, and follow them at a safe distance. Having overheard that the marshal's destination was Fort Worth, he knew there was no need to stay close—the road was well marked. His plan was a spur-of-the-moment one, but if he could wait until night when the big lawman and his boss were bedded down, perhaps he could carry out a rescue. If successful, such a heroic act would endear him to the old man forever.

Now here he was, crouched beneath the window of the farmhouse, shivering and doubting the wisdom of his plan, wondering what his next step would be.

He waited in the shadows, holding his breath, as the marshal finally appeared on the front porch, his arms loaded with blankets and a basket of food. He listened as the farmer said good night, and watched Singletary slowly walk toward the barn. It sounded as if he was whistling.

Hatchett remained motionless, his knees stiff and aching and his mouth dry, until the lantern inside the house was doused and the family was sleeping. He heard no sounds from the barn and slowly began to crawl toward its doorway.

Only after letting his eyes adjust to the darkened interior was he able to see the outline of two figures. The marshal lay on a mound of hay, his head resting against his saddle, his legs covered by the blanket provided by the farmer's wife. His boots sat nearby, his hat still on his head, tilted to cover most of his face.

If, Hatchett thought, he was the bold and seasoned lawman he'd claimed to be in his storytelling, it was likely he was a light sleeper, easily alerted by the slightest sound.

Opposite Singletary, his prisoner sat tied against a post, his arms behind him, wrists cuffed and his ankles bound by the same rope that was wound across his chest. A blanket was spread over his lap and the food basket lay at his side.

For several minutes Hatchett listened to the rhythmic snoring of the marshal before getting to his feet and putting the cold stock of the shotgun to his shoulder. His heart was pounding and he'd never felt more afraid. He considered turning and running toward the horse he'd tethered several hundred yards away, leaving Sinclair to fend for himself.

He stepped into the barn and pressed his body against the wall.

The marshal's snoring stopped. With a grunt, he rolled onto his side and pulled the blanket tighter. Only after he was settled and snoring again did Hatchett realize he was holding his breath.

The next thing he became aware of was Lester

Sinclair's piercing eyes. Even in the dim light, the saloon-keeper saw that they were staring directly at him. With Sinclair awake and aware of his presence, turning back was no longer an option. Hatchett took half a dozen quick steps toward the marshal and pressed the shotgun against his neck.

Singletary awoke and reached for his pistol with his right hand, but Hatchett knocked it away with the barrel of his gun. "Hands where they can be seen," he said. When Singletary attempted to rise to a sitting position, Hatchett pushed him back with the heel of his boot. "I don't mind tellin' you I've got little experience at this sort of thing," the nervous saloon-keeper said, "and for that reason I'm not likely to show much restraint."

From across the room, Sinclair spoke in a guttural voice. "Kill him."

The marshal's raised hands were shaking as Hatchett cocked the shotgun and pressed it harder against him. "I'll thank you to slowly unbuckle your gun belt."

"Kill him," Sinclair repeated, this time louder.

Hatchett felt a panic rising in his throat and feared he might be sick to his stomach. He'd never shot a man. But he breathed easier as Singletary's gun belt fell into the hay.

"Kill him . . . *now*," Sinclair yelled.

As his command echoed through the building, the farmer appeared in the doorway. Barefoot and still in his long johns, he peered into the darkness. "What's going on in here?"

The sound of another voice sent Hatchett over the edge. There was a loud boom, followed by a wisp of smoke, a guttural sound, and the sudden scent of burned flesh. He wasn't even aware he'd pulled the trigger until he saw the marshal fall back, his eyes wide-open in a blank stare. There was a gaping hole in his chest.

Hatchett turned the shotgun toward the unarmed farmer and ordered him to untie Sinclair. "Most likely," he said, "you'll find the key to the handcuffs in the lawman's pocket. But take care to keep your hands away from his pistols. I've just killed a man for the first time in my life and I'd prefer it be the last."

Once freed, Sinclair stood up and dusted his pants. He smiled and there was a renewed vigor in his movement as he collected the dead marshal's pistols. "You've done me a good turn, Isaac," he said. "I'm grateful."

He turned and shot the farmer in the thigh. "I see no need to kill him," he said, "but neither do we want him spreading the news about what's just occurred. At least till we're well on our way." He pulled the marshal's saddle from beneath his body. "I'll be riding his horse as we head back to the ranch."

Hatchett walked past the moaning farmer into the cold night air and took a series of deep breaths. He felt he was going to faint.

Chapter 26

While Blanca and Tracker watered the horses at a small spring, Coy Jennings sat on a nearby outcrop, watching a mother coyote as she leisurely cleaned her pups. He was far enough away that he posed no threat to the animals, and the sun's warmth felt good on his aching leg. He was feeling more relaxed than he'd been since he and his companions crossed the river and returned to Texas.

Tracker approached. "We should be on our way."

Jennings didn't move. "I know where Pete's likely to be headed," he said. "It came to me last night as I was trying to sleep."

When Blanca joined them, Coy shared his thoughts.

"The fool's headed home," he said. "Not that he seems to know his way, but that's his intent. He's unaware of what all's taken place at the Bend in his absence. To his thinkin', it remains a safe place to be, with his old man orderin' a bunkhouse full of hands to do his dirty work and provide protection. Pete had already gone into hidin' before Bagbee and his men raided the place and took back their cattle. He's had no way of knowing that his daddy's in the Phantom Hill Jail and likely to soon be taken away by a marshal."

He looked at Blanca. "Far as he's aware, you and your friends are still there, waiting for whatever instructions he might be inclined to give. I reckon he's in for a big surprise when he returns and sees what's changed."

Blanca was incredulous. "We should allow him to return?"

Jennings nodded. So did the Indian. "We can cease this tiresome trackin' and sleepin' in the cold," Coy said. "My thinkin' is we'll save ourselves time and additional saddle sores by determining us a direct route to the Bend of the River Ranch. I figure Tracker here can show us the way. Once there, we'll just sit and wait for him."

"And then kill him," Blanca said.

"Sooner'n you think, we'll be needin' to toss us a coin to see who gets the first shot," Jennings said.

Tracker was already scanning the horizon to determine the way.

Thirty miles away, so was Pete Sinclair.

After days of hard but aimless riding, he'd reached a river and believed he'd finally found the landmark for which he'd been searching. If he followed its course eastward, he thought, it would eventually lead him to the Bend. His spirits lifted, he briefly put aside concerns about his pursuers and walked his horse into the shallows to allow it to drink and cool its tired legs.

Pete kneeled and filled his hat with the rust-colored water and poured it over his head, smiling as the icy shower refreshed him. The weather had warmed considerably in the past few days. "Won't be long now," he said. It didn't occur to him that he'd been talking to himself a great deal in recent days.

He'd traveled only a couple of miles upriver when he saw two riders on the opposite bank. They were moving slowly in the opposite direction with a pack mule following along. Sinclair called out to them, then forded the river.

"Mornin' to you," he said as he approached. The men appeared to be about his father's age. Neither seemed friendly.

"I mean nobody harm," Sinclair said when he saw that both had their hands resting against their holsters. "Fact is, I've lost my way and was wondering if you might assist me. What brings you fellas to this unappealin' country?"

"Headin' toward New Mexico to do some prospectin'. Word we hear is there's claims waitin' to be made and riches to be had."

"Then I'll wish you luck."

The men dismounted. "We were about to rest our stock and make a fire for some coffee," one said. "You're welcome to join us." He cackled. "Unless, of course, you got somebody chasing you and can't afford to linger."

Sinclair forced a laugh. For the first time he could remember, hot coffee sounded even better than a shot of whiskey.

"And where is it *you're* headed?"

"Just tryin' to get home," Pete said. "I was down in Mexico, doing some cattle business, and once I got back into Texas, I met up with a terrible blizzard that caused me to get plumb turned around—embarassin' as that may sound. Thought for a time me and my horse was both gonna freeze to death."

"That manner of misfortune ain't uncommon out this way," one of the men said. "That's why we carry us a map. 'Fore I forget, let me fetch it and provide you some directions."

Pete kneeled next to the fire and fanned it with his still-wet hat. "Is this river called the Brazos?"

The two men laughed. "No, sir, it ain't," the one pouring the coffee said. "This sorry excuse for a river is the Pecos." He pointed to the northwest. "You'll find the Brazos a couple hundred miles in that direction, though you'll see the Colorado first. Here, lemme show you."

He unfolded his map and laid it in the sand, pointing a bony finger to the Brazos River. "You've still got a far piece to go," he said. "On a good horse, I'd say a week, maybe more."

"Then I'd best be on my way," Sinclair said. "I'm obliged for the coffee. And I hope you'll be men of considerable wealth next time our paths cross."

As the prospectors kicked embers into the river, Sinclair glanced toward their horses. He wondered if either might be stronger than the one he was riding.

It was the good fortune of the aspiring gold miners that their mounts looked no better.

"He seemed a nice enough fella," one said as they watched Sinclair ride away.

Miss Mindy was scrubbing the last of the pots she'd used for preparing dinner when she noticed April McLean was standing in the doorway, a forlorn look on her face. Now that Ira Dalton was up and about—well on his way to recovery, Doc Matthews had said—she had spent less time attending his needs and more in the kitchen. It had given Mindy an opportunity to observe her.

"Seems you're a million miles away," she said.

April turned and smiled as she brushed a stray ringlet from her face. "Just tired, I suppose."

Mindy dried her hands on her apron and walked from the kitchen. "Let's sit for a minute," she said.

They were silent as Mindy lit a cigar and blew a smoke ring. After watching it slowly float toward the kitchen ceiling, she spoke. "Now that things seemed to have settled and there's been a show of progress in Phantom Hill," she said, "I'm hoping you and your little girl—she's as polite as she is pretty, if I've not said so before—will plan on stayin' here. With Jakie now cookin' out at the Bend, I'll be needin' to take on a full-time partner, and you would be my first choice."

"I'm flattered at the thought," April said, "but we don't even have a place to call home. Penelope and I can't continue to intrude on the doctor's hospitality."

"If I'm right, I think the next thing you'll see happening in Phantom Hill is the building of additional houses. Could be there'll even be new businesses starting up. I've already heard talk from a couple of the men about opening a lumberyard. There's also a rumor that now that his pa's gone, Peter Sinclair might be of a mind to sell the saloon to a reputable buyer. Not that I care for the place, but I see its value to a community. Though I'd prefer they spend their money on the food I cook, men need somewhere for their occasional Saturday-night socializing.

"For the first time since I arrived here, I'm sensing a feeling of pride among folks who wish to see this little town grow to something more than it now is. I'd like to see us have ourselves a schoolhouse—maybe you could be the teacher—and even a proper church one of these days."

April smiled and reached across the table to place

a hand on Mindy's shoulder. "As every day passes, you're sounding more and more like a politician."

"I s'pose so. It goes with the business of bein' mayor. If I'm not optimistic, who will be?" She blew another smoke ring. "Another thing I'm hopin' is that with a bit of encouragement from you, once Coy Jennings returns he'll consider settling here and continuing to serve as sheriff. I'm not sure how we'll manage it, but we'll be needin' to offer him a salary for his work—"

"With *my* encouragement?"

"Unless I'm sadly mistaken," Mindy said, smiling, "that won't be a difficult chore for you to assume."

April McLean blushed. "Perhaps you're right," she said.

Part Three

Chapter 27

Peter Sinclair began to settle into the responsibilities of running things at the Bend. Every day he rode out to work the cattle, seeing that wagonloads of hay were delivered and scattered. Dallas, becoming his most trusted hand, had explained the need to do so until spring warmed the ground and the dormant grass again appeared to provide ample food for the herd. He was learning to spot an animal suffering from scours and how to treat the ailment, rising early to make sure that cows were being milked, pigs slopped, and Jakie was delivering breakfast to the bunkhouse.

The workdays were long and hard, but satisfying. They kept his mind off things he didn't wish to think about.

When Giles Weatherby arrived with his farrier wagon one morning to shoe some of the ranch's horses, Peter was pleased that the livery owner was friendly as he stoked the fire pit behind the barn.

"You need to be showin' yourself in town a bit more often," Weatherby said. "Your welcomed donations have caused the meals at the kitchen to be considerably improved. You should ride in and sample some of Miss Mindy's cookin'." When Peter didn't reply, Giles added, "Ain't no grudge being held against you in Phantom Hill. Folks know you had no part in your pa's business. He's gone, long since taken to appear before a judge up in Fort Worth. It's not likely he'll ever be seen in these parts again."

Sinclair asked, "Reckon what's become of my brother?"

"That I couldn't say. It's my understandin' there's folks looking for him, but it could be he'll not be found. And if you don't mind my sayin', that would be a relief to everybody, yourself included."

Peter watched Weatherby work for a while before leaving to make his rounds. "I've asked Jakie to see to it you get coffee and something to eat 'fore you leave," he said.

"Thanks. Be sure I remember to tell him Miss Mindy's been asking when he'll be visiting." He laughed. "Ain't that a pair?"

It was that evening, as he sat in the kitchen with his cook, when Peter thought to ask if Weatherby had passed along Miss Mindy's invitation. Jakie was warming a pan of beans and a slice of ham for his dinner.

"I don't mind tellin' you," he said, "that woman scares me more'n a little. Demanding as she is, I find her hard to please."

"From what I hear, they all are," Peter said.

Jakie cleared his throat as he placed a plate in front of his new boss. "On a different matter," he said, "Thanksgiving's approaching. Then soon after it'll be

Christmas. I was wonderin' if you had any special preparations you'll want me to make."

The question caused Peter's thoughts to flash back to his boyhood days, a time when life on the ranch had been simpler, even pleasant. His father hadn't seemed so driven, so hard and unhappy in those days, and his brother had yet to become a bully who delighted in making his life miserable. Jakie's question reminded him of crisp mornings when Lester Sinclair would take Pete and him to hunt wild turkey.

"Last time I was down that way," he said, "there seemed to be plenty of good-sized gobblers nesting in that stand of trees in the south pasture. My guess is the hands would appreciate a turkey dinner. You know how to prepare properly seasoned corn bread dressin'?"

"No, but I expect Miss Mindy could show me."

"Maybe that would be a good reason for you paying her a visit," Peter said.

He was still smiling as he made his way up the stairs to go to bed.

The room was in shadows, faintly lit only by the moonlight that filtered in from the open window. The curtains flapped gently as Peter closed the door and sat on the edge of the bed to remove his boots. He was too tired to bother lighting the lamp sitting on a nearby table.

As one boot fell to the floor, he heard a familiar voice that came from the corner of the room, causing an icy shiver to run through his body.

"Hello, son," Lester Sinclair said.

Peter squinted in the direction of his father.

"You seem surprised to see me," Lester said.

"I thought you—"

"Was on my way to face a judge and be locked away in prison. Or worse. Well, clearly, that ain't gonna be happening. I've returned home with some questions I'd like to hear answered."

He rose from his chair and walked toward Peter. "Why was it you never bothered to visit me when I was in that jail? Why didn't you try to break me out?"

His son had no reply.

"Where's my boy Pete? And that fella Coy Jennings, who I look forward to soon seein' dead?"

"You'll not like the answers I have for your questions," Peter said. "Truth is, I could see no good reason to visit you. Nor was there any logic to trying to help you escape. We'd both have gotten ourselves killed. As to Pete, I ain't seen him since you sent him away. And I don't know the whereabouts of Jennings. He's not visited here since the day he came and arrested you."

Lester sat on the bed next to him. His clothes were caked with mud and he smelled of sweat and rotted hay. His breath caused Peter to turn away as he spoke.

"You're not looking too good," the son said.

"I will, once I've cleaned up and had me a drink or two."

"Now that you're here, what are your intentions?"

"I plan to see things are put back the way they were, of course," Lester said. "First, there's some business needin' done to remind folks around here who's in charge. I'll want you to gather the hands tomorrow so I can speak to them. Then I'm thinking of watching Phantom Hill burn to the ground before it gets too big for its britches. Won't be a bunch of meddlin' Yankees to protect 'em this time."

He stood and looked down at Peter. "We'll have more talkin' to do at a later time," he said, "but for now all I need to know is that you won't be telling anybody in town that I'm here. That understood?"

Peter's shoulders slumped. "Understood."

His father returned to his chair.

"Now I've got a question," Peter said. "Had I been the one in jail, would you have come to see me or attempted to get me out?"

This time Lester Sinclair didn't reply.

In the dark hallway, Jakie slowly moved away from the door and crept down the stairway, still holding the coffee he had brought up for Peter.

It was well past midnight when Miss Mindy was awakened by pounding at her back door. She pulled her robe tight against her throat, picked up a boning knife from the table, and went to investigate the commotion.

"You drunk?" she said as she saw Jakie standing in the dark, shivering. He was still wearing an apron under his jacket. "Come in outta the cold, you ol' fool. A little late for calling, don't you think?"

He held his hat in his hand, nervously tracing its brim with his fingers. "I'm stone sober," he said, "and I'm fully aware of the lateness. But there's something I need to tell you, you bein' the mayor."

She waved him inside. "Sit yourself down and let me see if the coals are still hot enough to brew coffee."

"Has Sheriff Jennings returned?" Jakie said. One leg twitched as he spoke.

"Not unless he rode in durin' the middle of the night. What is it that's got you so riled up?"

"Lester Sinclair's back. Out at the Bend as we speak."

"You *are* drunk."

"I swear, I ain't had a drop. He's there, I'm tellin' ya." He described the conversation he'd overheard earlier.

"Sweet heavenly Jesus," Mindy said. "How could this happen? I watched with my own eyes as the marshal took him away. He was wearing handcuffs and looking about as pitiful as any man I've ever seen—includin' present company."

She banged three empty cups onto the table. "Since I'm not properly dressed, you'll need to go over to the livery and wake Giles Weatherby. Tell him coffee will soon be ready and to get his deputized self over here. We need to have us a discussion."

A few minutes later, Weatherby arrived in a foul mood. "Seems to me a mayor callin' a meeting in the middle of the night is stepping far beyond the bounds of her assigned authority." He was still grumbling as he reached for the cup of coffee Miss Mindy pushed toward him.

Only when she had Jakie repeat what he'd told her did the blacksmith calm.

"What could have happened?" Mindy said.

"Of more concern to me is what's *gonna* happen," said Weatherby. "Knowing Lester Sinclair, he's not returned home to live out a peaceful life. He's mad about what's been done to him and has already begun plannin' his revenge."

"And what do you figure we're facin'?"

"The greatest of my concerns at the moment is the well-bein' of Coy Jennings," Weatherby said. "It's him who was responsible for Lester being jailed and several other affronts. The only good I can think of at the moment is that Coy's currently away. But since Lester ain't likely to know that, there's a good chance he and some of his men will soon come to town lookin' for him. And we can trust they'll not arrive in a good mood."

"What 'men' is it you're speakin' of?" Mindy said.

"Don't think for a minute those hands who were set free to assist young Peter are still feelin' obliged for bein' released. The minute ol' Lester looks 'em in the eye and reminds 'em it's him paying their wages, they'll do whatever he asks."

The discussion went on into the wee hours, long after Weatherby urged Jakie to return to the ranch before his absence was detected.

The livery owner rubbed his face and stood to stretch his legs. "I'm mostly wishing that our sheriff was here to tend to this," he said. "Meanwhile, I reckon we should call a town meetin' for tomorrow to alert folks there might be trouble. As soon as it's daylight, I'll ride out to Buck Burton's farm and ask him to assist in spreading the word."

At noon the following day, Miss Mindy's kitchen was full as she and Weatherby explained the situation. Several men volunteered to return home and retrieve their weapons, then alternate standing guard at the edge of town.

Ira Dalton stood at the back of the crowd. He reached out for April McLean's hand. "Is Mr. Jennin's likely to be hurt?" he said. "If that's the case, I'd soon he never comes back, even with me missin' him like I do."

April squeezed his hand. "He'll be back," she said, smiling, "and everything will be okay. Don't you worry." She turned away and the smile disappeared.

Weatherby was lost in thought as he walked back toward the livery. Waiting for a wagon to pass, he glanced down the street in the direction of the saloon.

He noticed that it had reopened, but Isaac Hatchett hadn't bothered to attend the meeting.

Chapter 28

Thunder rolled angrily and lightning zigzagged across the night sky as Pete Sinclair rode along the swollen banks of the river. Drenched, he wondered aloud if the world might be coming to an end. He laughed at the thought. If Judgment Day was indeed on the way, he would at least be able to welcome it from the comfort of home.

When the flashes briefly lit the way, he caught glimpses of familiar terrain and pressed his hands against his head in an effort to think clearly. The route of the river, he knew, would eventually take him to the Bend. Somewhere, off to his right, was Phantom Hill, where one of his enemies was sleeping, warm and dry and unaware that he had returned.

Should he confront Coy Jennings before riding on to the ranch? He'd spent days thinking of ways he would kill the man he was sure had stolen April McLean away.

And what of April? Thoughts of her had seldom left his mind during his travels. Her soft voice had constantly played in his head. He'd only needed to close his eyes to bring her smiling face to mind. He wanted to see her, talk to her, convince her of his feelings. Once he took care of Jennings, she would again be his. But where was she?

He rubbed a hand against his throat. Before he could think clearly, he needed a drink to quiet the voices in his head and warm his insides. He turned his horse from its muddy course and slowly rode toward town.

As he reached the far end of Giles Weatherby's pasture, he was surprised to see several head of cattle bunched together in the pelting rain. He tied his reins to a corner post, dismounted, and crept toward them. As another bolt of lightning brightened the sky, he was able to see that the livestock bore the brand of the Bend. He added it to the growing list of things that made no sense to him.

Avoiding the street, he made his way through the shadows past the livery and the general store until he was at the back door of the saloon. Though it was locked, he had no trouble breaking it from its hinges as he pushed his shoulder into it.

The sound of splintering wood woke Isaac Hatchett. "That's far enough," he called out as he cocked his shotgun.

"Put the gun down, old man. It's me, Pete."

"I thought you was—"

"Whiskey," Pete said.

As Hatchett went behind the bar, Sinclair moved to the front window. Across the street he could see the faint outline of a building that was unfamiliar to him. At the far end of town he thought he saw movement.

"Be aware there's men guarding the entrance to town, even in this foul weather," the saloon-keeper said.

"Why's that?"

"They're thinking your pa and his men might ride in and cause trouble."

"For what reason?"

Hatchett moved to the window. "See that new building? It's a jail. After the considerable commotion raised out at the ranch by men who came to retrieve cattle that was stolen from their boss, the sheriff locked Lester up."

"The *sheriff*?"

Hatchett continued to stare out at the pouring rain. "Yep, that's what the Jennings fella is now bein' called."

Pete swore and grabbed the bottle, taking a long drink that sent a warm sensation down his throat and into his stomach. He moved away from the window and toward a table. "Sit and tell me what's been happenin' in my absence," he said. "I find it confusin', so start from the beginnin'."

Isaac sat across from Sinclair. He told him of the arrival of Will Bagbee and his men, of the raid on the ranch and the arrest of Pete's father and his hands. "I'm speaking, of course, of them that wasn't killed. And the cowardly Mexicans, who rode off soon as the shootin' started. That's talk I only heard, bein' as I wasn't actually there to see what took place. I do know for a fact that all but your pa were eventually let out of the jail to return to the Bend and help your brother." He paused. "And young Repete's been runnin' things as he's seen fit. Until recently."

He described the marshal's arrival to take Lester Sinclair to Fort Worth to be tried. In dramatic detail he described rescuing Pete's father and returning him to the ranch. The physical stature of the marshal had grown even larger in the telling and a frantic shootout had occurred before he was able to free the ranch owner. Hatchett made no mention of ever being unsure or afraid.

"What you did for my pa . . . I'm obliged." Pete took another long swallow. "Now tell me about Jennings."

"My understanding is that he went searchin' for you. Ain't seen him around here in a number of days."

Pete thought of the men who had been following him. It wasn't just Mexicans. Jennings was riding with them.

"It's unlikely your daddy is aware of his absence," Hatchett said. "I've thought of going out to the ranch to alert him, and tell him of the men currently standing guard. But it would be a difficult thing to do without bein' noticed."

"I'll see to that, directly," Pete said. "First, I've got another matter that needs tendin'. Where's April McLean?"

"I'd advise you not to allow yourself to be seen here in town," he said. "There's something happened in Phantom Hill lately. More'n building that jail across the street. People's thinkin' has changed considerable of late. Two men—Weatherby and Burton—have been deputized by Jennings, and they seem to be takin' their responsibility seriously. When there was talk your daddy could be coming to town, might near everybody with a shotgun showed up to stand watch. If you don't mind my sayin', folks seem to have made up their minds that they ain't gonna be bullied by your family."

Pete scoffed. "We'll see about that. Again, do you know April's whereabouts?"

"I occasionally see her walking over to Miss Mindy's kitchen," Isaac said. "I think she's been helping out there. She and her little girl are living over at Doc Matthews's place."

"I'll be needin' to borrow your shotgun," Sinclair said. He looked out the window to see that the rainstorm had ended. "I'll also want that can of coal oil you keep behind the bar. Then go to the shed and saddle your horse."

"You're plumb crazy," Hatchett said.

"That could well be," Sinclair said, and got unsteadily to his feet.

By the time the front wall of the jail was fully aflame, Sinclair was already back on the opposite side of the street, slipping through the pitch-blackness toward the rear of the doctor's house.

Those who had been standing watch ran toward the fire. "Lightnin's hit the jail," one man shouted.

The noise woke Doc Matthews, who stepped onto his front porch, hastily buttoning his britches and pulling up his suspenders. April rushed to the doorway, a blanket wrapped around her shoulders. Silently they watched the flames. From the shadows near the back of the house, Pete Sinclair saw Giles Weatherby run past, closely followed by Ira Dalton. The doctor hurried down the steps to join them.

April turned to go into the house. A large hand pressed against her mouth, and a powerful arm encircled her waist. The scream she attempted died in her throat. She was aware of the strong smell of whiskey on her attacker's breath as he placed his face against her cheek. "I ain't here to hurt you," he whispered.

Her knees buckled and the blanket slipped from her shoulders as she fainted.

The fire was put out quickly as a bucket brigade was established between the watering trough in front of the saloon and the jail. The walls, already wet from the nightlong downpour, had only smoldered once the initial flame died away.

"The damage ain't as bad as it coulda been," Weatherby said as he wiped soot from his face.

"It wasn't started by any act of nature either," the doctor said. He was holding a crock jug he'd found near the doorway of the building. It smelled of coal oil. "Somebody set this fire."

Weatherby asked several of the men who had been standing sentry if they had seen anyone come into town. No one had. Puzzled, the livery owner and the doctor walked together down the muddy street. They were nearing Matthews's house when they saw Miss Mindy standing on the porch, hugging Penelope McLean. The girl was crying.

"What's the matter?" Weatherby said.

"I was comin' to find out what all the carryin'-on was about," Mindy said, "when I seen little Penelope standing here, sobbin'."

The child lifted her face from Mindy's bosom. "Mama's gone," she said.

Chapter 29

Lester Sinclair stood in front of the men assembled near the bunkhouse, looking far better than he had the night before. He'd bathed and trimmed his beard, and wore fresh clothes and a pair of polished boots. The new cook, whose name he could not remember, had coffee waiting for him when he awoke, then prepared him a breakfast of eggs, ham, and wheat-grain flapjacks.

The rain had ended and the skies were filled with white, puffy clouds. The crisp morning air smelled clean.

"I suppose," he said, "there are those of you somewhat surprised to see me."

The looks on the men's faces were his answer.

"It's my understandin' that my boy Repete has done a fine job of looking after things in my absence, and I thank him kindly for it. But now that I'm back, it's me who is in charge. And I don't mind saying I'm more'n a little upset about certain things. Truthfully, mad is what I am."

He launched into a steaming tirade about the poor

defense that had been put up when the raid on the ranch occurred. He talked of the humiliation of being paraded into town "like a common thief" and locked in jail, of how his cattle had been "stolen." And when he spoke of Coy Jennings, his conversation became laced with curses.

"I'll not tolerate being treated in such a manner," he said, "and soon we'll make him and the rest of 'em know who runs this part of the country. If I have my way—and generally I do—Phantom Hill will soon be nothing more'n a bad memory."

Several of the hands took silent note of the fact that Sinclair's younger son was nowhere to be seen.

"I'm expecting Pete will soon be returning to again act as foreman," Lester said. "Once he's back, we'll consider a plan. In the meantime, you're to carry on as usual—except you'll want to stay alert for anything that might seem of an unusual nature. And if anyone from town sets foot on the Bend, shoot 'em."

The previous night's lightning storm had spooked their horses so badly that Jennings, Tracker, and Blanca took shelter beneath a rock overhang near Blue Flats. With their kerchiefs they blindfolded the frightened animals, then hobbled them with strips of rope.

Aware they were near the place where he and his men had briefly camped, Blanca had spent much of the night glaring into the pounding storm. "Though I cannot see it," he said, "I know it is very near. I had hoped never to see the cursed place again. If there is truly a gateway to hell, that's where it is to be found. Even this rain could not wash away its evil stench."

Tracker nodded. "Despite this delay," he said as he looked into the clear morning sky, "I believe us to still be ahead of the man we seek. He would have been a fool to travel in last night's weather."

Jennings was standing by Rodeo, stroking his mane. "We'll ride on toward the ranch house and determine a proper place to watch for his arrival," he said.

Blanca turned to the sheriff. "We will soon end this journey," he said. "And I wish to tell you something I never thought I would say to any lawman. You are now my friend. You have a good heart and are a man who seeks to only do that which is right. For you, killing is not an easy thing. I have no such problem. For me, avenging my son must be done. Putting this man Sinclair to death will only bring me great joy, so I ask that you stand aside when the time comes and allow me to do it."

Jennings looked into the Mexican's eyes for several seconds but said nothing.

"It will be the last request I make of you," Blanca said.

Even at first light, April had difficulty recognizing the man riding next to her. Only his voice assured her that it was Pete Sinclair who had abducted her. Since she'd last seen him he had changed dramatically. His eyes were sunken and had a wild look. He'd lost weight, and he was filthy. Though he had talked constantly since carrying her from the doctor's house, his thoughts seemed confused.

"Where are you taking me?" She attempted to speak calmly despite a fear that caused a painful knot in her stomach.

"Home," he grunted. He rambled about a trip to Mexico to check on some cattle, of how he'd missed her, and how it would be good to again spend evenings watching the mare and her colt in the corral. "I'll see you're happy and taken care of once we're back at the Bend."

"My baby will wake and wonder what's become of me," April said. He didn't seem to be aware of the raid that had occurred at the ranch, or his father's arrest, so she made no mention of it.

Pete reached across and touched her arm. He saw that she was crying again. "Not to concern yourself," he said. "We'll fetch her shortly, soon as certain things are taken care of."

Twenty minutes later, the sun was just peeking through the trees as they emerged from the riverbank on the back side of the ranch. Pete's face broke into a smile when he saw the house. "It's good to return," he said.

The routine at the Bend seemed normal as Jennings and Blanca made their way to the rear of the barn while Tracker hid behind a watering trough near the bunkhouse. Those ranch hands who weren't already in the pastures went about chores in the corrals and down by the pigpen. Two were hauling hay to be placed around the bases of the fruit trees in the orchard.

None noticed the three intruders as they crawled into position.

Except for Jakie, whom Coy could see through the kitchen window, the house seemed quiet. "Could be young Peter's out among the herd," Jennings said. "If so, that's good. We'll not want him in harm's way should Pete arrive wishing to put up a fight."

"Amigo, that is my hope," Blanca said.

Before the men working the orchard made their way back toward the barn, Jennings signaled to Blanca and they hurried inside and climbed a ladder leading to the loft. "From this position," he said, "we'll have a view in all directions."

They could see Tracker was making his way to the rear of the bunkhouse.

They had been in place for only a short time when Armando nudged Jennings's shoulder and pointed toward the river. "Two horses coming," he said as he raised his rifle.

Jennings put a hand on the barrel of Blanca's gun, pushing it away. "Things just got complicated," he whispered. His throat was suddenly dry and his chest tightened. What he was seeing puzzled him for a moment. "He's got a woman riding with him."

Only when they neared the ranch house could he see that it was April McLean. Dressed only in a night-gown with a blanket over her shoulders, she obviously had not accompanied Sinclair of her own free will.

"I am a good shot," Blanca said as he lifted his rifle back into position.

As he did so, Pete dismounted, pulled April from her saddle, and headed toward the porch steps.

"They're standin' too close," Coy said. "Too risky."

"But what . . . ?"

"We wait. I need to think out a plan."

A stunned look crossed Lester Sinclair's face as he saw his smiling son and a frightened April McLean enter the main room. Then it turned to anger and he hurled his coffee cup toward the fireplace.

"I swear, you're a bigger fool than any I've ever previously known," he said. "Whatever possessed you to bring this woman here?"

"Ain't you glad to see me back?"

Lester shook his head. "Look at you. All dirty and half-dead but grinnin' like a possum. Did you go plumb crazy in your absence?"

His son scowled. "You'll recall, old man, that it wasn't my idea to take my leave. The only fool thing about me is doin' what you told me. I've been sick and nearly killed since you sent me away." He attempted to recount the dangers he'd faced during his winding journey but found it difficult to focus, to keep things in proper sequence. As he spoke, his father glared at him.

Finally Pete's shoulders sank. "I expected a bit warmer welcome, is all I'm sayin'."

"You've not answered my question about the woman."

"I stopped in town," Pete said, "so she could return and be with me . . . with us."

April stood near the shattered pieces of the elder Sinclair's mug, shivering as she listened to the exchange between two men she believed to be insane, wondering how Lester had managed to elude the marshal and return to the Bend. She turned toward the kitchen and saw Jakie peeking through the doorway. She shook her head ever so slightly.

"Mr. Sinclair," she said, "I wish you to know I'm not responsible for whatever inconvenience my presence causes you. If you like, I can get you another cup of coffee while you continue your conversation with your son."

Lester looked at her. "Bring two," he said. "Me 'n' Pete got a lotta talking to do." He paused, then spoke in a gentler tone. "Did my boy do you any harm?"

"No, sir," she said as she turned toward the kitchen.

Jakie quickly moved to April's side. "How is it he's back?" she whispered. "And where's Peter?"

Jakie glanced toward the main room before replying, "Mr. Sinclair just showed up, lookin' about as bad as Pete does now. He's got his other son locked away in a bedroom upstairs after considerable shoutin' during the night. I delivered him breakfast and had to hand-feed him, since he was bound to a chair." His hands shook as he poured coffee. "I wish I'd never come to this place."

By the time she returned to the main room with their coffee, the men were seated in front of the fireplace. Lester was attempting to explain the events that had transpired while Pete was in hiding, but he wasn't sure his son was fully comprehending what he was saying. As he recounted the raid and being taken to jail, the only thing that seemed to register was the mention of Coy Jennings's name.

"The main reason I've returned," Pete said, "is to see him dead."

Lester Sinclair relaxed and smiled. "I'd be much obliged to see that done," he said.

In Phantom Hill, the search for April was frantic. Long before the rain ended, residents gathered at Miss Mindy's and were assigned areas to look. From one end of town and into the surrounding landscape, they rode and walked, calling out her name until daylight arrived. Ignoring the doctor's warning, Ira Dalton took his mule from the livery and joined in. Miss Mindy lit every lantern in her kitchen and made coffee for the searchers.

"Somebody's abducted her," Giles Weatherby said as he stopped in to check on April's daughter. "That business with the jail bein' set on fire was to turn our attention away."

"But by who?" Mindy said.

"Don't know for sure," Giles said, "but there's a fella that I'm on my way to speak with."

A few minutes later he was knocking on the back door of the saloon. On the way, he'd stopped at the livery to get his shotgun.

Isaac Hatchett peered through a narrow opening. "What'll you be wantin' this time of the mornin'?"

Weatherby pushed at the door, and it swung open easily. "Looks like you're needin' some repairs," he said. "Somebody bust your door down recently?"

Hatchett didn't answer as he retreated inside, followed by the livery owner.

"You've been actin' strangely of late, Isaac, and I've come to allow you an opportunity to explain why."

"What business is it of yours?"

"In case you ain't heard, I've been officially deputized by the sheriff. That's what makes what you and everybody else does my business. I noticed, for instance, that you were closed for a few days a while back and when I came to check on you, I seen your horse was missin'. Then, next thing I know, you're back open for business but didn't see fit to attend the town meetin' that was recently called. And last night, when there was a fire needin' to be put out across the street, everybody but you showed up to lend a hand."

"I've been feelin' poorly—"

"Just now, when I checked in your shed, you're horse is again missin'."

Weatherby raised the shotgun and pointed it at Hatchett, then lowered the barrel to his right knee. "I ain't here to shoot you, but if it takes that to force you to provide me the information I'm seekin', that's what

I'll do. You've only got one good leg left—wanna lose the other? Where's April McLean, Isaac?"

"Don't know her."

"Who busted down your door and set the fire over at the jail?"

Hatchett shook his head. "I got no knowledge of what you're asking about. I swear—"

"I've got little patience—or time—to spare," Weatherby said as he cocked the shotgun and raised it to Hatchett's chest. "I'm telling you nothing you don't already know when I say that there wouldn't be a tear shed in Phantom Hill if you was found lying dead on this floor."

Hatchett fell to his knees. "It wasn't none of my doin'," he said. "I swear I had no knowledge that he was gonna take the woman."

"Who is it you're speakin' of?"

"It was Pete Sinclair, and he was acting out of his head."

"And where was it he was headed?"

"To the ranch, I 'spect, to meet up with his pa."

"That can't be. Lester Sinclair's headed to Fort Worth, in custody of Marshal Singletary."

"No, he ain't."

In the kitchen, where Miss Mindy sat with Penelope McLean, assuring her that her mother would soon be returning, both jumped at the loud roar that came from down the street.

Mindy rushed to the door in time to see Giles Weatherby coming out of the saloon, his shotgun resting across his shoulder, a wisp of smoke floating from the mouth of its barrel.

"Oh my Lord," she said.

* * *

The hands working in the orchard saw Pete Sinclair's arrival and quietly slipped away. They recognized the woman who had once prepared their meals and assumed she had been taken from town against her will. Lester, they knew, would be unhappy, and they chose to get as far from the ranch house as they could. Instead of turning their wagon back toward the barn, they headed in the direction of the south pasture where others were working.

"We cannot just continue to wait," Blanca said as he watched them ride away.

Jennings's eyes had never left the front door of the house, even as he massaged his aching leg. The only movement he'd seen was a glimpse of April as she briefly appeared near the kitchen window.

"The lady, who I assume to be your friend, is not safe. If we do not do something soon, she will be in even greater danger than she already is," Armando said. "I need not tell you that Pete Sinclair is no gentleman."

Jennings slowly got to his feet, brushing hay from his clothes and adjusting his hat. "I'm gonna call him out," he said. "You stay here, and if a good shot presents itself, take it."

He slowly made his way down the ladder and to the doorway of the barn. He had his rifle at his side as he took a few steps into the sunlight. Placing a hand to the side of his mouth, he called toward the house, "Pete Sinclair, show yourself."

As he spoke, Tracker emerged from his hiding place and walked over to stand beside him. In the open doorway of the loft, Blanca rose and stood in plain sight, his rifle aimed toward the front door. Tracker turned to see him and whispered to Coy, "The more targets, the more difficult it will be for the man inside."

"You're sorely outnumbered," Jennings yelled toward the house. "There's no need for killin', so step out and surrender yourself."

A voice came from inside. "Who are you and what's your business here?"

"I'm Coy Jennings, now sheriff of Phantom Hill, and I've come to arrest you."

There was a lengthy silence before the front door slowly opened. The first person Jennings saw was April McLean. Pete Sinclair stood behind her, an arm around her throat and a pistol at the side of her head.

"I reckon you'll not want to cause this pretty lady harm," Pete said. "I'll politely ask that you and your friends discard your weapons and be on your way."

April struggled until Sinclair tightened his grip around her neck and she began choking. "She's feisty," Pete said. "That's one of the things that caused me to admire her when she first came to the Bend. Long before you was ever around."

Jennings tried to determine a way to handle the situation. "She's no part of this, Pete. Leave her be. If you do, I'll promise you won't be killed."

Sinclair laughed crazily. "How long you been trailin' me, Jennings? Was that you down in Mexico?"

"And me," Blanca shouted from the loft. "That was my son you shot, amigo. Mr. Jennings has already agreed to allow me to be the one who kills you. I can do it quickly—if you release the woman. If you don't, I will slowly cut up your body, piece by piece, and you will wish for death long before it comes."

Pete fired a wild shot toward the loft, the discharge causing April's right ear to ring. "That you, Armando?"

"Consider your odds, Pete," Jennings said.

Before he could respond, another figure appeared in the doorway. It was Peter and he too had a pistol positioned against his temple. The man standing behind him was Lester Sinclair.

"Our odds are good," he said. "Soon my men will be returning from the pasture. I've instructed them all to arm themselves and shoot anyone who trespasses on my ranch. Once they see what you're attempting, Phantom Hill will be without a sheriff and Mexico will be shy one cattle rustler. And one less Indian won't cause any distress."

Until he could think of something, anything, Coy's only plan was to keep the Sinclairs talking. "Last I seen you," he said, "you were bein' led off for prison, or a hanging."

"It's my understandin' that was the way Marshal Singletary was plannin' it," Lester said.

"And what happened to him?"

"Got himself shot dead."

"By you?"

"I can only wish," Sinclair said. "Let's just say a friend helped. I've got lots of friends, Sheriff Jennings."

As he spoke, a shot rang out from the loft, splintering a corner of the doorframe. "It's time you die," Blanca yelled. "I have reached the end of my patience."

"No," Jennings yelled. "No shootin'."

Tracker turned and aimed at Blanca. "I do not wish to kill you," he said, "but I will if you do not put down your rifle."

When the Indian looked back toward the house, the Sinclairs and their hostages had retreated inside. He pulled Coy back into the shadows of the barn.

Jennings gritted his teeth, then kicked at the dirt. "This ain't gonna be easy."

Chapter 30

"Somebody'll be needin' to clean up the mess over at the saloon," Weatherby said as he looked across the table at Miss Mindy. "I've got other matters on my mind." He had just told her that it was Pete Sinclair who took April, and that Lester had escaped from the marshal.

"Won't be me—that's for sure," Mindy said. "Truth is, I didn't much care for Isaac Hatchett even when he was livin'. What is it you figure to do?"

"I wish I knew. Last I heard, Coy and that Indian was attemptin' to locate Pete. I have no idea whether they found his trail and are followin' it. One thing's for sure—they didn't catch him soon enough."

"Could it be they're close behind and nearin' the ranch? And, if so, are they likely to run into trouble they're not expectin'?"

"That's my worry. If it's a fact that Lester Sinclair and his crazy son have been reunited, there's a good chance they'll be wishin' harm on a lot of people. Once they've tended to Coy, they'll be coming here.

And we don't have no Union army to help us this time."

It was the first time he'd ever seen Miss Mindy frightened. "I've got Ira saddling my horse as we speak," Giles said. "I'm gonna ride out toward the ranch and attempt to see what's goin' on."

"You'll need to take some men with you."

Weatherby shook his head. "I don't consider that wise. You 'n' me both know that the men here ain't gunfighters. They acted brave enough, standin' guard during the night, but truth is they're just farmers. I'll not be responsible for more people bein' killed."

As he spoke, the door opened and he turned, expecting to see Dalton. Instead it was Will Bagbee.

"Never thought I'd be seein' you again," Weatherby said.

"Never figured on returnin'," Bagbee said as Mindy hurried to the kitchen to get him a cup of coffee. "I've got business with Coy Jennings but wasn't able to locate him over at your livery." He sat down and leaned back. "And why are you lookin' so glum?"

"You'll recall," Giles said, "that it was his intention to go after Pete Sinclair once y'all settled matters out at the Bend."

Bagbee nodded.

"Well, him and your friend Tracker ain't yet returned. But Pete has." He told the visitor of the abduction of April McLean. When he finished, he drained the fresh coffee Miss Mindy had brought out.

"From what I'm hearin'," he said, "he's taken her to the ranch, and I've been sittin' here tryin' to figure how to get her safely back."

"We should head that way now," Bagbee said as he got to his feet and pulled his hat down tight.

Weatherby held up a hand. "There's more to tell. Seems the marshal you sent to pick up Lester Sinclair didn't make it back to Fort Worth."

"What?"

"I've just learned that Sloan Singletary was killed along the way, and his prisoner is also now back at the Bend."

Bagbee shook his head disgustedly. "I thought I was shed of that place and its craziness once we drove our cattle away. There's no time for me to summon help from up north, so it seems the only thing to do is for us ride out there and see what we can learn about the situation."

Ira peeked through the doorway. "Mr. Weatherby, your horse is ready so you can go 'n' get April. And I'm hopin' you're plannin' to bring Mr. Jennin's back as well. I been worryin' over 'em both."

"We all have," Giles said. "I'm leavin' you in charge of the livery till I return, okay?"

"Okay, Mr. Weatherby. You're the boss."

As the two men walked toward their horses, Miss Mindy moved to Bagbee's side. "Your friend Jakie's out there as well," she said. "He hired on to cook for Peter Sinclair after you left. I'd appreciate you seein' that no harm comes to him."

They rode in silence for the first couple of miles before Weatherby spoke.

"Though it's none of my business," he said, "I was wondering what it is you're needin' to speak with Coy Jennings about."

"I'm to pass on a message from my boss. Seems he was so pleased to get his cattle back that he made a kind gesture I wasn't expectin'. He's offered to provide me with a small corner of his land and a starter herd so I can try makin' it on my own." He smiled. "It's time I settled down. There's this gal in a little town up north that I've had my eye on. She ain't all that pretty, but she's a nice person and a mighty fine cook—close to as good as Miss Mindy. I'm thinkin' we'd make a pretty good team. Maybe even raise us some young'uns."

"Sounds like a good plan to me. Also, it seems you're workin' for a good man."

Bagbee nodded. "That I am. I've done told him I'm of a mind to take him up on his proposition, so he'll soon be needin' a new foreman. He asked if I had anybody to recommend and I gave him Coy's name. Even after I told him he was once a Reb, he said he'd like to speak with him. Said it's time to put war grudges in the past."

"I've no doubt that Jennings would do him a fine job," Giles said. "But I gotta tell you—I hope the position is of no interest to him. He's needed in Phantom Hill."

The wagon rattled into the south pasture, stopping near where several of the hands were watching over the herd. The driver removed his hat and began waving it, signaling for the men to gather.

Dallas was the first to arrive, soon joined by half a dozen others.

"There's big trouble up at the house," the driver said. "There's done been shootin'—we heard it as we drove away—and there's likely to be more. Pete rode in with the McLean woman at his side and the shoutin' started the minute they walked through the door."

"Was you able to see Peter?" Dallas said.

The driver shook his head. "Best I can determine, it's him, his brother, and their pa inside the house with April. And the new cook, I reckon."

Dallas turned to the men. "If it wasn't for the woman and Peter and ol' Jakie, I'd say we just let 'em get on with their business and hope they kill each other and be done with it. But with others in harm's way, I suppose we'll need to ride back and see what's happenin'."

After retreating into the house, Lester Sinclair went nowhere near the door or windows. He paced the floor, waving a pistol and glaring at those around him. April and Jakie stood near the fireplace while Peter sat on the floor with his back to the wall. Pete kneeled near a window, looking out toward the barn.

"How many of 'em you suppose there are?" Lester said.

"I've only seen the three," Pete said. "But there could be more around back. Some of Blanca's Mexican friends, who were likely following me, might be hidin' somewhere."

Beads of sweat dotted Lester's forehead. "My men will be arrivin' soon," he said, "and will make quick work of this situation. That Jennings fella is a fool to think he can continue messin' with me."

"He'll not attempt anything so long as we've got April here," Pete said.

Lester said, "It was you who brought all this about. When he was lockin' me away in that god-awful jail, he told me how mad he was over your beatin' of that half-wit and how he'd track you down and see you pay. Now you've only riled him more by bringin' the woman here. I was cursed the minute you were born." He turned to Peter. "By you as well."

Pete tried to shut out his father's anger. He balanced a rifle on the windowsill and aimed it toward the barn.

"Jennings," he shouted, "come out so we can have ourselves a meaningful conversation."

In the barn, Tracker gripped Coy's arm and shook his head. "He is only wanting an easy target."

"You first," Jennings called out.

In response, a shot ricocheted off the barn door.

Bagbee and Weatherby heard the sound of gunfire as they neared the ranch and whipped their mounts into a gallop. They'd ridden only a short distance before two of Sinclair's ranch hands appeared from behind a stand of trees, pistols drawn.

"That'll be far enough," one said. "You got no business here. And you should know we've been told to shoot anyone trespassin' on Bend of the River land."

"We just heard shots and feared someone might be in need of help is all," Weatherby said. "We had no intent to trespass."

"Climb down from your horses and see that you keep your hands away from your firearms."

Bagbee leaned toward Weatherby as he raised his arms. "I'm thinking maybe we shoulda had us a better plan."

As the hands tried to determine what to do with the intruders, Dallas and half a dozen hands from the pasture approached.

"Stand down," Dallas said. "Let's try sortin' things out 'fore anybody gets hisself shot."

He immediately recognized Bagbee. "It can't be good that you're here again," he said. "Or you, Mr. Weatherby."

"If you'll recall," Giles said, "it was me doin' you a sizable favor last time we met. Otherwise you'd still be sittin' in that jail. Now I'd like the kindness repaid."

"In what way?"

"First off, you can have your friends holster the pistols they've been pointin' at us. The reason for our bein' here is we're aware that Lester and Pete Sinclair have returned and are holding a friend of ours hostage up at the house. Could be young Peter, who you were set free to work for, is also bein' kept against his will."

"And my friend Jakie," Bagbee added.

"What is it you wish us to do about it?" Dallas said. "None of this is our doin'."

"Which is how it should remain. What I'm suggestin' is that you consider what's proper to do for Peter and the lady."

"Same goes for Jakie," Bagbee said.

"I beg your pardon," Weatherby said. "My friend here is right to again remind me. Jakie is also an innocent bystander in this foolishness and a good man. We aim to see to his safety as well."

Dallas motioned for his fellow hands to ride closer. They moved away from Bagbee and the livery owner and talked among themselves. A minute later they returned.

"Here's what I suggest," Dallas said. "We'll ride back south and then return to the bunkhouse, as if our day's work is done. While we're doin' so, you wait here. I'll approach the house to report our chores are complete and see if I can determine what it is that's takin' place, then ride back to inform you. Is that agreeable?"

Weatherby looked at Bagbee. "You reckon this man can be trusted?"

"I can't see we've got another option."

"I'd suggest you hide yourself and your horses over in that stand of trees till I return," Dallas said.

"If you don't," Bagbee said, "know that I'll come lookin' for you."

From their vantage point in the loft, Jennings and his companions watched as the hands slowly approached the compound. Things had been quiet at the house since Pete's single wayward shot. Blanca raised his rifle and pointed it toward the corral, where the men were removing saddles from their mounts.

"It is to our advantage that they don't know we're here," the Mexican said. "If we start shooting now, we can—"

"Wait," Jennings said. He pointed toward the rear of the bunkhouse, where one of the riders was tethering his horse, leaving its saddle on. He recognized the multicolored serape the man wore. "That's Dallas. Let's see what he's of a mind to do."

Once the last hand was inside the bunkhouse, Dallas walked toward the house.

"The men are back," Pete said as Dallas walked in. "Now we can put this matter to an end." He got to his feet and walked toward the front door.

Lester Sinclair shoved his son out of the way. "Can't tell you how proud I am to see you," he said as he grabbed Dallas's hand. He quickly began to describe the situation that had developed since they left for the pasture.

Dallas looked over at April as Sinclair spoke, and tipped his hat. "What's she doin' here?"

"My ignorant son brought her from town. Now we've got three men out in the barn, aiming their guns at us."

"Who?"

"That fella Jennings and a Mexican who once worked for me. You recall Armando Blanca?"

Dallas nodded. "He wasn't among my favorite people."

"And there's some Indian with 'em. If there's more, I don't know who they might be."

"And what is it you want?"

"Go tell the men to get their guns. Surround the barn. Shoot 'em dead."

Pete moved to stand next to his father. "'Cept for Coy Jennings," he said. "Just bring him out into the open and leave him for me to kill."

Dallas looked around the room, briefly making eye contact with Peter, then April. "What's to happen with the woman?"

"That," Lester said, "will be dealt with once this other matter is concluded."

"If there's to be as much shootin' as I fear," Dallas said, "it would be my suggestion you stay in the back of the house, away from any windows and doors."

"Yes, that's good thinkin', good thinkin'," Lester said. "We'll just wait it out while you and the boys do your business." He gripped Dallas's shoulder. "You can rest assured I'll show my appreciation."

"Right now," Dallas said, "I'd settle for a cup of coffee 'fore I go."

He walked into the kitchen, where Jakie sat at a table, his face in his hands. As he looked up, Dallas smiled and said, "Ain't this a fine mess you've got yourself into?" He glanced back toward the doorway, then quickly removed his pistol from beneath his serape and placed it in an empty pot. Laying a towel over it, he said, "Yessir, one fine mess. I'm guessin' with what all's goin' on there'll be no supper fixed tonight."

He poured himself a cup of coffee and returned to the main room. "You folks just stay out of sight," he said. "If I can make it back to the bunkhouse without bein' shot, we'll figure what needs to be done."

As he walked down the steps, he glanced in the direction of the barn and nodded slightly, then lifted his serape to show that his holster was empty.

It was nearing sundown when Bagbee saw a horse heading in his direction. He nudged Weatherby, who was sitting against a tree trunk, hat pulled down over his face. "I think our man's back."

Dallas was grim-faced as he dismounted. "Things are a bit more complicated than you described," he said. "You've got friends up there—and I'm not speakin' of the woman and Jakie."

Weatherby smiled grimly. "Coy caught up with Pete," he said.

"Him and two others—a Mexican and an Indian, from what I'm told. They're holed up in the loft of the barn, urging the Sinclairs to surrender."

"And that ain't gonna happen this time," Weatherby said. "Not with Pete now involved. So, what is it we're to do?"

"I've told the others to remain in the bunkhouse and take no sides," Dallas said. "We could easily rush the house and bring the matter to an end, but not without risking the lives of those bein' held. I was inside briefly and seen how desperate Lester and Pete have become. Unless they favor us by shootin' each other, I see little chance of this ending in a satisfactory manner."

Chapter 31

"What is it they're waitin' for?" Lester Sinclair said as he paced nervously. "It's near dark and there's been nothin' happening."

"I don't think those in the bunkhouse can be relied on to do what you instructed," Pete said. "They're cowards who have washed their hands of us."

Peter sat in a corner of the main room, a faint smile on his face as he watched the anger of his father and brother mount. The fear he'd initially felt had begun to wane, replaced by concern for the safety of April McLean.

"Perhaps if you was to allow her to go free," he said, "Jennings and his friends might be satisfied and take their leave."

Lester walked over and delivered a hard slap to his face. "I'll thank you to remain quiet," he said. "It's you who turned my men against me—caused them to betray me. You've made cowards of them all—ungrateful cowards like yourself."

April spoke from where she sat on the couch. "I only wish to see my little girl—"

Lester turned toward her and raised his hand. Peter jumped to his feet and grabbed his father's arm and pulled him away. "If you're planning to do her harm," he said, "it will be only after you've killed me. She's done nothing to deserve this treatment."

"Little brother, you surprise me. Didn't think you had it in you," Pete said. "Might be a good idea if she was to help the cook with fixin' us somethin' to eat."

Lester gestured toward the kitchen. "It would be a pleasure to have her outta my sight. Just see she don't attempt to go runnin' away."

"I'll keep a watch on her," Pete said.

Dallas was having a difficult time keeping Bagbee and Weatherby at bay. They had heard no shots fired since his arrival, and he was urging them to wait until nightfall to ride toward the compound. "I've no interest in gettin' shot," he said, "and if we can safely make our way to the back side of the barn, we can alert your friends to our presence. After that we can determine what we'll need done."

"What needs doing," Weatherby said, "is for us to get April safely out of that house. Her and Jakie. And Peter. Then I'm of a mind we set the miserable place to blaze and be on our way. Lester and his drunken sot of a son can learn themselves an early lesson on what hellfire is all about." Spittle shot from his mouth as he spoke.

April prepared corn bread while Jakie heated the stew he'd cooked earlier in the day. Neither spoke as Pete leaned against the doorway, watching.

"What causes you to admire that Jennings fella?" he said.

April ignored him.

"I'm askin' you a question."

"Truth is, I can't say I know him all that well," she said, "but from what I've seen he's a good man who is respected by all." She gave Pete a look. "Except for you and your father."

"We'll see how respected he is once he's dead," Pete said as April brushed past him with the pot of Jakie's stew. When she made a second trip with a basket of hot corn bread, Pete followed her into the main room. "I can't recall the last time I ate," he said as he reached for the ladle.

"While you're feedin' your ugly face," Lester said, "be sure you continue to watch for activity across the way."

Pete picked up the bowl and wolfed down the rest of his stew, wiped crumbs from his beard, and walked to the window. He looked into the darkness. In the loft, he could see a single lantern burning in the doorway. "They're still out there, demonstratin' their patience," he said.

After Lester and Pete had eaten and Peter declined the stew, April began gathering the pot and dishes. "There's fresh-made coffee," she said.

"Sweeten mine from the whiskey bottle on the shelf," the elder Sinclair said, "but see to it that Pete's is served black. I want him to remain sober till this business gets taken care of."

Jakie waited until April was at the washbasin before placing a finger to his lips. As he silently signaled her to remain in the kitchen, he took Dallas's pistol from its hiding place and slipped it into his waistband under his apron. It was the first time in longer than he could remember that he'd touched a gun, and his hands were shaking as he walked into the main room.

Lester had paid little attention to the elderly cook during the ordeal and was surprised when he saw him. "Where's the woman?" he said.

The coffee cups Jakie was bringing into the room slipped from his hands and fell to the floor as Pete pushed past him to make sure April had not attempted to escape. "She's right here," he called out from the kitchen.

As he spoke, the sound of a single gunshot rattled against the walls. Pete lifted his rifle as he turned to see his father on the floor, writhing in pain, blood pouring from a spot high on his chest.

Jakie pointed the pistol toward Pete but was unable to pull the trigger before a bullet tore into his abdomen. He sank to his knees, the gun clattering away on the floor.

Peter looked on in frozen silence. In the kitchen, April screamed.

Pete stepped over Jakie's body and kneeled by his father, leaning close to his face as he gently brushed his hand through Lester's hair. "Lie still," he said. "Don't try movin'. You're gonna be okay."

Lester looked up at him, grimacing. "No, I ain't," he said in a guttural voice. "Your foolishness has got me killed." He spat blood into his son's face before his eyes closed and his body went limp.

Weatherby and Bagbee were nearing the barn when they heard the shots. In the loft, Blanca and Jennings cocked their rifles. "We have waited too long," Tracker said as he rushed toward the ladder.

Jennings's stomach was in knots as he led them across the compound toward the porch. April's scream had caused him to put all caution aside. As he reached the locked door, he plunged his shoulder into it. The door gave way, and he burst into the main room.

His eyes first went to the two bodies that lay in the floor, then to Peter, slumped against the fireplace with a large gash over one eye.

"Where's April?" Coy said.

Peter, barely conscious, motioned toward the kitchen.

Jennings found her, curled into the fetal position and sobbing. He sat beside her, cradling her in his arms. "You're safe now," he said. "We'll soon get you back to town, where Penelope's waiting. Are you injured?"

She shook her head. "Just scared."

Blanca entered the kitchen. "The *viejo* is dead," he said. "And there is another, a man I do not know, in bad shape. Peter got hit in the *cabeza* and is bleeding, but he is coming around."

"It's Jakie," April said. "He's the other man you're speaking of. Will he be okay?"

Blanca turned back to the main room without answering. "Where is Pete Sinclair?" he yelled.

"After he tried tendin' to my father," Peter said, "he told me this was all my doin', then struck me in the head with the barrel of his rifle. I don't recall anything after that."

His eyes didn't leave his father's body.

Tracker and Bagbee searched the house but found no sign of his brother.

"He's gone," Jennings said. "Somehow he managed to slip away."

Outside, the hands emerged from the bunkhouse

and were gathering around Dallas, hoping to learn what had occurred.

"Get the wagon hooked up," he said. "They'll be needin' to get Jakie to the doctor and deliver the woman to her daughter. The Indian is bandaging Peter's head and says he'll be okay. We'll watch after him here."

April had regained her composure and was applying damp towels to Jakie's wound and whispering encouragement. "Doc Matthews will see that you survive this," she said. "If I have but one prayer left to be answered, that will be the case. And Miss Mindy, she's been asking after you every day. She'll be waiting to see you." There was a catch in her voice. "Please, Jakie, don't die."

She bent forward and kissed his forehead. "What you did was a brave thing," she said, "and I thank you ever so much for it."

Bagbee placed a hand on her shoulder. "He's an ornery ol' cuss," he said. "Trust me when I say he'll live to do more bad cookin'. For now, though, we need to load him into the wagon for the ride into Phantom Hill."

"I'll sit by his side," April said.

It was pitch-dark when the wagon left, driven by Weatherby and accompanied by two hands whom Dallas assigned to ride along. "Just in case you run into Pete and some fool plan he might have," he said.

Those who remained gathered on the porch.

"Which way you think he might head?" Bagbee said.

"I got no suggestion to make," Jennings said. "I'm so tired I can't hardly move."

"Reckon there's someplace he might think he'd be safe?"

"Desperate as he now is, I'm thinkin' he has other concerns."

Tracker had already been at work, and now he approached the gathering. "He left from the back of the house and took a horse from the corral behind the bunkhouse, then walked it to the river," he said. "He is riding without a saddle."

"Let us find him and put him out of his misery," Blanca said. "Any man who would do us the favor of killing his *padre* deserves one in return."

"Dallas," Jennings said, "you take some of your men and travel south. I'd suggest you stay close to the bank, at least for a time, then move on to see if he's crazy enough to try hidin' out at Blue Flats."

He nodded toward Blanca and Bagbee. "We'll head upriver, with Tracker leading our way." He smiled wearily. "I reckon it was foolish of me to think I'd get some rest."

At the river's edge, Tracker kneeled and examined boot tracks and hoofprints. He pointed north.

As the wagon neared Phantom Hill just before dawn, one of the hands rode ahead to alert Doc Matthews. By the time it arrived, the anxious doctor was standing in front of his house, Mindy and Penelope McLean at his side. Weatherby hadn't even reined in the horses when the child climbed aboard and fell into her mother's arms.

Mindy rushed past the happy reunion to Jakie and did something no one had ever seen before. As she placed her hands to his face, she began to sob, tears running down her weathered cheeks. Jakie was unconscious, his white apron soaked in blood.

The doctor gently moved Mindy aside. "We need to get him into the house quickly," he said.

"If you ever did miracle doctorin'," she said as she

pulled a handkerchief from her pocket to wipe her face, "I'd wish it to be now. Don't allow him to die."

By sunup, people were already gathering near the singing tree. Several held Bibles, their heads bowed in prayer. Some were humming hymns. When April and Penelope emerged from the house and walked toward them, arm in arm, those keeping vigil began to cheer.

As the townspeople gathered around, April recounted what had taken place at the Bend. When she finished, she said, "I'm thankful for the prayers you've said for me and my daughter. Now I'd appreciate your saying them for Jakie as the doctor tends him. And for Coy Jennings and his friends who are in search of Pete Sinclair. Hopefully they will soon return and this nightmare will be at an end."

Off to one side, Ira Dalton stood silently, his face drawn. April moved toward him. "Your friend will be returning soon," she said as she patted his shoulder. "He asked that I relay that message to you."

It was a falsehood for which she felt no remorse.

In an effort to leave no trail, Pete led the horse into the shallows of the river and slogged through the cold water until his feet were numb. He'd fallen several times and his clothes were soaked. His head pounded and he was having difficulty breathing. His thoughts came in bursts, jumbled and confused.

All he knew for certain was that he was again being chased, and this time he knew by whom. How close were they? Why couldn't they leave him be? He needed to stay ahead of them long enough to find a hiding place, somewhere to rest and collect his thoughts. Above all, he needed to find a way to kill Coy Jennings. Everything had been good until the day he showed up at the Bend and began poking his nose into things that didn't concern him, then getting friendly with April McLean the way he did, causing her to run away.

Coy Jennings had ruined everything.

His father was dead, lying on the floor back at the house with a hole in his chest. Pete hated Lester Sinclair, just like everybody else. Not a good man—evil and mean. And he'd passed those genes right along. But dead? Pete couldn't get the picture out of his mind. Nor could he even remember who it was who killed him. No matter, it was all Jennings's fault that so much bad had occurred. He spoke his name: "I curse you, Coy Jennings."

And in a fleeting moment of sanity, a plan took shape.

Chapter 32

Riding bareback for the first time since he was a child added to Pete Sinclair's discomfort. With no reins to direct the path of the horse, he clung to its mane, jerking it in the direction he wished to go. Spells of dizziness made it necessary for him to repeatedly close his eyes tightly until the spinning stopped.

When the sky turned from black to predawn gray, he was finally able to get his bearings and turned his horse in the direction of Phantom Hill. With luck, he could arrive before his pursuers.

There, he would end it.

Bringing the matter to a conclusion was also on Coy Jennings's mind. Tired from the sleepless night and the anxiety of the events at the ranch, he had said little as they followed Sinclair's trail. Tracker had easily recognized the point at which Pete left the river and began riding cross-country.

Finally Coy broke the silence. "What with all that's been goin' on," he said to Bagbee, "I haven't thought to inquire about your suddenly showin' up. Wasn't expectin' to ever see you again, much less involve you in this trouble."

Bagbee explained the purpose of his return. When he finished, he said, "Now's clearly not the time, but maybe in the near future you can think on it."

"I've got but one thing I'm thinking at present."

"Which I can fully understand. Seems you've taken responsibility for seeing to the safety of Phantom Hill folks as a serious matter. It's my observation that you have a right proud feelin' for the place and those livin' there."

Jennings couldn't see the slight smile on Bagbee's face.

"'Specially that lady we just removed from harm's way."

When Coy didn't respond, Bagbee continued. "It's peculiar to me how the lives of so many good folks can be spoiled by a few. That ol' man lying dead back at his ranch coulda done himself—and others—a favor by bein' a good neighbor, showin' some kindness, doin' his part to see the town grow. But all he wanted was to fill his own pockets and deal out misery. Now we're chasing his son, who seems full of the same meanness."

"Was it not for the young son Peter being good-hearted," Jennings said, "I'd figure it was just in the family blood. Truth is, all I can say is that the world has seen considerable improvement with the passin' of Lester Sinclair. And it'll get even better once his boy Pete is also dead and gone."

Tracker and Blanca rode back to join them. "He is headed toward town," the Indian said.

The tiredness Jennings was feeling vanished as he tried to think what Sinclair might be planning. "We need to catch up to him before he gets there," he said as he dug his heels into Rodeo's ribs.

The vigil being held by the townspeople continued to increase in number as the sun rose. Miss Mindy walked out onto Doc Matthews's porch to announce that the bullet had been removed and the bleeding seemed under control. Jakie was still unconscious, she told them. It was far too soon to say if he would recover.

Seeing that there was little she could do to aid the doctor, April opened the kitchen and, with Giles Weatherby and her daughter helping, prepared biscuits and coffee for those gathered near the singing tree. After tending the livestock, Ira Dalton positioned himself on the bench outside the livery, his eyes fixed on the end of the street as he waited for Coy Jennings's return.

Aside from the whispered prayers and occasional singing of hymns, the town was eerily quiet as Pete Sinclair left his horse behind and crept toward the back of the saloon.

He was surprised to find the door off its hinges and that Isaac Hatchett was not asleep in the bedroll he kept behind the bar. Mumbling to himself, Pete took a bottle from the shelf and smiled. His luck was changing. He'd managed to stay ahead of those he knew were pursuing him, managed to get into town undetected, and his insides would soon be warmed by whiskey.

Can't drink too much, he warned himself. *Just enough to steady the nerves and stoke some fire in the belly. Gotta be alert when Jennings arrives. Gotta be ready to do what I've come to do.*

He slowly moved to the front window and was surprised to see the number of people gathered down the street. *No matter,* he thought, *they'll not get in the way. Neither will the half-wit sitting in front of the livery. Shoulda killed him when I had the chance. Maybe, once I'm done with Jennings, I'll finish that job as well. Maybe I'll do a whole lotta killing before I get done. Just as well to shoot April, should the opportunity present itself. If I can't have her, nobody will. That would show folks they ought not to mess with a Sinclair.*

He took another drink. *Just a sip, not too much. Can't afford to dull my aim.*

Still shivering, he searched the room, found Hatchett's old blanket, and pulled it over his shoulders. It smelled of sweat and stale beer but felt good. *Lord, that river water was so cold.* He removed his sodden boots and dried and massaged his sock feet.

Though the front window afforded him close proximity to the street, it was difficult to see all the way to the end of town, where he expected Jennings would soon appear.

He sat on the floor, the bottle between his legs and his rifle at his side. He was staring at the ceiling when the idea struck. His ideal vantage point, the place from which he could be assured his best shot, was the roof of the saloon. *It'll be cold waiting. But it's the perfect location for what I want to do.*

At the rear of the building, next to the damaged doorway, was a ladder leading to the wooden framework that held the canvas roof in place. *Only problem I've got is seeing I don't fall and break my neck,* he thought as he made the climb.

He felt good about his decision to leave the whiskey bottle behind.

It was Tracker who discovered Sinclair's abandoned horse. Blanca muttered a stream of Spanish curses as he measured the short distance to town. "He beat us here," he said. "He'll be hiding somewhere, waiting to ambush us—like the coward he is."

Jennings's first thought was the livery. Then the safety of Giles Weatherby and Ira. "We'll ride around and enter town from that way," he said as he pointed. "Once we're near, we'll separate and begin searchin'. Unless he's taken himself another hostage, shoot to kill as soon as you lay eyes on him. I want this settled quickly, with no harm to bystanders."

He told Blanca to make his way toward the rear of the kitchen and Bagbee to approach from behind the general store and saloon. He would ride directly into town.

As he neared the settlement, Coy was shocked to see such a large gathering of people near the singing tree. He quickly rode toward them, yelling for everyone to take cover. "Get yourselves inside the kitchen," he said. "You're in danger out here in the open. There's likely to be shootin'."

The prayers and hymns stopped as people rushed toward Miss Mindy's. A couple of children were knocked to the ground but were quickly helped to their feet by Weatherby, who had rushed outside to see what was happening. Several of the women screamed as they ran.

When Mindy and the doctor came onto the front porch, Jennings waved them back inside.

The first shot from atop the saloon went over Jennings's head and splintered a limb of the singing tree.

Coy returned fire as he dismounted and swatted Rodeo's rump, sending him galloping away. As he raced to the tree for shelter, he saw Ira running in his direction, calling his name. Jennings fired several rapid shots to distract Pete until Dalton reached him. "Stand behind me and don't dare to move," he said.

"Yessir, Mr. Jennin's. You're the boss. I'm mighty glad you're back. But it appears you've got somebody really mad at you."

Another shot buried itself into the trunk of the tree. "The feelin's mutual," Coy said as he squinted toward the roof of the saloon. All he could see was the top of Sinclair's hat.

"Hey, Coy Jennings," Pete yelled, "those was only shots to show my seriousness. I got plenty of ammunition up here and all the patience that's needed. You can make this easy by showin' yourself so we can be done with our business."

Ira grabbed Coy's arm. "Don't give him satisfaction, Mr. Jennin's," he said. "Don't do somethin' that'll get you killed."

Blanca had moved away from the kitchen and was crouched behind the livery's watering trough. "I have no clear shot until I can get closer," he yelled.

"Stay put for now," Jennings said.

Meanwhile, Bagbee was making his way toward the rear of the saloon. Once he reached the corner of the building, he waved his hat to signal his position. When Jennings and Blanca fired a volley of shots toward the roof, he slipped inside and pressed his body against the wall.

Once the gunfire from below stopped, Pete peeked through the log slats providing his cover and was surprised to see a cloud of dust rising on the early-morning horizon.

As it got closer, he saw that it was being raised by approaching riders. Leading them was his brother, head bandaged and a rifle in his hand.

"You're now far outnumbered, Pete," Coy shouted. "Time you give yourself up."

As Pete replied with two more shots, the hands from the Bend were dismounting and racing for cover. Soon half a dozen rifles were aimed toward the saloon.

From behind a wagon, Peter cupped his hands against his mouth and shouted, "Pete, hear me out before you do more shootin'. You've done far too much harm already and there's no cause for makin' things worse. All's gonna happen is you gettin' yourself killed. Climb down and give up this foolishness."

Pete aimed toward the wagon and fired a shot that kicked up dirt near where his brother was kneeling.

"I don't want to," Peter yelled, "but if need be I'll shoot you myself."

As he spoke, Bagbee quietly put one boot on the ladder and began climbing up to the roof. He removed his hat before reaching the top rung, and he lifted his head enough to see that Sinclair lay in a prone position at the edge of the roof.

Bagbee was preparing to shoot when a rung of the ladder gave way with a loud crack. Sinclair whipped his rifle around, aiming toward the sound. Two shots, sounding like one, were fired, followed by a single scream.

Sinclair clutched his thigh as blood poured from a hole in his britches. He crawled toward the trapdoor where the ladder had been and looked down into the saloon. On the floor below, Bagbee lay dead, a gaping wound where his right eye had once been.

As Pete tore strips from Hackett's blanket to make a makeshift tourniquet, he heard Jennings's voice calling out, "Will . . . Will Bagbee. Speak out and tell me if you're okay."

Sinclair groaned as he slowly made his way back to the front of the roof. "If the man who just tried to sneak up and shoot me had the name Bagbee," he yelled, "he's in no condition to be talkin'."

As the morning passed, the standoff was reduced to only an occasional shot from atop the saloon. Pete would fire in the direction of his brother, then toward Coy. The shots were becoming increasingly wild and off the mark.

In the kitchen, Weatherby clutched his shotgun as he looked out on the street from the edge of the doorway. Behind him, people lay on the floor, hiding behind tables that had been turned on their sides to shield them from the gunfire.

The livery owner pulled his hat tight on his head. "I'm of no use here," he said, then stepped off the porch and ran toward the singing tree. He was surprised when no shots were fired.

Jennings rubbed his aching leg as Weatherby, breathing heavily, kneeled beside him. "Our best choice seems to be to wait till dark," Giles said. "Earlier, I seen some of the ranch hands position themselves toward the back of the saloon. That'll make Pete's escapin' unlikely."

Jennings nodded. "Once he can't easily see our movement and take sure aim, we can move closer."

"What of Bagbee?"

"I fear he's dead or badly wounded," Coy said.

Still standing behind him, Dalton whispered, "Mr. Jennin's, you're the sheriff. I'm scared. Can you make this be over?"

"Soon," Jennings said. He turned to signal for Blanca to remain in place. But the Mexican was no longer behind the watering trough.

* * *

Pete Sinclair was unable to stop the bleeding. His injured leg was numb and he repeatedly bit down on the brim of his hat to keep from fainting. The dizziness he'd experienced on the ride into town was back, only now worse.

He was having moments of darkness long before the sun began to set. In lucid moments he would grit his teeth, utter a curse, and fire another shot. And he would mutter to himself. "I'll not die before you do, Coy Jennings," he said in a raspy voice that sounded as if it were coming from far away. As he stared down at the shadows that were forming in the street, his mind revisited the times when he'd won fistfights in front of the saloon. "I was properly respected then," he said.

Blood had soaked the leg of his britches, making the place where he lay sticky and smelling faintly of copper. When he thought he heard movement in the saloon below, he fired a series of quick pistol shots into the canvas roof. "That you, Isaac?" he said. "If so, I'd appreciate you're bringin' me up a bottle."

Blanca clung to the saloon wall, avoiding the shots, then began pouring the coal oil he'd taken from Weatherby's livery. He splashed it against the bar, onto the tables, then the floor. Retreating toward the back door, he emptied the final drops into a moist trail.

"Adios, senor," he called out as he lit a match and set the building on fire. As he left, he dragged Bagbee's body away.

In minutes, the twilight was brightened by the flames that rose from inside the saloon and burst through the door and windows. Soon the canvas roof began to burn.

Pete smelled the fire before he saw its flames and struggled to his feet. Balancing on the roof beams, he swore and began to shoot wildly. "Show yourself, Jennings," he yelled, "so I can shoot you dead. I'm runnin' short on time."

Jennings stepped from behind the tree and took careful aim at the madman standing on the roof. There was the crisp sound of a rifle shot, and Pete Sinclair doubled over, clutching his chest before falling in a somersault toward the street below.

"You've ended it," Blanca said, slapping Jennings on the back. "If it wasn't for all the whiskey bein' burned up, I'd buy you a drink to celebrate."

Coy let his weapon fall to his side. "It wasn't me," he said.

Standing in the middle of the street, Peter Sinclair still had his rifle braced against his shoulder and aimed toward the burning rooftop. A gentle man, he had now killed two people.

Chapter 33

People began to slowly emerge from the kitchen. A few approached Sinclair's body. One farmer kicked at it, as if to make certain he was dead. A woman quoted Scripture about the Lord demanding vengeance. Most, however, seemed satisfied with silently watching the flames and tinder sparks that floated into the night sky.

"Looks like fireflies," Ira Dalton said as the weary Jennings put his arm over his shoulder. After a minute, he walked down the street to where Peter still stood.

"It wasn't your place," the young Sinclair said. "It was my family that caused all this misery. And it was my responsibility to see it ended. I ain't proud, but I did what I had to do."

Coy couldn't think of anything to say that might comfort him. Instead he just shook his hand.

"I just wish I coulda known what made my pa and my brother such bad people," Peter said as he stared toward the fire. It was much smaller, more smoke than flames. "I guess it's something that'll never be known." There was pain in his voice.

"You and your men oughta get on back to the ranch and take care of things there," Jennings said. "There'll be matters that'll need sortin' out, but they can wait till later."

"I'll send a wagon to fetch my brother," Peter said. "Seems right that he and our pa be buried at some peaceful place on the Bend."

Jennings turned and walked toward the doctor's house. The night was getting colder, and Miss Mindy and April stood on the porch with blankets wrapped over their shoulders. Mindy held a lantern.

"Is Jakie gonna make it?" Jennings said.

"Doc says he's got a fair chance," Mindy said. "He's not yet awake, but his breathing seems normal. He's gettin' the best attention that can be provided."

Jennings looked at April. "I'm sorry for what you and your daughter have been put through," he said, then turned to find Blanca.

As he walked away, April called out, "Sheriff Jennings . . . please know that I appreciate what you've done."

Weatherby joined him as he made his way to the back side of the burned-out saloon. He found Armando kneeling beside Bagbee, draping his serape over the body. Soot and ashes covered the Mexican's face. "He was a fool to attempt what he did," Blanca said as they approached. "He was a good man with too much courage."

Jennings stared down at Bagbee, then looked up into the ink-black sky. "I wish he'd not returned," he said. Weatherby put a hand on Coy's shoulder.

"Once it's light, we'll need to prepare him properly," Jennings said. "Then I'll see he's taken home where he belongs. I'll have Tracker lead the way. "

"If you're of a mind," the livery owner said, "I'd like to join you on the ride."

Blanca looked up at the two men. "I do not think I would be welcome to come along, since I stole his boss's cattle and was one of the causes for him coming here in the first place."

For the first time since the nightmarish events began, Jennings smiled and again shook his head at the strange relationships he'd recently formed. "Your business is down south," he said. "Go see to your boy."

Weatherby leaned down to grip the dead man's shoulders. "Help me carry him up to the livery," he said, "Ain't right to leave him out here in the cold."

The following day, they prepared to leave for the ride north to the Red River. Weatherby and Trapper had wrapped Bagbee in coal and salt, then tied a tarp tightly around him. Ira insisted that his mule be used to carry the body.

April restored things to order at the kitchen and prepared food for their trip.

As the three men slowly rode from town, they saw that several hands from the Bend were already busy cleaning away the debris of the burned-out building. Others were replacing the scorched logs on the jail. Dallas had already arrived with a wagon and taken Pete's body away. Aside from the sounds of the men working, Phantom Hill was quiet.

"You do know that the saloon will need replacin'," Weatherby said as they rode past the piles of ashes. "No town can be seen as respectable unless it's got a place a man can purchase himself a drink."

Jennings grinned. "I think we can worry about that sometime in the future."

Weatherby was in a talkative mood. He complained of the winter weather, voiced concern that Dalton would properly care for the livery in his absence, and wondered how Peter Sinclair would do now that he was finally free of Lester and Pete. "Speakin' of times ahead," he said, "was Bagbee able to tell you his purpose for comin' back this way?"

"We briefly spoke about it."

"And?"

Coy said, "We'll need to make a stop in Fort Worth and alert Marshal Singletary's people to what happened to him. Since Isaac Hatchett told you about it, I think it best you do the talkin'."

For the first time since their ride began, Weatherby was silent.

After a night of sleeping beneath a stand of live oaks, Jennings peeked from his bedroll to see that Giles and the Indian had already stoked the fire and were making coffee. "Even with the slowness of Ira's mule," Tracker said, "we should arrive at Fort Worth before noon."

"I'm sorely dreadin' what we gotta do," Weatherby said, " but at the same time I'm looking forward to seein' what a real town looks like. It's been a while."

Despite the sharp wind and constant howling of nearby coyotes, Jennings had slept soundly. He hadn't realized how tired he'd become in recent days. He promised to buy his traveling companions a drink once they found the marshal's office and delivered their message. "That's if they have a saloon that's not been burned down," he said, "and will allow us to hitch a dead man and a mule outside."

Weatherby laughed. "I'm proud to see your sense of humor's returnin'," he said. "You bein' a sheriff and me a fully sworn deputy, I expect they'll allow us to do as we please."

The first signs they were approaching their destination were the endless stretches of fences—something Lester Sinclair had never felt need of—that marked the boundaries of the farms and ranches they passed. Then, on the flatland horizon, they saw rows of buildings. "Lord help me," Weatherby said. "How big you figure this place to be?"

"It could probably fit Phantom Hill in its hind pocket," Coy said.

They were welcomed to Fort Worth by a bustle of activity. Wagons and buggies made their way along the main street, and owners of shops visited with people on the board sidewalks. There was a fine-looking hotel, several eateries, a grocery, and plenty of saloons that didn't appear to have been visited by fire. The livery they rode past was far more impressive than Weatherby's. A blacksmith waved as they went by. There was a sign on one building announcing that its proprietor purchased all manner of animal hides.

They passed a telegraph office, a post office, a church, and what appeared to be a schoolhouse. When a breeze rose, they could smell the stockyards on the far end of town.

"I think I'd appreciate livin' here," Weatherby said. "If it wasn't for there bein' so many people."

"Yonder it is," Coy said as he nodded toward a small frame building ahead. Above the doorway was a wooden sign: MARSHAL'S OFFICE.

Inside, a portly man wearing a hat that seemed too big for him greeted them. His boots, polished to a high sheen, were propped on the edge of his desk. "You boys got business here?" he said.

"A minute of your time," Jennings said. "We've come to speak with you about Marshal Singletary."

The man got to his feet. "Name's Bootsy Lansdale . . . *Marshal* Bootsy Lansdale. What is it?"

"He'd dead."

Lansdale eyed the sheriff's badge on Jennings's coat. "Where is it you're from and how is it you know Singletary's dead?"

"He came to Phantom Hill to escort a prisoner back this way."

"And I've been awaiting his return."

Jennings turned to Weatherby, who began retelling the story he'd been told by Isaac Hatchett. When he finished, he said, "He didn't say where the killin' took place, only that it was in a farmer's barn somewhere between Phantom Hill and here. As I understood him sayin' 'fore I shot him, the marshal and a cattle thief named Lester Sinclair was stayin' the night there."

"And what's become of the prisoner?" the marshal said.

"He's been shot dead too."

"That him strapped to the mule outside?"

"Nope," Jennings said. "That's the man who alerted Singletary that we was holdin' Sinclair in our jail."

Lansdale pushed his hat back. "Sounds like you fellas have had yourselves a busy time." He pulled a kerchief and wiped his brow. "I'll send some men out to look for the marshal directly, though I got to admit I'm neither surprised nor all that saddened that he got himself killed. The man could talk the bark plumb off a tree. And most of what he had to say was untruthful boastin'."

"Just felt you should be informed," Jennings said. "We'll be takin' our leave now."

As they turned for the door, Weatherby stopped. "Is

there a place in town a fella can get himself a drink without bein' robbed or shot?"

"I suggest you go down the street to the Lucky Dollar," Lansdale said. "And be sure you show your badge. Lawmen ain't required to pay for whiskey in Fort Worth."

Tracker had waited outside, keeping watch over Bagbee's body.

As he climbed into the saddle, Weatherby said, "The man inside didn't seem all that broke up by our news. I'm guessin' that once Singletary's found, it ain't likely there'll be too big a crowd at his buryin'."

"We done what was needed," Jennings said. "Let's have ourselves that whiskey and be on our way . . . but let's make it quick."

They were leaning against the bar when two men appeared in the doorway, slapping dust from their hats. "We've just delivered a herd of cattle," one said, "and our throats are mighty parched." Though he announced his arrival loudly, neither Jennings nor Weatherby looked up. It was obvious that the Lucky Dollar wasn't the first saloon the cowhands had visited.

"There's a swaybacked mule tied outside that appears to be carryin' a man who's dead. What kind of crazy place might this be?"

Weatherby turned to face the men, his jaw set. "I'll thank you to mind your own business," he said. "If it's whiskey you're wanting, order it quietly and keep to yourselves."

The cowboy, a smallish man with a waxed mustache that curled at its ends, smiled at his partner before replying. He moved his hand toward the holster that hung low on his hip. "I take it you must be the one that sorry excuse for a mule belongs to."

Jennings moved a hand toward Weatherby's arm. "Let's just finish our whiskey and move along," he said. "This little man's just lookin' for a fight we have no time for."

"Little man? You calling me a 'little man'?" He drew his pistol—and immediately felt something cold against his throat.

Tracker stood behind him, his knife pressed against the man's Adam's apple. "Drop your pistol and have your friend do the same."

The man's cockiness vanished. "We wasn't meanin' nothing . . . just jokin' . . ." His gun made a clunking sound as it hit the floor. His partner unbuckled his gun belt and let it slide away.

Tracker signaled for Weatherby to pick up the pistols. "We will carry them to the edge of town," the Indian said, "and leave them in plain sight. Your horses will be there as well. If you're not too drunk, you should be able to soon find your belongings."

The two men nodded.

"There's one more thing you'll be needin' to do before we take our leave," Jennings said. "Remove your boots and throw them into the street. Then unbutton your britches and let them fall to your ankles."

Quickly they were standing on their sock feet, their long johns exposed. Both were red-faced.

"Now I guess it's time we get on our way," Coy said. As he walked past the men, he said, "I wouldn't think about rushin' out in an attempt to follow us, exposed as you are. There's ladies on the street."

As they rode from town, Weatherby looked at Tracker. "Would you really have cut that man's throat?"

Tracker didn't reply.

*   *   *

It was near dusk the following day and a gentle snow had begun to fall as they arrived at the entrance to the Blue Norther Ranch. A large bull looked lazily in their direction, showing them no interest before sauntering away toward a small pond where a herd of cows were gathered. In the distance, there was activity in the barn as men were still loading hay onto a wagon. The ranch hands showed no more interest than the bull until they recognized Tracker.

"These men are here to speak with the colonel," the Indian said.

One of the workers stabbed his pitchfork into the hay, gave a glance toward the mule, then motioned toward the nearby house. "'Bout now Colonel Swindle's likely to be sittin' down to his supper."

A tall angular-faced man, white-haired and with a well-kept goatee, met them at the door. The starched shirt he wore matched the color of his hair. "Gentlemen," he said, "may I ask the purpose of your visit?"

Coy removed his hat. "Name's Coy Jennings, sheriff of Phantom Hill. I'm afraid we've come with bad news."

"I'm not pleased to hear that, but perhaps you should come in from the cold." He extended his hand. "Colonel Benjamin Randolph Swindle," he said, then motioned them toward chairs near the fireplace. In one corner of the room was a Christmas tree, gaily decorated.

"I'd plumb forgot it was near Christmas," Weatherby said.

"It's late enough for a taste of whiskey if you gentlemen are so inclined," the colonel said. "Perhaps it would be the proper thing to do before you share what you've come to tell me." He looked at Jennings. "You're the man Will spoke to me about."

"And one of the reasons he's now dead," Coy said.

"Tracker's taken his body into the barn," Weatherby said.

"As you can imagine," Colonel Swindle said, "this news distresses me more than I can say. I admired Bagbee, both as a soldier when he served under me, and as my foreman. I've never had children, you understand, but I thought of him as a son."

He fell silent, as if lost in thought. "Once the sun goes down, the weather promises to get ugly, so I must insist that you spend the night as my guests. That will give you ample time to tell me how this unfortunate situation came about. What happened in the town you've come from must have gotten even worse than what Will described to me after returning with my cattle."

Jennings sipped at his whiskey as he explained the series of events that led to Bagbee's death. He made sure that the colonel understood that he had died during an act of bravery. He also told him that his former cook, Jakie, had been seriously wounded.

"Good men, both. It is no surprise to me that Will Bagbee met an honorable end," Swindle said as he poured more whiskey into his visitors' glasses. "I saw him act bravely on the battlefield many times before the war ended. He was a fine man, and it is kind of you to bring him home. I'll see to it that he is given a proper burial.

"Now, we should talk of another thing before you get your rest. Am I to assume Will was able to explain the purpose of his return visit before he died?"

"We talked briefly about it," Coy said.

"He explained, I assume, that my feelings toward those who fought for the Confederacy have changed as I've grown older and a bit wiser."

Coy nodded. "I reckon my thinking about the blue-coats ain't what it once was."

"All that's now ancient history that needs to be put behind us. Time we all moved on."

"I agree," Coy said.

"So, based on Will's recommendation, I had hoped to meet you—under better circumstances, of course—to judge your interest in coming to work here on the Blue Norther."

Weatherby inched to the front of his chair. "Colonel Swindle," he said, "I should admit to you that I invited myself along on this ride for a selfish reason that had little to do with Will Bagbee, may God rest his soul. My intention was to persuade my friend here not to accept your offer. While we were on the trail, I just never found the proper words to say."

"Why don't you wish him to come here?"

"Because he's badly needed in Phantom Hill, which I doubt you'd ever heard of till Bagbee told you about it. It ain't got much to offer but some good people."

"I assume you're talking of those who haven't yet been killed," the colonel said.

"It was all that commotion that has now given our town a chance to be something better'n it once was. Some of the things Coy's done since his arrival have caused considerable improvement. And I'm not speaking just of him bein' sheriff. Folks, myself included, looked up to him long before he was wearing the badge. What I'm sayin' is that with folks like Coy, Phantom Hill can one day grow itself into a fine town."

The colonel raised his hand. "I think you've stated

your case admirably. My thinking is that the decision is not up to you or me, but Mr. Jennings." He raised his glass. "Perhaps he would like to sleep on it."

Swindle showed them the way to the bunkhouse. "I'd like to welcome Tracker back, then show my respects to Will before I retire for the evening," he said. "I'll expect you gentlemen to join me for breakfast."

Before daybreak the dining room table was filled with platters of eggs, grits, ham, and biscuits. A large pot of coffee awaited as Coy and Giles joined the colonel.

They ate in silence before Weatherby spoke. "Appears you found yourself a fine cook to replace ol' Jakie."

"Truth be known, ol' Jakie was never much at cooking, though I'd rather you not tell him I said so," the colonel said. "I do, however, ask that you wish him a speedy recovery when you next see him." He poured milk into his coffee and looked across the table at Jennings. "Have you given thought to my offer?"

Coy swallowed a last bite of biscuit. "I slept on it, like you asked, and I thank you kindly for your consideration," he said, "but if you don't mind, I'll decline. I've got reasons for wanting to return to Phantom Hill."

"Understood. You now know the way should your mind ever change."

It took three days of hard riding to get home. There was no stop in Fort Worth, since the colonel had given them a bottle of whiskey as they prepared to leave. "Something to keep your innards warm," he'd said. They had bade good-bye to Tracker and thanked him.

Trail weary and subdued, they talked little until they neared Phantom Hill.

"I wasn't sure you'd make the decision you did,"

Weatherby said as they stopped near a stream to allow their horses and Ira's mule to drink. "I wish you to know I'm glad you'll be stayin' in Phantom Hill. Folks will be pleased to learn you're planning to call it home." He scratched the mule's ears. "Ira will be but one of them."

Dalton was standing outside the livery as they entered town. Running toward them, he seemed momentarily confused, not knowing whether to greet his mule, Bell, or Coy Jennings first. He chose Coy.

"Mr. Jennin's . . . Mr. Jennin's . . . happy to see you back."

"Good to see you as well," Coy said. "Bell did us a fine job and will likely appreciate some oats and a considerable amount of rest."

As Ira led the mule toward the stable, Jennings and Weatherby continued toward Doc Matthews's house. Miss Mindy was sitting on the porch, smoking a cigar. She seemed in good spirits.

"Was wonderin' if you boys would ever find your way home," she said. Before they could ask, she told them that Jakie was awake and feeling much better. "Though he still seems a bit out of his head. Last evenin', the fool proposed we get married, but said he'd only consider it if I promised to quit smokin' cigars."

Weatherby laughed. "And what was your response?"

"I told him I'd not marry him till he became a better cook. Which means it's not likely we'll ever get hitched."

April McLean appeared on the porch, Penelope at her side. Jennings tipped his hat.

"It's Christmas Eve, Mr. Jennings," Penelope said, hurrying down the steps toward him. "People will soon be coming to town to sing carols over by the tree."

Coy smiled at the little girl and lifted her into his arms. "If you'll allow me to join you," he said, "I just might try singin' myself."

Chapter 34

If there was a single thing that caused Phantom Hill to grow, it was the announcement made by Peter Sinclair one morning as he stood in front of Weatherby's livery soon after his ranch hands had begun construction on the new saloon.

He'd hired a surveyor whom Coy Jennings mentioned and had him travel from San Antonio to determine the actual size of the Bend of the River Ranch. Once the job was done, Peter decided that it was far too much land to continue watching over. He fenced the land he wished to keep and parceled the rest into small-acre farms for which he charged settlers only a minimal price.

Word spread quickly, and wagons began to arrive almost daily, filled with new families and new hopes.

Soon the number of children in the community had grown to a point that the building of a school was being discussed. Rather than put the matter to a town vote, Mayor Mindy simply decreed it should be built and called on the men of the community to cut wood, haul it into town, and begin construction. After promising that a small cabin would be built next to it, she persuaded April McLean to serve as teacher.

Taking April's place at the kitchen was Jakie. He still moved slowly and was no longer able to ride, but he'd healed well enough to cook corn bread and biscuits and occasionally make the coffee. Mindy wouldn't allow him near her stew pot or to help prepare the main courses she served.

She didn't quit smoking, but Jakie finally agreed to overlook her habit, and they were married by a traveling preacher in the shade of Phantom Hill's singing tree. Mindy renamed her eatery, having Giles Weatherby build a new sign that read MINDY & JAKIE'S TOWN KITCHEN.

One of the newcomers in town, a young man who had worked a chuck wagon for road builders in Louisiana, took Jakie's place, cooking at the Bend. Buck Burton, having grown weary of the hard life of farming, paid Sinclair a ten-dollar gold piece and became owner of the saloon.

One day a few years after the troubles, Peter Sinclair sent a rider into town with a message to Jennings, asking him to visit the ranch. The sheriff was apprehensive about making the trip. There were too many bad memories. Finally he saddled Rodeo early one morning and rode out to the Bend.

Peter was standing on the porch when he arrived, looking every bit the ranch owner. There was a new air of confidence about him and a peace that Coy was pleased to see.

He asked that Jennings walk with him after they'd had coffee. They first headed toward the river, where trees and grass were again green and cattle drank along the bank. He showed Coy the headstones that marked his father's and brother's graves. The sheriff said he thought that the grave sites somehow offered a peaceful ending to such violent lives.

When they reached the corral, a beautiful bay mare looked toward them with large brown eyes, snorting and pawing at the ground. Peter had broken her himself. It was the young colt that April and her daughter had once made their nightly visits to. Sinclair asked if Jennings would deliver the horse to Penelope McLean.

Then he pulled a piece of paper from his shirt pocket and handed it to the sheriff. Jennings unfolded it and read. It was a deed to two hundred acres on the northern part of the ranch. The river served as one if its borders, and Peter assured him the soil was deep and fertile. When the sheriff said he was in no position to afford it, Peter explained that it was not for sale. It was a gift. He wanted them to be neighbors.

As he rode back toward town, Penelope's new horse prancing behind, Coy pondered the changes that were occurring. Giles Weatherby was right. Phantom Hill had a future.

Yet for all that was new, some things hadn't changed. The livery was the same, though a bit busier, and Weatherby had found it necessary to enlarge his stables. Ira still worked there, and he'd resumed his nightly rides to visit the grave of his dog, his shirt pocket always filled with peppermint sticks. His aging mule moved more slowly but still seemed to look forward to the journey. Occasionally Coy and Rodeo accompanied them.

And on Sundays, people still gathered at the singing tree. They sang the same hymns and listened to the same Scriptures, but they'd begun talking of the need for a real church, and a real preacher. Mayor Mindy assured people it would soon happen. She said it would be built near the tree.

Once it was completed, Coy and April planned to have Penelope and their newborn son, Will Bagbee Jennings, baptized there.

National bestselling author
RALPH COMPTON

THE MAN FROM NOWHERE
SIXGUNS AND DOUBLE EAGLES
BOUNTY HUNTER
FATAL JUSTICE
STRYKER'S REVENGE
DEATH OF A HANGMAN
NORTH TO THE SALT FORK
DEATH RIDES A CHESTNUT MARE
RUSTED TIN
THE BURNING RANGE
WHISKEY RIVER
THE LAST MANHUNT
THE AMARILLO TRAIL
SKELETON LODE
STRANGER FROM ABILENE
THE SHADOW OF A NOOSE
THE GHOST OF APACHE CREEK
RIDERS OF JUDGMENT
SLAUGHTER CANYON
DEAD MAN'S RANCH
ONE MAN'S FIRE
THE OMAHA TRAIL
DOWN ON GILA RIVER
BRIMSTONE TRAIL
STRAIGHT SHOOTER
THE HUNTED
HARD RIDE TO WICHITA
TUCKER'S RECKONING
CHEYENNE TRAIL
DOUBLE-CROSS RANCH
THE DANGEROUS LAND
VIGILANTE DAWN
THE EVIL MEN DO
STRAIGHT TO THE NOOSE
THE LAW AND THE LAWLESS
BROTHER'S KEEPER
TEXAS HILLS

"A writer in the tradition of Louis L'Amour and Zane Grey!"
—*The Huntsville Times* (AL)

Available wherever books are sold or at
penguin.com